Uncommon Lives

Uncommon Lives

Gay Men and Straight Women

by

Catherine Whitney

With an Afterword by
Christine Henny, Ph.D.

NAL BOOKS

NEW AMERICAN LIBRARY

A DIVISION OF PENGUIN BOOKS USA INC., NEW YORK
PUBLISHED IN CANADA BY
PENGUIN BOOKS CANADA LIMITED, MARKHAM, ONTARIO

NAL BOOKS TRADEMARK REG. U.S. PAT. OFF. AND FOREIGN COUNTRIES
REGISTERED TRADEMARK—MARCA REGISTRADA
HECHO EN BRATTLEBORO, VT., U.S.A.

SIGNET, SIGNET CLASSIC, MENTOR, ONYX, ROC, PLUME,
MERIDIAN and NAL BOOKS are published *in the United States* by
New American Library, a division of Penguin Books USA Inc.,
1633 Broadway, New York, New York 10019, *in Canada* by Penguin
Books Canada Limited, 2801 John Street, Markham, Ontario L3R 1B4

LIBRARY OF CONGRESS CATALOGING-IN-PUBLICATION DATA
Whitney, Catherine.
  Uncommon lives: gay men and straight women / by Catherine Whitney.
      p.   cm.
  Includes bibliographical references.
  ISBN 0-453-00715-5
  1. Gay men—United States. 2. Women—United States. 3. Unmarried
couples—United States. 4. Married people—United States. I. Title.
HQ76.2.U5W46 1990
306.73—dc20   89-38282
                                                                CIP

Designed by Julian Hamer

First Printing, March, 1990

1   2   3   4   5   6   7   8   9

PRINTED IN THE UNITED STATES OF AMERICA

Dedicated to men and women who:

wrestle with tradition
invent new options
take risks
live creatively

Contents

Acknowledgments

I am grateful to the many people who have supported me during the period this book has taken shape.

My friend and literary agent, Jane Dystel, has concentrated her customary energy and business savvy on the success of this project from the first day. Jane always pushes me a little farther than I think I can go, and I'm glad to have her in my life.

In a time when books about relationships seem to feed the neediness in society rather than presenting visions of possibility, I have appreciated the way that my editor, Alexia Dorszynski, has consistently cut through glib assumptions to help me articulate the honest issues. I also appreciate her continued confidence in the project.

I would also like to thank Nancy Shiner for her copyediting, and Judy Courtade, Maryann Palumbo, and Lee Hochman of New American Library for their help.

I wish that I could thank personally every man and woman who took the time to participate in the study. I wish they could know how often their stories moved me, and how impressed I was with their depth of insight and their willingness to confront difficult issues.

Finally, I would like to thank the many friends and colleagues who have contributed their ideas and support, and tolerated my work schedule. In particular, I am grateful to those people who have been a primary part of my personal community: Lynn, Ron, Ellen, Jerry, Jane, Tom, Priscilla, Paul, and the many others who have enriched my life. And always, I am grateful to my parents, who remain my role models for loving honestly and well.

* * *

AUTHOR'S NOTE: To protect the privacy of the men and women who participated in this study, I have changed names and other data in telling their stories. In some cases, stories are composites drawn from the lives of several people. Any similarity to real people and circumstances, except where specifically noted, is coincidental.

''Know the white
Yet keep to the black:
Be a pattern for the world''

Tao Te Ching

CHAPTER ONE

Finding Love
in Mysterious Places

The meaning of life differs from man to man,
from day to day and from hour to hour. What
matters, therefore, is not the meaning of life in
general but rather the specific meaning of a person's
life at a given moment. To put the question in
general terms would be comparable to the question
posed to a chess champion: "Tell me, Master,
what is the best move in the world?"

—from *Man's Search for Meaning*,
Viktor E. Frankl

IT HAS BEEN more than three years since I started writing this book, and it has changed course so many times that I hardly remember what it is I set out to do in the beginning. For the most part, I have not directed its course as much as it has directed me, and I am pleased by this. Writing a book about real people is a discovery process that would be hampered by too many rigid restrictions or preconceived notions. People never say or do what you expect; they're always baffling the "experts." As I've written this book, I have found the unpredictability of responses exhilarating but frustrating. Often, just when I've seemed to discover the core of some truth, I've found another layer to peel away. Human beings defy labels—and the participants in my study have repeatedly demonstrated this. More than anything, this book is about the impossibility of defining human behavior with labels.

The book started out as a simple research project to study

the ways that men and women find love and commitment beyond the consideration of their sexual identities. They live, as the title suggests, "uncommon lives." I have always been curious about people who choose to exist on the far side of what's obvious or "normal." Perhaps by living in New York City, I've encountered more examples of this than one ordinarily would. Big-city life requires many compromises—families are not as "nuclear" here as elsewhere. People come together for many different reasons. A big city can be frigid and indifferent, and it's not a pleasant environment in which to be alone.

I have often wondered: If we fear loneliness so much, why are we so determinedly alone? It is easy to imagine, looking out into the glittering lights of New York's skyscrapers, that behind the shades of hundreds of thousands of tiny windows, single people exist by dint of stoic grit—hoping to find a commitment but feeling sad and stunned by too many defeats along the way. Most of them have been raised on a fiercely romantic ideal about what constitutes a valid and satisfying partnership and feel that to accept anything less would be "settling." Better, they reason, to live alone.

And yet we crave community. We fight to locate meaningful connections. And deep down, we all know, or at least suspect, that the roots of our satisfaction lie in a far broader range of emotions and experiences than the romantic ideal allows. If this were not true, holidays would not be such a time of despair for those who are alone. It is not romance they are looking for—at least, not in its idealized sense—but community. As Alvin Toffler says in his extraordinary book *The Third Wave*, "Individuals need life structures. A life lacking in comprehensible structure is an aimless wreck."

There are certainly many people who feel aimless in the absence of close ties that bind them in communities and families. In his book—written ten years ago!—Toffler says that at least one fifth of the American population lives alone. But looking toward the future, he warns that the answer is not to recover old nuclear family ideals that are no longer in sync with broader societal changes. Rather, new forms of community and family that meet the specific needs of present and future generations must be encouraged.

In this book, I will share the stories and reflections of more than a thousand men and women across the country who have struggled in unique ways to forge meaningful connections in a society where loneliness and lack of commitment are central themes. These are people who want to be committed, who have chosen to be related—even though their choices often seem ludicrous and deeply troubling to outsiders. For the most part, the men in the survey profess to be homosexual or bisexual, while the women are heterosexual. Many are married by choice, lured into commitment by a mysterious blend of love and commonality. Others have formed a new paradigm of contemporary community—relationships that reach beyond the label of platonic friendship into a realm that might, inadequately, be termed "committed friendship." These men and women share homes, possessions, friends, and plans for the future, and though they may not express their love sexually, they call each other "significant others." Their relationships are forged of love, respect, and an understanding that each partner does and will care for the other.

There are also, of course, the many homosexual men who entered marriage because of the tradeoffs—or who only came to grips with their homosexual feelings after years of living in a traditional marriage and having children. This scenario sounds more familiar, but it turns out to be startlingly different from the negative stereotype, for most of these couples have chosen to remain together and confront their uneasy dilemma in a responsible and caring way, rather than splitting apart.

I have chosen to focus on these particular matches because there are so many of them. That might surprise some people. It surprised me, too, when I began my investigation. I had known such couples myself, but I imagined that since I was living in New York City—and Greenwich Village at that—it was to be expected. What I didn't expect was the tremendous flow of response from all corners of the nation—small towns, large cities, places I had always viewed as conservative strongholds.

The other reason I decided to focus on these couples was that they were so interesting sociologically. We have all heard the traumatic side of the gay-straight match, in which the man's revelation of homosexuality (usually to his wife) is followed by a storm of tears and rage and finally dissolution of the relationship. But we hear very little about the couples who choose to be together in full confidence of their love, or about those who solve the problems that arise from differing sexual needs with the gentle touch of compromise.

In presenting these people's experiences and points of view, it is not my intention to be an advocate of the way they live as much as a reporter of their choices and the consequences. Some stories only serve to demonstrate how frustrated people are by the absence of acceptable options for finding committed and loving relationships. Other stories show how determinedly some people can deceive themselves when they become desperate enough for companionship.

Some of the survey respondents appear to be living rewarding, albeit unusual, lives. Others are clearly unhappy or confused. But the common thread is that all have found more traditional partnerships unworkable or unavailable, and they have tried to meet their needs for partnership, family, and love in other ways.

Even when the choices my respondents made seemed questionable, I was often impressed with the thoughtfulness of their responses as well as with the brutal honesty with which they articulated their hopes and fears. It has been refreshing to meet people who understand and accept the consequences of their actions and who try to be responsible both to their inner selves and to those they care for.

In the process of examining these people's lives, I have also been forced to ask how valid some of our most dearly held assumptions really are. It is possible that some of our important cultural myths have actually served as barriers to people seeking to find their place within the community. For many who live different lives, the struggle to justify their choices against the perceived norm is most difficult. Nearly everyone is comfortable with the idea that conforming to the norms—particularly in sexual expression and family styles—is more satisfactory (read ''healthy'') than deviating from them. Ask any ten people what is ''normal,'' and at least eight of them are likely to give the same answer—and with great force of conviction.

But what is normal? According to social psychologist Stanley Schachter, whose research on the subject in the 1940s has become the basis for further investigation by psychologists, sociologists and anthropologists, the majority of individuals who conform to a set of accepted beliefs and practices usually perceive those who deviate to be sick, immoral or dangerous, regardless of what the beliefs or behaviors are. Richard W. Smith, a psychologist at California State University, describes the ''Schachter effect'' in this way:

> Some version of the Schachter effect seems to occur in all fairly cohesive human agglomerations, from the smallest face-to-face discussions to the largest ongoing civilizations—no matter how naive, sophisticated, religious, atheistic, or whatever, the human collectivities are. The executive who wears nothing but jockey shorts in his office, the Marine who insists on always keeping his pants on in the barracks, the orthodox Jew who eats lobster, or the Englishman who keeps two wives, are equally targets of the effect. The phenomenon does not depend on whether the disliked activity is objectively harmful, neutral, or beneficial.

In this way, norms are frequently arbitrary or limited, and they are often subject to change over time. Therefore, a judgment about the validity of a person's beliefs and behavior cannot be based solely on whether or not he or she conforms to a current norm. Smith also observes that most scientists and clinicians who have done studies on sexual options—including homosexuality and bisexuality—are not entirely neutral, and their studies often reflect the bias of the majority against minority expressions. (For example, while many theories attempt to account for homosexuality, there is no corresponding research that examines why people become heterosexual; heterosexuality is simply considered "natural.") Further, most research has been devoted to finding ways of helping the nonconformists to conform, rather than studying the legitimate bases of their nonconformist behaviors and speculating about their positive influence in society. This tendency is described by Schechter, who states that there is always pressure from the majority to make the minority fall in line.

On the other hand, there seem to be dangers inherent in making too great a point of the beleaguered minority being subject to challenge by the majority. Sometimes nonconformists tend to place too much value on the act of nonconforming, defining it as courageous and progressive simply because it is different. They try to avoid dealing with real issues by arguing that they are misunderstood, finding prejudice around every corner and viewing every study with suspicion. After all, a certain amount of conformity is necessary to make societies function—people cannot justify driving on the wrong side of the road simply on a whim, or choosing not to pay taxes, or forbidding their children to attend school. The result of such actions would be chaos. We must consider whether nonconformist positions are damaging to the overall fabric of a society, whether they are neutral, or whether they might lay the groundwork for the development of positive new norms.

This examination is fundamental to any discussion of alternative family styles. And it's quite relevant, for we are all aware that there is a crisis occurring with regard to family.

Nuclear Family: Collapse or Transformation?

As I worked on this book, I encountered many different reactions from the people I told about it. The most common was a conviction that those who responded to my survey were weird, misguided, or pathetic. In describing the lifestyles of my respondents, I frequently used the term "nontraditional," which most people took to mean "not normal." But what *is* the family norm?

When I was growing up in the 1950s and early 1960s, we knew what was normal. There was a standard model for postwar families, and we zoomed in on that model with such intensity that we managed to erase all that had come before from our consciousness. When people speak of returning to "traditional family values," they are often thinking of a very narrow strip of history, from about 1946 to 1964.

Ironically, my maternal grandparents, who were born at the turn of the century, had a much broader view of nuclear family than my own parents did. Although marriage was the norm (and certainly the only permissible context for sexual activity), the family itself was a more flexible unit. For one thing, it wasn't viewed solely as a vehicle for procreation. My grandmother, an accomplished seamstress, worked outside the home all her life. When I was young, she used to tell me stories about life in the factory, always making it sound like a close-knit and high-spirited community. She told of how the young married women shared a conspiracy to avoid pregnancy. With no reliable methods of birth control available in the early 1920s, they used their imaginations to invent their own, and shared their discoveries with one another. My grandmother took great pride in the fact that she had only two children—the number she wanted—allowing her the freedom to seek other forms of fulfillment in addition to family.

In contrast, my own parents, who married at the end of World War II, joined a culture in which the family was the only important thing. My father sacrificed without hesita-

tion his desire to be an artist because he realized he probably could not raise a family on an artist's earnings. He
worked very hard at a number of uninspiring occupations,
and he never complained. I don't think it would have occurred to him that he had cause for complaint; where he
came from, young men supported families, they didn't pursue dreams.

My parents were Catholic, and their priorities were neatly
set—to have and raise as many children as possible. They
had nine children and this was considered a moral accom-
plishment. Indeed, in Seattle, where we lived, there was a
Church policy that if a family managed to have *twelve* children, the bishop himself would preside at the baptism of the
twelfth, and the family would be congratulated in the local
Catholic newspaper. Imagine—twelve children! Catholics of
that era had a mandate to build an ''army of youth,'' as they
called us, to fight for faith and moral values. Unlike her
mother, my mother never even considered birth control an
option.

But it wasn't just the Catholic families who were living
this way. What strikes me most when I reflect back on those
years is the sense that all the families I knew were exactly
like ours. There was an absolute commonality of values and
experience. Those of us who grew up during that period,
no matter in what part of the country, can meet today and
know what each other's lives were like.

During the past twenty years, I have heard my parents
and other parents of that generation ask with great bewil-
derment and sorrow, ''What went wrong?'' What they wonder, of course, is how it came to be that the family culture
they had worked so hard to build has fallen apart so completely. Underlying their dismay is a very real belief that
once people began to pursue personal fulfillment—in the
workplace, in lifestyle, in spirituality, and in sexual expression—there were no longer any tried-and-true controls to
keep things humming along at a steady pace, impervious to
the danger of freedom. (By contrast, my grandmother, who

died in 1982 at the age of eighty-two, said of the new freedoms, "It's about time!")

To be sure, as young adults in the late 1960s and early 1970s, my generation sometimes carried our newly found freedom to extremes. It was a revolution, and revolutions are cataclysmic events. If our parents believed that the family, the Church, and the community should take priority over self-fulfillment, we did our best to hold the other extreme and our motto became "supremacy of the self." We were the "Me generation"—self-indulgent, self-involved, and without respect for custom. Today, the almost hysterical stampede back to "traditional family values" is considered a judgment on the "Me generation." For some, the ills of society—drugs, crime, disease, and so forth—have been caused by the collapse of the family that we set in motion during those days.

For those who see human history in a linear fashion, it makes sense to conclude that the problems that plague our society today can be resolved by returning to the postwar culture. But history is not a straight line; it is dynamic, with many loops and curves. The family culture of the 1950s existed in support of an industrial/agricultural society; why should we assume it would work as easily for the global information society we have become? There has never been any other age like ours. For example, for the first time in known human history, majorities of adults are living into their seventies and beyond. What new community and family structures must be created for them? It seems that what is required is not a flight to the past, for there is no place left to return to. Rather, the imperative seems to be to find the new forms of family and community that fit these times.

In 1981, social psychologist Daniel Yankelovich published *New Rules: Searching for Self-Fulfillment in a World Turned Upside Down.* In it, he documents the dramatic shift that occurred in American attitudes about family over a thirty-year period. Yankelovich recalls asking young women in the 1950s why they cherished marriage, family, and children as their inevitable destiny. "My question struck them as unanswerable, meaningless,'' he recalls. ''Asked why she wanted to get married and have children, one woman replied, sarcastically, 'Why do you put on your pants in the morning? Why do you walk with two feet instead of one?' '' But, says Yankelovich, a mere generation later, the normative premise had shifted completely. During the 1950s, a University of Michigan study asked a cross-section of Americans what they thought of a man or woman who rejected the idea of marriage. A full 80 percent of respondents criticized such a person as being ''sick,'' ''neurotic,'' or ''immoral.'' But in the late 1970s, another Michigan study found that only 25 percent of respondents held this view.

Recent statistics have confirmed that, in spite of the fact that many people still consider the traditional 1950s-style nuclear family as the norm for families, a shockingly small percentage of Americans still live in two-parent-households with their own children. According to Sar Levitan, research professor of economics and director for social policy at George Washington University in Washington, DC, only 10 percent of the more than 90 million households in America fit the model of the ''Fifties family.'' And over 7 million men and women live in households where they are single parents.

Further, it has been found that men and women alike are spending fewer years of their lives in marriages. Research conducted by Thomas Espenshade, a demographer from Princeton University, has shown that the proportion of their lives that women spend married declined from 54 percent (1945–1955) to 43 percent (1975–1980). United States Census Bureau statistics show that many more people are postponing marriage. In 1987, 42 percent of men between the ages of 25 and 29 had not married, compared with 19 percent in 1970. Of women, 29 percent had not married, compared with only 9 percent in 1970. The interval between marriages has also lengthened. In 1985, divorced women waited an average of 3.6 years before remarrying and men waited an average of 3.2 years, an increase of about 1 year since 1970.

Researchers at the University of Wisconsin published evidence in 1989 of a "serious underreporting" of divorce and separation statistics by government and private demographers. Larry Bumpass, who coauthored the report with Teresa Castro Martin, reports that close to two thirds of all first marriages end in divorce or separation.

During the past thirty years, as we've watched the family norm change dramatically, we have focused most of our energy on finding ways to return it to its prior dominance. But norms are neither stable nor permanent. Rather, they are markers that move societies from one point to the next along the historical landscape.

It is scary for many people to find that the "meaning" once ascribed to family is no longer so clear. A friend in her forties who chose not to have children told me how she and her husband wrestled with the decision for almost ten years. "We didn't want children," she said, "but it might have been easier to just go ahead and have them than it was to figure out who we were as a family with just the two of us. And my mother has always been very upset that we didn't have children. She asked me once, 'What's to stop Jay from leaving you?' I thought, My God, is that all it's about? Others have asked me if I wasn't afraid of being alone and not having anyone to take care of me when I get old."

For many people, the primary function of family is to insulate them against the world, and they find the "collapse" frightening. They wonder: *Who is going to take care of me when I get old? Who is going to be there for me when I'm needy?*

But if we look beyond our fears, we might find that the family has not collapsed so much as it has expanded in context to reflect who we are at the end of the twentieth century: A population whose average life expectancy stretches to seventy and eighty years, a society where nearly 70 percent of women work outside the home, a people whose technological advances expand our options for movement and communication. Think of it—a married couple in their fifties, whose children are grown, might have a full thirty years of active life ahead of them. They no longer need the same type of stable environment that was important during the years they were raising their children. They can literally re-create their relationship from scratch. But many couples are afraid to risk change and instead they watch their twenty-five- and thirty-year marriages cease to hold any meaning or give any joy. In this context, divorce might be the only way some people know how to move from one stage of life to another.

We can also speculate that once we get past moralism and fear one of the real crises in the frequency of divorce is that there is no readily available community for those whose primary partnerships dissolve. People remain relatively isolated until they marry again or find another permanent partner. Those who don't remarry are often dissatisfied and lonely. The demand for post-nuclear family forms has grown faster than our ability to conceive what these forms might be, resulting in a crisis of isolation that has broken the spirit of many people. We haven't discovered new ways to be together, even though the old ways only work for a relatively small percentage of the population.

This is not a new idea, of course. During the past twenty years we have seen many examples of groups of individuals organizing themselves into family-style communities. In our early twenties, my former husband and I participated for several years in one such experiment that is still going on today. The premise was developed by a group of Methodist ministers in Texas, who proposed that the contemporary family was victimized by its romanticism—in other words, by the idea that people ''fall in love and live happily ever after.'' Historically, these men pointed out, the family has been both internally and externally focused; thus, a family with no other ''mission'' but to keep itself afloat would atrophy. The group's founders were also intent on stretching the identity of family beyond the nuclear unit, postulating that the smaller units of individuals and couples must exist in the context of a larger community. The experiment they

ultimately developed was what they termed a "secular, ecumenical religious order." Located in a crumbling black
ghetto on Chicago's Westside, the Ecumenical Institute
brought together hundreds of families and individuals from
across the nation and around the world. While the sanctity
of individual families was maintained (this was not a promiscuous community), there was a common life of study,
conversation, celebration, and shared tasks, as well as an
external mission to revitalize the ghetto. The group was involved in catalyzing the neighborhood people to rebuild
burned-out buildings, establishing a health center and a pre-
school, and creating a community-run shopping center.
Eventually, the group expanded into other cities and to other
parts of the world in a grass-roots renewal effort that is still
going strong today.

The Ecumenical Institute was an interesting model, sharing with traditional religious orders and community move-
ments like the kibbutz the basic understanding that the
family's identity must be linked to the world around it in a
socially responsible fashion. Structures like these might ultimately become the direction of the future but, for now,
they are perceived as oddities. By and large, people view
family as being an internal structure that serves as a protec-
tion from, rather than an outreach to, the world at large.

Apart from these rare examples, there remain no accepted
"family" structures—legally, physically, or emotionally—
except those that exist among blood relations or within a
male-female marriage.

Those who live in the homosexual community are criticized for their promiscuity and inability to form committed
partnerships. But most states in our country have firmly denied them the opportunity to become families by making it
impossible for homosexuals to legally marry. This rigid morality, according to one expert, ignores the basis of what
family is meant to be. Writes Thomas B. Stoddard, the executive director of the gay rights organization, the Lambda
Legal Defense and Education Fund, "Those who argue
against reforming the marriage statutes because they believe

that same-sex marriage would be 'anti-family' overlook the obvious: marriage creates families and promotes social stability. In an increasingly loveless world, those who wish to commit themselves to a relationship founded upon devotion should be encouraged, not scorned.''

Finding New Ways to Be Together

To argue that there exists only one acceptable way of being family is to trivialize our human history. Why force old styles into new realities? Human beings are more adaptable than that. I once asked a gathering of gay men and their wives to consider this situation: ''Suppose there were no preconceived notions, either in your own minds or in the minds of those around you about what was normal or acceptable or preferable or right or wrong. Suppose you had no measure for the validity of your relationship other than whether or not it met your needs and held up in the face of your priorities. Suppose you didn't even have to consider what your mothers would think, or what your friends would say, or what consequences there might be if others determined there was something wrong with you and the way you were living. Would you feel any differently than you do right now?'' And they laughed and nodded, and I could see in their faces that many of them were thinking that things would be very different. The pressure of the need to conform was such a constant, heavy weight that it made it hard to evaluate the validity of their relationships with anything even approaching objectivity.

That question was wishful thinking on my part—just a little fantasy. For, of course, we do set norms and there are always face-offs between the majority who conform to them and the minority who do not. But it seems to me that our community morality must transcend the ideals that have outgrown their usefulness, and we must find new ways to identify ourselves in relationship to others.

My purpose in writing this book was to begin to raise

questions about what these new forms might look like. It was not my intention to suggest that the lifestyle choices my study participants have made are necessarily valid. But neither do I think we can ignore the fact that they are occurring, or automatically assume there is something wrong with them because they are different.

Many of the people who participated in the study assumed that I was their advocate; they may be disappointed to find that I haven't been that. My advocacy is for the dialogue their choices make possible, not for the choices themselves.

Doing this research has been a personal journey for me, for I have had to examine my prejudices as well. My own life has been largely traditional, in spite of my interest in people who have chosen other options. Writing this book has been the same exercise in awareness for me that I hope it will be for those who read it. In the past three years, my eyes have been opened in many ways. In some cases, I have seen people find satisfaction in relationships I might have thought to be intolerable, and this has forced me to consider the value of their insights. In other cases, I have witnessed all the sad, misguided, and destructive things people do when they are desperately lonely or separated from the mainstream. In the process, I have learned things I never knew before about love and commitment and the tenacity of the human spirit. Sometimes, in the middle of an interview, I would find myself experiencing both distaste and admiration at the same time.

For me, the work of the past three years has started in motion an exploration process that I plan to continue in future writings. At the back of this book is a survey titled *Ties That Bind: A National Survey of Family Living Styles.* Its aim is to identify the many different ways that people today are living. In addition to its appearance in this book, it will also be made available to thousands of other Americans through periodicals and organizations. Once we begin to discover and accept the multitude of family styles that are being lived out all around us, we can start the task of formulating a new model for what family might look like in the next century. The most important thing is to keep the dialogue moving forward.

CHAPTER TWO

The Study:
Love Between Gay Men
and Straight Women

It is only in relations of the deepest intimacy that we
can allow to another person the same complexity of
nature which we know to be our own. That is, with
such individuals, we can stop making
presuppositions and merely accept, as we do with
our own selves, that there is no need to define them,
no need to seek for patterns or shapes, no need to
say that he or she is such and such a type.

—from *Incline Our Hearts*,
A. N. Wilson

I AM NOT a scientist, and mine is not a scientific report.
Nor is it a definitive study of sexuality and modern relationships. Many times in the course of talking to individuals
and groups, I have been asked for answers and assurances
I was not qualified to give. Mostly, people have wanted to
know if they were doing the "right" thing. Or if their mixed
feelings would ever go away. How could I possibly answer
those questions? I could only tell them what other people in
similar situations had told me.

At first, this inability to be definitive troubled me. There
is a comfort in having a statistical analysis to support a
clearly posed premise. But over time, I reached the conclusion that maybe we have depended too much on statistics to
define who we are in our relationships. Statistics only seem
to appeal to the deeper fears we have that ask, "Am I normal?"; they lead people to seek validity not in their own

experiences, but in their conformance to norms. It is better, sometimes, to listen to and absorb the honest human expressions, without the distraction of trying to fit people into predetermined slots on a chart.

In reviewing the information on the questionnaires, which included both multiple-choice and reflective questions,* I frequently found that there was a disparity between the points checked off in the multiple-choice sections and the more descriptive explanations that followed. This further demonstrated to me that there is a natural ''accuracy gap'' when people are asked to select one of several responses to questions about deeply felt emotional issues. Many respondents reported being frustrated by the limitations of the multiple-choice questions; many included several pages of added commentary.

For these reasons, it is my feeling that the statistical results outlined in this chapter are perhaps less illuminating and useful to discussion than the lengthier interviews and responses that are described in the rest of the book.

Finally, as many social scientists have observed, it is impossible to be completely scientific, in the objective sense, when evaluating human behavior, since those who do the evaluating are human as well, and approach the research with a particular point of view. In that respect, I have written this book from a highly personal position, talking to and getting to know many of the respondents. What I report on here is not only what they have told me, but also what I have seen and heard and felt. It has never been my intention to prove a point—that would be impossible, given the diversity of the people and circumstances I have encountered. Rather, my goal is to open a window on the lives of people who have chosen to stake their commitments in unusual territories. My expectation for the ultimate value of this document is that it will encourage a more open-minded view of the scope of legitimate options available to people who

---

*See Appendix A for a complete summary of the research methodology, the questionnaire, and the statistical results.

seek personal fulfillment and loving partnerships in our chaotic times.

But how representative is this research of current patterns? Do the respondents characterize a trend or an aberration? It is impossible to ascertain how statistically representative the respondents might be. It is very difficult—if not impossible—to accurately measure the scope of behaviors that are so often cloaked in secrecy. However, the research, conducted over a period of nearly three years, was designed to generate the highest possible response using both random and defined samplings. These are the results:

RANDOM SAMPLING:
The random research was conducted this way: Advertisements were placed in ten popular national magazines (some of them more than once), requesting responses from gay or bisexual men in "committed" or "love" relationships with women, or from women in "committed" or "love" relationships with gay or bisexual men. Publications were not selected in an entirely random way, as some consideration was given to the likelihood that readers would be responsive to the topic of the survey.

The publications used for research included:

The Advocate	(2 ads)
Bisexuality	(1 ad)
Harpers	(1 ad)
Mother Jones	(2 ads)
The Nation	(1 ad)
New Age	(1 ad)
The New York Review of Books	(2 ads)
The Progressive	(2 ads)
Psychology Today	(2 ads)
The Village Voice	(2 ads)
Total advertisements:	16

The exact text of the ad varied according to the publication; in all, I used six different texts in an effort to elicit a broader variety of responses. The ads appeared under the heading "Relationship Research" and read:

AUTHOR SEEKS INPUT FROM "NONTRADITIONAL" COUPLES; GAY MEN/STRAIGHT WOMEN, BISEXUALS, SEXUALLY NON-MONOGAMOUS, CELIBATE BUT COMMITTED COUPLES . . .

WRITER SEEKS COMMUNICATION WITH WOMEN WHO LOVE GAY MEN AND GAY MEN IN LOVE RELATIONSHIPS WITH WOMEN . . .

ARE YOU A WOMAN WHO HAS LOVED A GAY MAN OR A GAY MAN WHO HAS BEEN IN A LOVE RELATIONSHIP WITH A WOMAN? WRITER NEEDS INPUT FOR BOOK RESEARCH.

AUTHOR SEEKS COMMUNICATION WITH GAY FATHERS FOR BOOK RESEARCH.

GAY MEN AND STRAIGHT WOMEN: DO YOU HAVE A GAY/STRAIGHT LOVE MATCH?

AUTHOR SEEKS INPUT FROM GAY OR BISEXUAL MEN WHO ARE IN HETEROSEXUAL RELATIONSHIPS.

Those who responded to the advertisements were sent a lengthy questionnaire. Of those who filled out the questionnaires, a sampling was selected for further personal or telephone interviews.

The demographics of the random survey are as follow:

TOTAL RESPONDENTS FROM RANDOM SAMPLING: 722

Male Respondents from Random Sampling:
Number of responses: 375

Age range of male respondents:

18–25:	39
26–35:	115
36–50:	147
Over 50:	55
Not known:	19

Current marital status of male respondents:

Married:	174
Separated:	65
Divorced:	32
Widowed:	12
Committed partners:	78
Not known:	14

Occupation of male respondents:

Professional:	75
Business/service:	87
Industrial:	39
Education/ social services:	98
Arts/entertainment:	24
Government/ military:	17
Clergy:	4
Student:	10
Not known:	21

Residence of male respondents:

Alabama	8
Alaska	4
Arizona	15
California	40
Colorado	12
Connecticut	12
District of Columbia	23
Georgia	5
Florida	16

Illinois	19
Indiana	14
Kansas	12
Louisiana	10
Maine	2
Maryland	6
Massachusetts	11
Michigan	7
Missouri	1
New Hampshire	3
New Jersey	31
New Mexico	5
New York	32
North Carolina	5
Ohio	13
Oklahoma	6
Oregon	3
Pennsylvania	15
Texas	13
Washington	5
West Virginia	10
Wisconsin	2
Canada	4
Europe	1
Unknown	10

Female Respondents from Random Sampling:
Number of respondents: 347

Age range of respondents:
18–25:	62
26–35:	87
36–50:	130
Over 50:	41
Not known:	27

Current marital status of respondents:
Married:	185

Separated:	28
Divorced:	40
Widowed:	13
Committed partners:	60
Not known:	21

Occupation of female respondents:

Professional:	89
Business/service:	62
Industrial:	18
Education/ social services:	85
Arts/ entertainment:	26
Government/ military:	7
Homemaker:	25
Student:	19
Not known:	16

Residence of female respondents:

Arizona	10
California	44
Colorado	18
Connecticut	8
District of Columbia	15
Florida	22
Illinois	16
Indiana	10
Kansas	4
Louisiana	8
Maryland	13
Michigan	15
New Jersey	26
New Mexico	3
New York	44
North Carolina	2
Ohio	21

Oregon	6
Pennsylvania	12
South Carolina	2
Texas	14
Utah	1
Vermont	1
Washington	9
West Virginia	8
Wisconsin	7
Canada	7
Europe	1

SELECTED SAMPLING:
In addition to the random research, I selected a number of
established groups, contacting more than 50 organizations
nationwide. Those who agreed to participate in the study
included:

Gay Married Men's Association—GAMMA
(Washington, DC)

GAMMA Wives
(Washington, DC)

Review—Bisexual and Married Men
(Westchester, IL)

Gay Married Men's Support Group
(St. Louis, MO)

Gay Married Men's Association—GAMMA
(Minneapolis/St. Paul, MN)

Bisexual and Married Gay Men
(Cleveland, OH)

Wives of Gay/Bisexual Men
(Cleveland, OH)

Bi-Ways
(Washington, DC)

Bi-Social Center
(Van Nuys, CA)

South Bay Gay Parents
(San Jose, CA)

Gay Fathers of Greater New Haven
(New Haven, CT)

The involvement of these groups included:
1. Questionnaires distributed to members
2. Notice of research published in newsletters
3. Focus group workshops
4. Personal interviews with members

TOTAL RESPONDENTS FROM DEFINED SAMPLING: 288

Male Respondents from Defined Sampling:
Number of male respondents: 195

Age range of male respondents:
18–25:	21
26–35:	70
36–50:	74
Over 50:	22
Not known:	8

Current marital status of male respondents:
Married:	113
Separated:	26
Divorced:	29
Widowed:	2
Committed partners:	15
Not known:	10

Occupation of male respondents:
Professional: 61
Business/service: 43
Industrial: 12
Education/
  social services: 36
Arts/
  entertainment: 7
Government/
  military: 22
Clergy: 2
Student: 3
Not known: 9

Residence of male respondents:
California   39
Connecticut   27
District of Columbia 22
Illinois   21
Maryland   17
Minnesota   18
Missouri   15
New York   9
Virginia   27

Female Respondents from Defined Sampling:
Number of female respondents: 113

Age range of female respondents:
18–25:   12
26–35:   41
36–50:   36
Over 50:   11
Not known: 13

Current marital status of female respondents:
Married: 85

Separated: 10
Divorced: 6
Widowed: 2
Committed partners: 4
Not known: 6

Occupation of female respondents:
Professional: 20
Business/service: 27
Industrial: 3
Education/
    social services: 18
Arts/
    entertainment: 3
Government/
    military: 3
Homemaker: 25
Student: 6
Not known: 8

Residence of female respondents:
District of Columbia   24
Illinois   14
Maryland   15
Minnesota   17
Missouri   16
Virginia   27

Beyond strictly demographic information, the participants in the study also represented a number of partnership types and circumstances. As I began to see the diversity of the respondents, I established a number of categories as a starting point for evaluating the responses. These were:

- Gay men and straight women in committed long-term or married relationships where the man's homosexuality was known from the beginning

- Gay men and straight women in committed long-term or married relationships where the man's homosexuality was revealed later in the relationship

- Gay men and straight women in committed long-term or married relationships where the man's homosexuality was not known by the woman

- Gay men and straight women in committed long-term or married relationships that were sexually monogamous

- Gay men and straight women in committed long-term or married relationships that were not sexually monogamous

- Gay men and straight women in committed long-term or married relationships that did not involve a sexual relationship

- Gay men and straight women in both sexual and nonsexual partnerships that were perceived to be a temporary means of achieving certain goals

- Gay men who chose marriage or committed relationships with women because of tradeoffs, which included the desire to have children, a preference for traditional family styles, and safety from discrimination in the community or the workplace

- Gay men who chose relationships with women because they found them more emotionally satisfying

- Gay men who chose relationships with women because they were not able to accept their own homosexuality and found gay life threatening

- Men who identified themselves as bisexual and had been in many relationships with both men and women, although sexually they preferred men. (Rarely, among study respondents, did self-identified bisexual men profess a sexual preference for women.)

- Women who didn't know that their husbands and lovers were gay or bisexual until they were deeply involved

- Women who preferred being with gay men and sought out relationships with them

While the focus of my research was not to examine lesbian relationships, I also heard from a number of lesbian couples, and in several cases, straight men who were involved in relationships with lesbian women. These respondents wondered why my focus excluded them. It is not my intention to communicate that these relationships are not important or worthy of study. However, I purposely focused my research in one arena of nontraditional relationships so that I could explore it more thoroughly.

By utilizing both random and selected sources to collect the data for this book, I feel that a representative cross section of the population has been researched. The respondents cover a wide span of age groups, professions, and geographic locations. Those whose stories are told in greater detail were selected for further interviews with an attention to finding a variety of circumstances and points of view.

Even as I write, I continue to receive mail from all over the country. Some of it will come too late to be included in this book. But the enthusiasm of the response reflects the possibility that this book only begins to scratch the surface of a far greater population of men and women. All along, that has been the most satisfying thing for me: the outpouring of response from those who want to talk about their uncommon lives and uncommon loves and in some way contribute to the ongoing dialogue about finding committed love in our times.

The Survey Responses

Through their answers to the survey, which included separate sets of questions for men and women, the respondents

articulated their thoughts and feelings regarding fundamental issues. These included: the meaning of sexual identity;
the roots of attraction; the relationship between sexuality
and love; the extent to which respondents experienced ambiguity about their choices; the attitudes of both respondents and their partners about central issues such as
monogamy, safe sex, family responsibility versus personal
freedom, and the importance of establishing long-term
versus short-term relationships.

The portrait that emerged was complex and, as I mentioned earlier, difficult to measure with any kind of "scientific" precision. However, when all of the responses were
calculated, a number of themes prevailed.**

THE MEN

**More than half the men said they had
known they were homosexual for many years.**

Of the male respondents, 52 percent said they had known
they were gay for many years, even preceding their relationships with women, while only 26 percent said they had
realized more recently the fact of their homosexual identity.

However, the way one knows or doesn't know one's homosexual leanings is not always cut and dried. For example,
John, a thirty-three-year-old Tennessee lawyer, talked about
having feelings very early on that he simply dismissed because they were so out of sync with his environment. "It
was so unthinkable in my conservative Southern family that
I never believed my feelings were real," he said. "I always
figured I'd fall in love and get married to a woman, and
that's what I did."

If the motivation is strong enough, denial can be complete, and, like John, many of the men responding to my
survey simply closed their minds initially to the possibility
of their homosexuality. For them, true self-disclosure came

**Response percentages do not always total 100 since some questions called for respondents to check more than one answer.

later, but they were more or less content with their family lives in the meantime.

Eighteen percent of the respondents reported that they would like to establish a sexual relationship with men, but were afraid to pursue such a relationship. These men usually reported their reasons as fear of disclosure that might lead to the collapse of family, career, or social position. A smaller group—8 percent—said that they were uncomfortable with and had not yet come to terms with their homosexual leanings. The context for their discomfort was often a "moral" one; for example, a number of clergy and religious fundamentalists admitted to having homosexual attractions, but said they believed it would be morally wrong to act on these attractions.

Although nearly all of the respondents had experienced at least one homosexual encounter in adulthood, they did not necessarily consider this to be compelling evidence that they were homosexual—especially when they were also involved with women.

**Most men reported feeling at least
some attraction for both men and women.**
It is commonly believed that if a man is homosexual, he cannot possibly feel sexually attracted to a woman. But 64 percent of the men said that although their sexual attraction to men was stronger, they had also experienced satisfying sexual relationships with women. However, of these, only 22 percent actually identified themselves as being "bisexual." Another 11 percent said they were not sure whether they were homosexual or bisexual.

One man, who was typical of respondents, wrote: "I first considered my sexual orientation when I was sixteen and was very upset over the possibility that I was gay—I thought I needed help. An eighteen-year-old friend, with whom I was sexually involved, suggested that I was bisexual and therefore not 'sick.' Another friend arranged a sexual encounter for me with a twenty-two-year-old woman, and she and I had sex many times. As a result of these experiences,

I considered myself bisexual for many years. I was always very open about my sexual orientation. It became clear that most men self-identified as 'gay' had also had sex with women. At the same time, I'd had sex with many men who considered themselves 'straight.' I later discovered that Alfred Kinsey had the same problem. His continuum of sexual orientation was a tool that made sense of my life—sort of a sexual compass. It made it easier for me to have a satisfying love/friend/sex relationship with my wife, and also understand my need to have men in my life.'' (See Chapter Three for a description of the Kinsey sexual continuum.)

Another man, who identified himself as a biologist and geneticist, said, ''Far too many people think you're 'gay' or 'not gay.' I don't think that's the way of nature. Human beings are much more complex than that.''

In identifying themselves as homosexual or bisexual, many respondents often made distinctions between preference and behavior. In other words, a man might identify himself as homosexual, but in practice be bisexual. The distinction had to do with the clarity of one's preference. ''Someone who is truly bisexual might be equally content having relations with either men or women,'' proposed one man. ''It would be like being sexually ambidextrous. That doesn't describe me. I prefer sex with men. I can be sexually satisfied with women, but I don't seek them out.''

Men were threatened by the prospect of admitting their homosexuality openly.

Only 32 percent of the male respondents admitted to being openly homosexual, and of these, many qualified the word ''openly'' by noting they were only open with certain people. And 68 percent said they lived publicly as *heterosexuals*. While the men articulated an almost universal acceptance of their own sexuality, they believed that public disclosure would hurt them in their professions, families, or communities.

Twenty-two percent of the men were involved with or married to women who did not know they were homosexual. These relationships often seemed characterized by problems with communication and intimacy, with the men reporting sexual frustration, resentment, a feeling of being trapped, and fear of disclosure. When the truth was not known by the women in their lives, 92 percent of these men agreed with the statement, ''I feel as if I am living a lie when I am with her.''

The most commonly expressed fear was that the woman would not understand and would end the relationship, making it impossible for the man to have contact with his children. One man wrote, ''I am not proud of myself for keeping this a secret. But in past relationships, I found that being open and out front about my sexuality just led to bitterness, hurt, and the end of the relationship. Because of these previous experiences, my justification for not telling my wife is that it is the best thing for our marriage.''

Another said, ''Keeping my homosexuality from my wife is obviously duplicitous. I would like to have a truly open and free marriage with no hidden areas. But frankly, I can see no way of making it work. My wife has been happy with me (or gives every evidence of being so) and I have been happy with her for the past twenty years. I cannot compromise our continued happiness. Seeing friends and relations go through messy relationships and many divorces makes me see how lucky we are.''

There were many viewpoints on the issue of telling or not telling spouses and loved ones about one's homosexuality. But typically, men who were not honest with the women in their lives found it very difficult to maintain the deception over time. ''I used to think,'' one said, ''that what she didn't know wouldn't hurt her. But as our marriage becomes increasingly strained, I have to face the fact that my hidden life may be somewhat responsible for that. I have concluded that it will be necessary for me to tell her the truth, and I am currently working with a therapist to help me handle her reaction.''

Because we are inclined to stereotype homosexuals and homosexual behavior, many people might wonder how the women could not have known or guessed that their partners were gay. But most of these men described their partnerships and sexual behavior within the relationship as being "normal"; as with most people, their sex lives went through ups and downs. Furthermore, the stereotypical behavior evidenced in the effeminate male is more a cultural style than the natural outcome of sexual orientation. Homosexual men do not necessarily "look gay" or "act gay."

Most men reported that women responded positively when informed of their partners' homosexuality.
Fifty-eight percent of the men said women who learned of their homosexuality after they became involved were open to pursuing the relationship, although most also said the women felt hurt or confused when they learned the men were sexually attracted to other men. Twenty-four percent of the men reported that the women with whom they were involved could not accept their homosexuality and were not willing to maintain the relationship; 12 percent of them said that their partners, upon learning of their homosexuality, agreed to maintain a friendship, but on a more casual, less committed basis.

When women agreed to pursue the relationship, men reported that the process of reaching satisfactory compromises was often more difficult than they had expected. For example, 27 percent said their partners insisted on sexual monogamy, something that was often hard for the men to accept.

It appeared from their related comments that men who characterized their relationships as close and honest were also those who found it possible to reach satisfying compromises. When the relationships were strained and characterized by little free and open communication, the women were less able to come to terms with the revelation and more likely to want out of the relationship.

Most men agreed that decisions about commitment were based on more than sexual preference.
Only 12 percent of the men said they felt that sexual attraction was the most important factor in establishing a relationship. And only 4 percent believed that their physical attraction to men was so all-encompassing that they had to pursue a partnership with a man. (I do not intend this to imply in any way that this is indicative of most gay men. It only says that for some gay men, sexual preference has a lesser pull. All people differ in the amount of importance they place on sexual activity.)

There are many different factors that enter into a decision about which course of life to pursue. For 68 percent of the respondents, the most important issue was love for the individual person. These men acknowledged that they could have a committed relationship with either a man or a woman, as long as there was love.

Another factor in making partnership choices was the perception that the tradeoffs were worth the sacrifices. For 50 percent of the men, the benefits outweighed the negatives, as they considered their personal needs and priorities. These needs included the desire to have children; the attraction of a "traditional" lifestyle; the need to have a close, permanent companion; and the belief that strong emotional attachments were preferable to strong erotic attachments. Some men reported feeling more emotionally fulfilled with women, even though their primary sexual attraction was for men.

Twenty-six percent of the men admitted that they might prefer to be with a man, but they could not tolerate what was perceived to be the "gay lifestyle." Said one man, "I am very traditional in my wants and needs. I prefer to live a quiet life with a permanent partner. My sexual attraction to men may be strong, but my attraction to the homosexual life is zero."

Sex wasn't necessarily the primary measure of love and attraction.

Forty-nine percent of the men agreed with this statement about the women they were involved with: "I love her and I want to be with her. Sexual preference is secondary." However, with that in mind, 80 percent said their ideal would be to remain with their female partners and also be free to pursue close relationships with men. In considering the idea of dual commitments, almost all men voiced a preference for having a single, permanent or semi-permanent male lover, as opposed to pursuing casual sex. This preference was related to concerns about AIDS as well as to the sense that casual affairs were less satisfying over the long term. A man who admitted to having had as many as 300 different sex partners before he met and married his wife, said, "AIDS hasn't caused my desire to be more monogamous. Rather, the awareness about AIDS came along at a point when I was already feeling the emptiness of casual sex. I now seek only relationships with people who are willing to relate to me on all levels and know me as a human being, not just an object for sexual gratification." Another 27 percent of the men said that the relationships they had with women fulfilled certain needs, but were not perceived as "permanent."

Many men reported being confused by the meaning of their attraction to women, particularly when they did not identify themselves as bisexual. Sometimes the conflict was resolved when they became more accepting of their own homosexuality. For example, one man wrote, "An intense, intellectual attraction led us to a whirlwind courtship and marriage that took us both by surprise. We seemed fabulously matched—were wonderful partners in travel, work, and school. But eventually, sex became a problem, and we danced around it for about five years. I see now that my attraction to her stirred my libido. Maybe I thought she could make me straight. It didn't last."

In other cases, respondents reported that strong emotional and intellectual attractions led to increased physical attraction to the women they were with—although most of these felt a need to have physical relationships with men as well. In male-female partnerships where sexual fidelity was practiced, men often said they were comfortable with the choice because they so strongly believed that it was "right." As one said, "I am free to make a commitment to whomever I choose. No one is holding a gun to my head. But once I make that commitment, it would be wrong for me to compromise it through casual sex outside the relationship."

**Love relationships with women
varied in their sexual context.**
The largest group of men—45 percent—reported that their love relationships with women were sexual, but not exclusive. This number included the 6 percent who said they did not view their sexual relationships with women as being permanent. Only 28 percent reported having sexually exclusive relationships with women that they also considered to be permanent partners. Those in sexually exclusive relationships agreed with the statement, "I prefer men, but am content to limit my sexual relationship to this woman because I love her." Those in nonexclusive relationships agreed with the statement, "It is also necessary to have sex with men."

Twenty-eight percent of the men said that they were content to have sex with either men or women, although bisexually motivated relationships rarely remained permanent, since there was a reluctance to choose one or the other.

Thirty-four percent of the men reported having intense, "intimate," nonsexual relationships with women. In these relationships, intimacy was defined in a number of ways. Among them were various forms of physical intimacy which included kissing, hugging, touching, and sleeping together but not genital or oral sex; primary emotional attachments in which partners were considered "significant others"; and very strong feelings of warmth, love, and desire that were not expressed physically.

The intimate nonsexual relationships were the most difficult for men to understand and come to terms with. Those

who were definite about being homosexual, rather than bisexual, often had trouble identifying the ''pull'' of emotions
that did not translate into sexual desire. Some of these men
admitted to convincing themselves they were bisexual, if
only to better explain their attraction to women, realizing
later that the bisexual label was a fabrication. The intimate,
nonsexual relationships that appeared to be most satisfying
were those in which the women understood and accepted
the terms of the relationship, and in which both partners
believed they were gaining substantially from being together. But even when compromises were successfully
negotiated, unexpected issues emerged.

"Geraldine and I had what I would term a very enlightened
relationship,'' one man said. ''We were closer in mind and
spirit than either of us had been with any other people in our
lives. But the strength of our relationship was never understood or accepted by our lovers. It always came down to
making a choice: 'him or me,' 'her or me.' I think this is
unfortunate, because I really believe that as humans we are
capable of filling different needs with different people. But
most people are too insecure to accept anything but a completely exclusive attachment that seems more like ownership
than love.''

**Many men said that the closest people
in their lives had always been women.**
For the 36 percent of men who agreed that the closest people in their lives had always been women, there were a variety of explanations. Among the perceptions about women
that led the men to form strong attachments were:

- Women were seen as deeper and more reflective, men
  as more superficial.

- Women were better at friendship because they were
  more willing to make commitments.

- Women were more open about sharing their feelings

and less judgmental when the men expressed deeply
felt doubts and fears.

- Women were more willing to make sacrifices for the
  sake of the relationship.

- Compared with other gay men, women were less concerned with physical appearance, sexual performance,
  and age.

- Women often shared more interests in common with
  the men.

In fact, 54 percent of the men said they had been seriously involved in relationships with women in the past; the
average number of these relationships was three.

As we will discuss in a later chapter, these perceptions
sometimes lead homosexual men to choose relationships
with women as a way of hiding from the more emotionally
threatening idea of pursuing a relationship with a male lover.
Relationships that are formed as a means of escape rarely
turn out well in the long run. Unconfronted fears do not
disappear; they only grow more threatening, as illustrated
by one man's story:

"Every time I felt strongly attracted to a man, my attraction turned into a monster. I got swept up in my emotions
and couldn't control them. Usually, I became very possessive and fearful of losing him. When the relationships ended,
as all of them did, I was thrown into such despair that I
couldn't function for weeks or even months. It seemed that
I was always suffering. When my desire wasn't reciprocated, I was miserable because I wanted him so much; when
my desire was reciprocated, I was miserable because I was
afraid I would lose him. Eventually, I began to withdraw
and block my feelings. They were too dangerous for me."

Most people would probably agree that the stronger the
desire, the greater the loss when it goes unmet. For some
gay men, choosing to be with women allowed them to cir-
cumvent the unruly and painful feelings surrounding love

and loss. These heterosexual relationships were comfortable and devoid of "sexual tension." But since so many areas were off-limits, and since they seemed to be based on escape rather than enrichment, it is questionable how "good" these relationships really were. On the other hand, men seemed to benefit more fully from attachments to women based on honest attraction, whether they were close friendships or committed partnerships.

Couples struggled with commitment, monogamy, and safety.

Men who were married or involved in serious relationships with women reported that the meaning of commitment and the importance of monogamy topped the list of issues couples struggled with, with 47 percent listing commitment and 45 percent listing monogamy. The specific issues included:

- The possibility of a committed relationship without monogamy

- The woman's fear that the man might someday leave her for a more permanent partnership with a man

- The maintenance of a nontraditional partnership on a permanent basis

- The balancing of family responsibility with personal freedom

Some men claimed to have no doubts about the relationship, but reported that their partners needed regular reassurance that the relationship was solid. "Sometimes I get angry with my wife, because she doesn't believe me when I tell her I'm happy in the marriage," complained one man. Another took a more sympathetic view, saying, "I wish she could relax, but I can understand her concerns. How many women have to deal with their husbands attending gay social groups twice a week?"

Next on the list of primary concerns was the prevention

of sexually transmitted diseases, with the threat of AIDS being at the forefront of respondents' minds. Forty-two percent listed "safe sex" as being a primary issue; even those who were sexually monogamous with their wives maintained a concern that they might already have contracted the AIDS virus. Nearly all the men made a point of saying that they were taking the threat of AIDS seriously. In addition to specific sexual practices, this meant seeking a permanent male sex partner and being regularly tested.

Finally, 22 percent of the men listed moral values and religious beliefs as being the primary concern of their relationships. Included in this group were:

- Couples affiliated with religious institutions that considered homosexuality immoral

- Couples affiliated with religious institutions that considered sexual relations outside of marriage immoral

- Couples with long-held moral beliefs that made them uncomfortable with relationships of sexual ambiguity

- Couples who struggled with each other's strongly held values about monogamy and commitment

It is not surprising that the more rigidly dogmatic the belief system, the more serious the crisis. One man, a Fundamentalist Christian minister, described a constant battle with his "good" and "evil" sides that, he said, was tearing him apart. For the most part, those whose behavior or desires were inconsistent with their belief systems were tremendously unhappy and, in at least two cases, reported being suicidal. They seemed to feel that there was no way to reach a satisfying solution.

THE WOMEN

Many women chose homosexual men as partners.
Only 36 percent of the women reported not knowing their

partners were homosexual until they were deeply involved in the relationship or even married. Forty percent said they knew when they met their partners, while another 24 percent said they learned of their partners' homosexuality in the early stages of the relationship.

This seemed to be one of the more meaningful revelations of the study, for it dispelled the myth that most women who are involved with homosexual men have been "tricked" into the relationships. "He was very honest with me," said one woman. "I knew there would be complications if I got involved with him, but it seemed to be worth it, since we had so many other things going for us."

The majority reported never before having had a (known) relationship with a homosexual.

Sixty-seven percent of the women said that they had not been involved with homosexual men in the past. These women were either surprised by their mate's homosexuality long into the relationship, or surprised by their own attraction to a gay man early in the relationship. "When I met him, I knew Peter was gay," said one. "When he expressed a sexual interest, I was very surprised. He told me he had had a number of relationships with women in the past, but he usually preferred to be with men. Ultimately, the fact that he could enjoy sex with me, combined with all of the other positive aspects of our relationship, convinced me that I would be happy with him."

Of the 26 percent of women who said they had been involved with other homosexual men in the past, 17 percent of these had only had one other relationship. But 9 percent reported having repeated relationships with homosexuals. As we discuss in Chapter Six, the minority of women who prefer involvement with homosexual men over involvement with heterosexual men usually have false expectations or are using the relationships to avoid what is perceived as a more threatening intimacy with a heterosexual man. Some women admitted to having had frightening encounters in childhood with a sexually abusive relative or violent father. For them, homosexual men represented a safe, gentle alternative to what they believed to be the violence of heterosexual men. Their approach to relationships was similar to that described for homosexual men who said they had their most important relationships with women.

Many women found themselves attracted to "qualities" they believed gay men to have.

Fifty-four percent of the women admitted having a special attraction to gay men. These women said they believed that gay men possessed certain positive qualities that the women were drawn to. These qualities included sensitivity, humor, warmth and compassion, creativity, interest in women as being more than sex objects, willingness to express emotions, spiritual and intellectual depth, and liberated behavior. Of course, all homosexual men do not possess these qualities, any more than all heterosexual men treat women like sex objects. But when asked about the specific qualities that attracted them to their partners, these women often listed some or all of these characteristics.

Levels of intimacy and sexual activity varied among relationships.

Thirty percent of the women claimed to have sexually exclusive, permanent relationships with homosexual men. It might be more accurate to describe this as their "perception" rather than as fact. In some instances, men whose wives or partners had termed their relationship as being sexually exclusive, revealed that they were secretly engaging in relationships on the outside. In the most common scenario, the woman demanded sexual fidelity and the man agreed in order to save the relationship, justifying his duplicity by arguing that it was better to keep the marriage or partnership solid than to reveal the truth. I have little doubt that these relationships contain ticking time bombs.

Another 18 percent of the women reported having sexual relationships that were not exclusive. These "open" terms were usually initiated at the man's request, and the women rarely took advantage of them to have outside relationships of their own. In later questioning, women in non-monogamous relationships said almost across the board that they would have preferred monogamy, but believed it was the only way to keep their relationships intact.

Twenty-eight percent of the women said that their relationships did not include sex, but could be characterized as "intense" or "intimate." This intimacy included much physical contact such as kissing, hugging, and touching; the ability to talk freely about deeply felt issues; sharing of common interests and values; and the intense desire to be together. In some cases, these relationships became permanent or semipermanent "platonic marriages."

Women tended to be understanding about their men's homosexuality and to try to make the relationships work.

A full 70 percent of the women agreed with this description of their attitudes about a partner's homosexuality: "I accept it and it doesn't affect my love or commitment." However, of these women, 28 percent admitted that they were still "very pained" by the situation. And 8 percent said that they had accepted the situation, but were afraid that their acceptance was theoretical—if confronted with the fact that their partners were seeing men, these women said they would probably be very upset.

Twenty-eight percent of the women said they could not accept their partner's homosexuality. Of these, 10 percent said they were bitter about the situation—for the most part, they had only become aware of the truth long into the relationship and felt that they were in some way cheated. Said one, "He says he didn't realize himself that he was gay until last year, but how can I believe that? How could he not have known? I sometimes think he has arranged things so he'll have everything he wants . . . a wife, children, security, and his freedom, too. But what about me? I'm the one who is trapped."

The remainder of those who could not accept their partners' homosexuality did not express bitterness as much as regret that they could not stay with their partners permanently. ''I know this is not what he wants,'' wrote one woman sadly. ''I could never be at ease, knowing he might be feeling unhappy with me. It's better that we go our separate ways now, even though I love him very much and I know he loves me.''

Many sexual issues concerned women.
Even when the marriage or partnership was strong and satisfying, almost every woman expressed concerns. Asked to express their feelings about the sexual aspects of their relationships, 35 percent said they believed their sex lives to be satisfying, but almost the same percentage—34 percent—characterized them as being lacking. Nineteen percent worried that their partners might only be pretending satisfaction. ''I am haunted by that worry,'' said one woman. ''My husband's attraction to men is something I can't understand, but I do understand that I'm not a man. How can he desire men and also desire me?'' Beneath this concern, there was the deeper fear, expressed by the 24 percent of the women who agreed with the statement, ''I am happy with him, but deep down I have the fear that he will someday leave me for a man.''

Forty percent of the women said they were afraid that their husbands and possibly themselves might get AIDS. Although most said they trusted their husbands to practice safe sex, they were aware that some danger still existed. And some resented having to practice safe sex themselves—''Imagine!'' said one. ''I have to have safe sex with my husband of twelve years!''—because it meant sacrificing some of their pleasure so their partners could have sexual relations with others outside the relationship. ''I wonder about my self-esteem sometimes,'' a married woman told me. ''I have been hearing for years that it's wrong for women to give up important parts of themselves to please their men. I ask myself if I've only agreed to go along because I'm afraid he'll leave me and I'll be alone.''

In spite of their concerns, 55 percent of the women agreed with the statement, "I believe that true love can exist apart from sexual preference."

"There are so many nuances to love," observed one woman. "So many shades and colors. This relationship has given me a chance to experience things that are new to me. Sometimes I get scared, but those feelings never last, because I believe what we have together is so good."

These are the reactions of some one thousand men and women who answered the questions posed by the study. This information gives us a foundation for looking more deeply into the nature of these relationships. In the following chapters we will meet many of these men and women and become close-up observers of their lives as they struggle with fundamental questions of love and commitment.

CHAPTER THREE

Living Amid the Ruins of the Sexual Revolution

Life is aimless: a little love, a little hate, and then—
good day! Life is short: a little hope, a little
dreaming, and then—goodnight!

—Leon Montenaeken

THERE ARE MILLIONS of refugees from the sexual revolution—nomads who have long since tired of the journey and who no longer thrill to the chase. The bloom has been off the rose of sexual freedom for a while, and sometimes it seems that a deep-rooted cynicism has replaced the giddiness of an earlier liberty. Talk to anyone and you hear stories not of enlightenment and contentment but of hurt, guilt, and disappointment.

We need only to peruse the titles of the best-selling self-help books to recognize that something has gone terribly wrong with relationships. We expected so much and got so little, and we wonder all over again what it is we are really looking for when we look for love.

In one way or another, everyone is afraid of being left to maneuver the rough terrain of life alone. We seek someone who has a knowledge of us, who sees us as we are—or at least as we think we are. Perhaps once we believed that this knowledge would grow naturally from sex, since physical intimacy takes us so deep inside another person's private territory. But as we gained the freedom to express ourselves sexually, we also learned how to have sex without intimacy and found it easy to close our eyes and make our partners faceless. We could blithely share our most private physical selves with people who were not our friends—people we may not even have liked, much less loved. Strangers. Sex became an act that was separate from intimacy, rather than an acknowledgment of mutual respect and trust. And this so-called freedom took its toll.

In *Alone in America,* author Louise Bernikow speaks poignantly of the cultural dilemma we face, saying of the people she interviewed:

> People talked about the feeling of belonging to something, the feeling of membership. Older people missed the feeling of belonging to communities and to families. Younger people missed the Sixties. A large segment of the population now has a memory of membership. Some mean simply the tribal feeling that existed among their generation in the Sixties—shared styles in clothing and culture. Some mean something more profound and more active. They remember civil rights marches and feminist actions and student protest and ending the war in Vietnam. They remember acting in concert with other people for a common goal they believed in. Their present lives have little of this feeling.

In the gay community, the bewildering spectre of AIDS enhanced the feelings of loneliness and disappointment. AIDS became like salt in the wound of an already-empty intimacy, just one more cruel legacy from a sexual revolution that suddenly seemed to be doing no one any good.

But with or without AIDS, there would have been disappointment, loneliness, questioning. As one couple's therapist said,

> We are sexual beings. But our mistake lies in simply equating sexuality with sex in an erotic way. Our sexuality is the sum total of who we are as individuals—the result of a series of genetic circumstances. But we have reduced ourselves to the erotic in a destructive way. When we express love of any kind—be it to a lover, friend, child, brother—we are acting out our sexuality, even though we are not necessarily acting erotically. When we

confuse the two, we place values on love that may be false. For example, who would ever say that the love a wife has for her husband is a *greater* love than that which she has for her child simply because the love of husband and wife also includes a certain physical intimacy?

It might be fair to say that sex has been a huge stumbling block for an entire generation of men and women who have lost a sense of "belonging" as they've discovered that sex can't create love and intimacy where it doesn't already exist.

Most of the people who participated in this study started out their adult lives with one ideal of love and sex, and ended up—usually to their surprise—choosing a different way altogether. Many ended up in relationships that felt right and filled certain needs, even when they didn't "compute" on any traditional compass. Others found that they could live happily with the kind of compromises they never would have dreamed were possible. Their stories are rich with insight, often moving, and sometimes shocking. They raise new questions about sexuality and lifestyle, the role of celibacy in loving relationships, the complexity of sexual identity, the value of sexual exclusivity in committed partnerships, and about what it means to "find" oneself in the aftermath of the sexual revolution.

Sexuality versus Lifestyle

Rick is a very straightforward man, tall and thin, with deep-set brown eyes that peer curiously at the world from behind thick glasses. We sat beside each other at a business seminar three years ago, talked, and decided to meet for lunch.

In the course of that first lunch, Rick let me know that he was gay. He had recently moved to New York from Philadelphia—in part to put an end to his twelve-year marriage, and in part to start a new business as a marketing consultant. He mentioned a man he had met at a party and who had become his lover. Rick was uneasy because the man was pressuring him to move in with him. "I lived with my wife for twelve years," he said. "I'm not ready for a committed relationship. I need a chance to be on my own for a while and figure out what I'm going to do."

Rick and I became friends and we met occasionally for dinner. I was curious about his lifestyle and I asked him a lot of questions. He was thirty-six years old, had been married most of his adult life, and was the father of two children—yet, now here he was, trying to become part of a gay world that afforded him little frame of reference. It scared him to death. He told me that the day he told his wife he was leaving was the worst day of his life. "I had been keeping this big secret for so long, but I knew once I told her, there would be no turning back. She was completely devastated, and so were my children. Ann insisted that I keep my reasons for leaving from them because they were too young to understand. But in a way that made it more traumatic for me. I had nothing to tell them—no excuses. I was just a cad."

"How long have you known you were gay?" I asked, and was surprised when he told me he first realized it when he was only fourteen.

"You knew you were gay when you married your wife?"

"I know it sounds like maybe I was trying to hide out and be straight, but it wasn't like that. I was never ashamed of being gay. It's more accurate to say that I was intimidated by what I'd call 'gay culture.' I decided to marry Ann because I was attracted to her and found that I really loved her. And also because I wanted all the things that went with a straight lifestyle—particularly having children. I desperately wanted to have children. At the time, being gay didn't seem to matter as much as marrying Ann and creating a home life with her and children."

"But it didn't last."

Rick sighed. "Midlife crisis, I suppose. I began to feel restless. There were parts of myself left unexplored. That's why I came to New York. I'm searching."

"And what are you finding?" I asked.

"Nothing I like very much," he laughed ruefully. "I'm too old to be playing this meat-market game. Most of the time, I feel ridiculous, and other gay men can sense it. It's like I'm not one of them. And in many ways, I'm not. I'm more comfortable at a backyard barbecue in suburban Philadelphia than I am in a gay bar."

I smiled. "Don't feel too bad. You're no different from any other single person. Everyone is looking for a relationship that's real—one that will last."

"I miss my kids so much. It's so stupid." His voice caught. "Sometimes I wonder, what am I *doing* here? I had a good marriage with Ann and I gave it up. I hurt her, I hurt my children, and I feel like I'm hurting myself, too. What's the point?"

I had known Rick nearly a year when he told me he was going back to his wife. "I'm lucky that she's taking me back," he said. "She's been great about it. Of course, I haven't told my gay friends yet, which is very funny—it's like I'm *sneaking* back to my wife. On the surface, it looks like a cop-out: I should stay and fight it out, find my 'true' self, whatever that means. But I think my true self is in Philadelphia with Ann and the kids. I simply don't enjoy life without them. And isn't that just as important? Nobody could accuse me of hiding. I'm simply making a choice that I have every right to make."

Initially, Rick's decision to return to his wife made me feel sad. It had taken great courage for him to set out on his quest, and he had failed. But later, as I thought more about it, I wondered if that evaluation was really accurate. As Rick put it, he had a right to make a choice about how he would live. And what had he chosen? Life with the people he loved and who loved him, rather than life in a world where he did not feel at home and where he was lonely. Maybe he had found himself after all.

A gay friend echoed this sentiment. "Being homosexual doesn't necessarily mean that you can tolerate the gay scene," he told me. "It isn't a very easy way to live. And different things are important to different people. We're not all cut from the same mold.''

"But isn't it a form of 'gay bashing' to suggest that men like Rick are better off with a woman?'' I asked, disturbed by the implications of his thinking.

"Sure, if you make a blanket statement, as some people do, and say that it's better for gay men in general to be with women and put aside these 'silly' ideas of being with men,'' he said, laughing. "That would be ridiculous. But every individual has to find his own way, and it's possible that Rick is better off. Who are we to say? He is free to choose his own path, whether *we* like it or not.''

I met a number of men like Rick as I was doing this research, and it was a learning experience for me. I had always assumed that if you were gay, it meant that you had an unfaltering set of antennae directed to gay life; in effect, you *had* to live in gay society—unless, of course, you were living in denial. Rick represented neither of these poles.

Homosexuals like Rick may be products of their times as much as anything. Homosexuality and homosexual behavior does not manifest itself apart from culture. Although most scientists are in agreement that the predisposition to homosexuality involves genetic factors and is not therefore a choice, it is also true that knowing this tells one little about how to live, whom to choose as a partner, or how to "be" in the world. Those choices are influenced as much by culture and personal priorities as they are by sexual identity. For example, in a society where living openly as a homosexual means forfeiting many important things—such as the opportunity to live with and raise children, or the social and legal protections of marriage—it is logical that some homosexuals would choose not to pursue that lifestyle.

Many people share the idea that being homosexual is primarily an erotic thing—that homosexuals exist as driven sexual beings, while heterosexuals are more reined in and more capable of living in nonsexual modes. But, while human beings may be sexual beings, they are not solely erotic beings, and it is absurd to suggest that other needs—for art, say, or good conversation, or religion, or the pleasures of parenting—are less central to the human condition.

From a social point of view, many of the men in this study made a clear distinction between being "homosexual" and being "gay." To them, the term "gay" referred to a certain set of lifestyle choices that had less to do with sex than with community. Perhaps what we've forgotten, in our eagerness to place labels on people, is that homosexuals are human beings first.

The Sexual Continuum

Goethe said, "Nature goes her own way, and all that to us seems an exception is really according to order." This point comes to mind when we examine human sexuality. In our desire to create a "rule" of behavior, we spend a lot of time listing exceptions, but these "exceptions" pile up eventually, straining the premise that the rule even exists. Naturally, some things are more the "rule," in that they are more common, but in doing this research, I learned that many common assumptions about sexuality simply don't hold true.

Many of the men who responded to my study used the Kinsey scale as a reference point for describing their sexual preference. Alfred Kinsey's concept of a sexual continuum caused a great deal of controversy when it was first published in his 1948 work, *Sexual Behavior in the Human Male.* The reasons for the controversy are obvious when we look at the findings of Kinsey's major survey. Kinsey blew apart the safe categories of sexual behavior (and, even more taboo, sexual *desire)* among men when he reported that 37 percent of the men interviewed had engaged in "some overt homosexual experience to the point of orgasm between adolescence and old age." This was a tremendously threatening discovery in 1948—and still might be today. When heterosexual men can separate themselves completely from

homosexuals, it is easier to justify a wide range of prejudices. Such a separation has also protected men from a
weakening of the heterosexual macho myth so central to our
understanding of family, social behavior, and the very
structure of power in our society.

Newer studies conducted by national research groups
in 1970 and 1988 appear to support Kinsey's 1948 data. The
1970 study was conducted by the Kinsey Institute for Sexual
Research, which surveyed 1,450 men in 1970. The 1988 report surveyed 638 men as a pilot project for a national study.
The data, which is not available as of this writing, will re-
portedly reveal a relatively high percentage of "bisexual"
behavior—men who have had homosexual contacts "occasionally" or "fairly often."

From his research, Kinsey developed the idea that sexual
preference, rather than being fixed, must be defined on a
continuum. He created a scale that ranged from 0, which
indicated *exclusive heterosexual behaviors and interests,* to
6, which indicated *exclusive homosexual behaviors and interests.* This scale helped loosen the restrictions felt by many
men in trying to explain the puzzling ambiguity of their
sexual natures. A man who termed himself a 0, using Kinsey's scale, might never have had any conscious desire to
be with another man sexually, while a man who termed
himself a 1 or 2 on the scale might view himself as primarily
heterosexual, while occasionally engaging in homosexual
fantasies or having two or three adult homosexual experiences. A man who viewed himself as a 4 or 5 on the scale
might be primarily homosexual, but have had sexual relationships with women on several occasions or even regularly. (It is likely that men on this end of the scale would
have more sexual experiences with women than men on the
other end of the scale would have with men, simply because
it is far more "acceptable." No doubt, with our society's
attitudes, primarily heterosexual men who have homosexual
fantasies or experiences are horrified by and fearful of
them.) A man who termed himself a 6 on Kinsey's scale

might never entertain any fantasies about women or feel any desire for sexual relations with them.

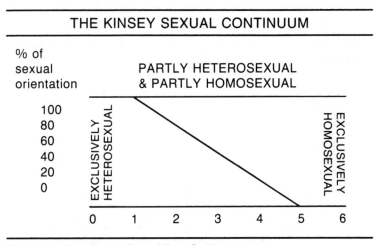

THE KINSEY SEXUAL CONTINUUM

(Kinsey scale; adapted from Alfred C. Kinsey et al.,
Sexual Behavior in the Human Male.)

Kinsey's premise blew the lid off the idea that sexual preferences and roles could be easily slotted into gay or straight. This is why a man who says that he is a 3.5 or 4, according to the Kinsey scale, might call himself homosexual, yet be able to have a satisfying sexual relationship with his wife; although his identity and preferences are homosexual, his sexual interests are not exclusively homosexual.

Kinsey's work also gives permission for humans to be human—that is, to be people who behave intentionally, rather than simply by reflex action. In *Sex Hormones and Behavior: A Critique of the Linear Model*, Ruth G. Doell and Helen E. Longino note that "there is a difference in character between the more stereotyped behavior of animals and many of the behaviors studied in humans, such as play activity, career choice, some higher cognitive performances, and choice of sexual partner." This distinction between intentional choice and reflex action does not deny inherent biological and genetic factors, say Doell and Longino, but it does acknowledge the unique capacity that humans have to exercise free will and choice in their lives.

Is a person who is capable of having sexual relations with both men and women actually *bisexual?* I was initially surprised that so few men in my study chose to identify themselves as bisexual. But there is little clarity about bisexuality and even the experts disagree about what it means to be bisexual—or even if the distinction exists. Humans have the capacity for bisexual *behavior* (witness prison populations, for example), but that does not necessarily make a case for bisexuality as a third "identity" on the sexual scale. Many social scientists believe that bisexuality is a repressed form of homosexuality and does not exist as a separate category. But bisexuality commonly exists among animal species, even though heterosexuality is the predominant—and the only reproductive—form. Exclusive homosexuality and exclusive heterosexuality appear to be unique to humans.

In a survey conducted with more than two hundred psychiatrists, editors of the 1987 book *The Bisexual Spouse* found a difference of opinion about the validity of bisexuality as a third category. In response to the question, "Is bisexuality a bona fide classification?" 63 percent replied "Yes," 17 percent replied "No," 17 percent replied "Not sure," and 3 percent had no response.

To further illustrate just how complex the nature of sexuality is, consider certain tribes of East Melanesia and New Guinea, where all boys go through a period of exclusive homosexual activity between the ages of nine and nineteen, as part of their passage into manhood. At twenty, they get married and become heterosexual. John Money, a noted sex researcher at Johns Hopkins University, explains that this behavior is rooted in a cultural and mythological premise. "They have their own folk medical story, which is that a child needs its mother's milk to thrive when it's born, and then, to become a man and a head-hunting warrior he has to have a man's milk," Money explains in *Psychology Today.* "It's tremendously important that any theory of how people become heterosexual or homosexual or bisexual be able to account for this phenomenon of cultural bisexuality.''

Further work by Carl Jung proposes that the ontology of male-female sexuality transcends the label of male or female. That is, every human being has both male and female qualities—the ''animus,'' or the male spirit, and the ''anima,'' or the female spirit. Individuals will present themselves according to the norms of the predominant identity. Jung's view is sometimes used to promote the idea that all men and women are bisexual or have the capacity for bisexuality. But again, having the capacity for bisexual behavior does not necessarily imply that bisexuality would ever be a primary form of behavior in American society. There is a pressure to choose a single form of committed sexual expression, be it homosexual or heterosexual. Those who openly practice bisexual behavior are viewed with suspicion in both heterosexual and homosexual circles.

The idea of bisexuality troubles many, from a sociological point of view, since it appears to support non-monogamous and unstable patterns of behavior. Those who are committed to their identities as bisexual beings, giving themselves permission to engage in sexual relationships with both sexes, might never feel pressure to choose one partner and live in a stable family unit.

In doing my research, I encountered two types of self-proclaimed bisexuals. The first type identified themselves as predominantly homosexual, although capable of having sexual relationships with the opposite sex. These men did not normally seek out partners of the opposite sex; they were more inclined to describe their marriages or committed relationships with women as phenomena or deliberate choices (as opposed to ''urges'') that occurred for a variety of reasons. In the typical scenario, a man who knew or suspected he was homosexual became emotionally involved with a woman and developed a committed relationship with her that included sex. If his homosexual feelings were strong, he was more likely to identify himself as bisexual in order to explain how he could find satisfaction with a woman while retaining the desire to be with a man. But since under different circumstances, this man might have lived exclusively as a homosexual, the circumstances may be responsible for the bisexual label.

The second, more vehement group might be termed "militant" or dedicated bisexuals who often belonged to bisexual organizations and favored Margaret Mead's view that "we shall not really succeed in discarding the straight-jacket of our own cultural beliefs about sexual choice if we fail to come to terms with the well-documented, normal human capacity to love members of both sexes." These people formed partnerships based on the self-understanding that they were bisexual, and they were eager to express themselves in both same-sex and opposite-sex partnerships. For them, love and intimacy seemed more intricately tied to sexual behavior; sexual expression was the natural ful-fillment of a close relationship with either sex. Many of these bisexuals voiced frustration with the way society judged them. They complained about being misunderstood and maligned in both the straight world and the gay world. They told me that because there was little scientific support for the validity of bisexuality, they were often accused of being sexually irresponsible or even "wishy-washy," straddling the middle to avoid defining themselves and making firm choices. I spoke with many of them and read their literature and tried to understand. I didn't question the sincerity of their struggle, but they appeared to be deal-ing with different issues than most of the people who re-sponded to the survey. Unlike the majority of respondents, whose focus rarely seemed to be on sex itself, the members of these organizations were very focused on the partner-as-lover. They seemed less willing than others to settle for a single permanent partner. They spoke often of the impor-tance of being free to explore their sexuality with men and women, without being bound by restrictions. On the whole, their lives seemed less settled and less commitment-oriented than others'. This may have been due to the fact that their primary focus was more sexual than others in the survey. They were more often non-monogamous; many were married to other bisexuals and had "open relationships." Some of them had practiced serial monogamy throughout their adulthoods—that is, one partner at a time, male or female, followed by another partner who was not necessarily of the same sex.

To add to the confusion, their descriptions of their goals and lifestyles were filled with many contradictions. For example, almost without exception, the bisexual respondents articulated a preference for a member of their own sex. Sometimes this was expressed in terms of being "male-identified" or "female-identified" in their bisexuality. Here are some of their comments:

I prefer women, and hope for a monogamous, long-term relationship with a woman, but I still have fantasies about men. I don't always act on these fantasies, but I feel much happier with both of my "halves" acknowledged.

—Donna, 38

I express myself primarily heterosexually, since I'm married. But I am also attracted to women and am involved in a lesbian organization. My husband does not know about my bisexuality. I am not sure what my true preference is, but it is very important for me to be free to express myself with both sexes.

—Barbara, 24

I practiced as a bisexual during the fifteen years of my marriage, but found that it was a societally dissonant expression that caused me much suffering. Ultimately, I divorced my wife and moved in with a gay man. I

believe that 'bi now, gay later' is the rule. Most
bisexual people will eventually evolve into gays.

—Jerry, 44

I am primarily attracted to members of my own sex,
and am in a committed relationship with another
woman. But both my partner and I continue to have
erotic encounters with men. I have found that I respond
erotically to people who share my erotic interests,
regardless of sex. Politically, socially, and emotionally I
identify with women. Men are mostly of interest for
sex.

—Cheryl, 28

I never let being "different" bother me. In fact, I
consider it an attribute. It makes life interesting and
fun. I like to show people how silly some of their
preconceived notions about sex are. I like people who
have open minds and live-and-let-live attitudes. For
example, my sister was married for about ten years, but
now she's divorced and lives with a woman. I think
people should be free to pursue what's right for them at
certain times in their lives.

—Bill, 35

I formed a partnership with my best friend. We are both
bisexuals. We both have other relationships with
members of both sexes. This arrangement works very
well for us. One of the biggest problems that I face is
that when men discover I'm bisexual, they assume that
means I'm "easy," which is a misconception of
bisexuals.

—Eleanor, 27

I asked members of bisexual organizations to answer a series of questions specifically related to their bisexual lifestyles. They responded as follows:

What Is Your Current Partnership Status?
(check those that apply)

Statement	Percentage of Affirmative Responses
I am married or committed to a member of the opposite sex and am sexually monogamous.	6%
I am married or committed to a member of the opposite sex and also have sexual relationships with people of my own sex.	31%
I have a strong love relationship with a person of my own sex and also with a person of the opposite sex.	6%
I have a committed relationship with a person of my own sex, but have had important heterosexual relationships in the past.	18%
The freedom to explore sexual relationships with both sexes is important to me.	37%
I see myself eventually choosing one sexual pattern.	4%
My sexual preference is homosexual, but there are aspects of a fully homosexual lifestyle that do not suit my needs.	13%

Some respondents admitted that bisexuality was a transitional phase for them, and that they expected eventually to lead lives that were almost entirely homosexual. Others said they lived almost exclusively as homosexuals or heterosexuals, but maintained the identity of bisexual because they felt the need to keep the option open.

It is possible that for many people, nontraditional sexual expressions are closely related to life stages. Same-sex "crushes" are common in childhood and early adolescence, for example, and many men and women have experienced isolated episodes with same-sex partners. Their having done so, however, does not necessarily make them bisexual or homosexual. The theme of life stages might go even deeper when the aspects of companionship and sharing are added. In her book, *The Eternal Garden—Seasons of Our Sexuality,* Sally Wendkos Olds cites a Consumer Union Study suggesting that a small percentage of older women might turn to female lovers to cope with the impossible imbalance between men and women in their age group. (United States Census Bureau statistics show that there are approximately 3.3 women for every man over the age of sixty-five, and nearly half of all women are widowed before they reach the age of fifty-six.)

It is not my intention to try to resolve these questions here—nor am I capable of doing so. But an understanding of the complex nature of human sexuality and sexual behavior is necessary to an understanding of the so-called "uncommon lives" my research subjects have chosen.

Finding the Self Beyond Sex

Patty and Greg used to be roommates. "My boyfriend left," she explained, "and Greg answered my ad for someone to share the apartment. I needed help with the rent. He seemed nice. So I rented him the spare room."

I was sitting and drinking coffee with Patty in the spacious kitchen of the two-bedroom house she and Greg had purchased together the year before. Patty was nearly forty now, but looked much younger. Her expressive brown eyes moved around the room as she talked, and she had a habit of twisting one long strand of dark hair around her finger almost continually.

Patty was proud of her new house and her newfound stability. But she told me how different things were when she met Greg seven years earlier. "That was a truly awful time for me," Patty said. "I lived with my boyfriend Jack in this crummy apartment. We didn't have any money. But we'd talked about getting married, and I really thought everything would work out. Well, it didn't. Jack started getting moody and complaining a lot, then withdrawing. Finally, he told me, 'I just can't *do* this.' I said, 'You just can't *do* what?' " She grimaced and shook her head. "We'd been together for four years, and he said he couldn't be committed. It was so stupid and I was so angry. I didn't believe he meant it. And when he left and the truth started to sink in, I practically fell apart. I was thirty-two, which felt old at the time, and I thought I would be alone forever."

"Yes," I said, nodding. "That's a familiar story. From all the people I've spoken with, one theme keeps getting repeated. They felt disappointed and cheated—as though they'd been guaranteed something that never came to be."

"Well, weren't we? I mean, when I was in my twenties, there was so much freedom. Everyone said it was a great thing because we'd never get trapped like our parents were. But what did we get? Living alone in lousy apartments? Pretending this was supposed to be a better way to live?" Patty sighed. "I felt completely cheated."

"So, then Greg moved in," I said.

Patty smiled. "Yes. I didn't really want a roommate. It made me feel even worse, like I was going backwards. But I couldn't afford the rent and I couldn't face moving. I hadn't considered having a male roommate, but I liked Greg and since he was gay, I figured he'd leave me alone."

Greg wasn't around, but Patty showed me a picture of a tall, smiling man, surrounded by children. "He's a social worker," she explained. "Those are some kids he took to a basketball game last year. It's the type of thing he does, one of the neat things about him. He cares so much about everyone, and how often do you see that anymore? He's a great storyteller, too. During the first year we were room-mates, he always had me either laughing or crying with stories from his work. It was good to *feel* something again—I had shut myself down emotionally after Jack left.

"Everything about the first year of our being together was an escape," Patty admitted. "I was in hiding from men who might hurt me, and Greg was in hiding from the gay scene because he had been hurt, too. We did everything together. We talked about 'us' and 'them' as if we were different from everyone else. It was one of the nicest years of my life."

"Did either of you go out with other people?"

"Oh, sure, a little. But then we'd come home and trash them completely. Neither of us could deal with the threat of getting involved with anyone, so we'd look for all the things that were wrong with them. I know, for me, I always found a million ways that other men weren't as good as Greg."

"What about having a family? Did you want children? Did you imagine that some day you would marry someone besides Greg and have children?"

"It was definitely a decision I put off," she admitted. "I wasn't sure if I wanted children. Actually, Greg wanted them more than I did. He was frustrated by that. We talked once or twice about having children together, but it was more like daydreaming than making real plans. We weren't sleep-ing together, but it wasn't as though we *couldn't,* if we chose to."

"Since Greg wasn't your partner," I said, "you must have thought about the fact that you'd both eventually move on."

"I tried not to," Patty said. "I just didn't want to think about all the implications. And we never discussed it."

"It was hanging in the air between you, unspoken?"

"Right," she said, laughing. "By the second year, it sure was. One night Greg brought a gay friend over for dinner, and I could tell they really liked each other, and this guy kept giving me funny looks all evening. I remember after he left, I went into the kitchen and started banging around

pots and pans, and Greg came in all agitated and said,
'What's the matter with *you?'* And I didn't know—or I
couldn't say it—but I guess I was jealous. So I realized this
had to stop. It was obviously a dead-end situation. We finally talked about it, and we both sort of said, 'Okay, let's
be adults now and behave the way we're supposed to.' Greg
moved out to his own apartment and we both started meeting other people, but we still saw each other a lot. I really
missed having Greg around. He was the only person I had
ever felt comfortable living with, and people can say anything they like about that, but it's the way I felt.''

"So, how did you come to buy this house together?'' I
asked.

"Oh,'' she shrugged, ''we always gravitated back to each
other. Greg used to say—especially when I'd get frustrated
with the people I was seeing—that if I never found anyone,
he'd marry me. It was a little joke between us. He didn't
mean it, and I never took him seriously and yet, to be perfectly honest, it didn't really seem like such a horrible idea.

"This house?'' She paused to glance around the kitchen
with obvious pride. ''I could never have afforded this alone,
and neither could Greg. We looked at things and said, 'Why
should just the married people get all the good stuff?' So
we bought it together. And that's the end of the story.''

"But surely it's not,'' I protested. ''You bought a house
together. Are you a couple?''

"Well,'' she said, tugging absentmindedly at that strand
of hair, ''that's kind of tricky. We bought this house together because we didn't see any point in waiting to have
the things we wanted in life until we'd both found the so-
called right partners. But there are obvious complications.
What if Greg finds a partner—would they live here? Or what
if I do? It's like we're a couple, but we're not. Fortunately,
as time goes on, we've each become less anxious about the
future. I'm sure we'll always be related in some way.

"Here's something that's very revealing,'' she said as she
laughed. ''When we were living apart and pursuing other
relationships, we used to talk about meeting back up when

we were in our sixties and spending our old age traveling around the world together. It's almost as though we were saying that now, while we're relatively young, we have to have more socially acceptable relationships, but it won't matter when we're older.

"Of course, my friends and family don't understand at all what I'm doing with Greg. They think I'm procrastinating to avoid taking charge of my life. I know people talk about us behind our backs, and they probably feel sorry for me. I try not to worry about what other people are thinking.

"I don't know what will come of all this, but for now I can only say that I'm glad I've had a chance to get close to Greg, that we were able to buy this house together, and that I wasn't sitting around waiting for something to happen in my life before I started really living. I'm living now."

It's easier to characterize nonsexual partnerships if we assume that the participants have unusually low sex drives and are simply less interested in sex than other people. Or we might conclude that, for psychologically complex reasons, they find sexual intimacy so threatening that they gravitate toward situations in which they can avoid its pressure. It is certainly true that sex doesn't place equally high on the priority scale for all men and women and that many are threatened by the unquestionably powerful force of physical intimacy in a relationship. But, in reviewing the responses of the study participants, I found little evidence that the men and women didn't care about sex or were afraid of it. To the contrary, many people admitted that they had placed too much emphasis on sex in the past and were now responding to a growing realization that sex did not have the power they once believed it did to heal crumbling relationships, save them from loneliness, or assure them the development of a deeper emotional intimacy. In this respect, they were articulating what many people have discovered in recent years—the expectations of the new sexual revolution have often come to disappointing conclusions. Today we hear the refrains of the loneliness of promiscuity;

the fear of diseases that can kill; the shattered expectation that good sex naturally leads to enriching relationships. In her book, *The New Celibacy,* Gabrielle Brown interviewed many men and women who had deliberately chosen physical celibacy for periods of time in an effort to rebalance themselves. Many of those she interviewed reported that the absence of sex allowed other parts of their lives to blossom and come into sharper focus. Says Brown, "They concluded that sex is vastly overrated; that throughout the nation people are no longer repressed and, therefore, the 'media hype' of sexiness and sexual attack is no longer valid; that a sense of a more spiritual rising consciousness is the emerging trend, and that the pendulum is now swinging the other way."

For couples like Patty and Greg, the decision to set aside sex for a time represents a comfortable compromise in their partnership. The celibate choice is rarely a permanent one, but a number of the people who were surveyed for this book articulated their great relief at having the sex issue out of the way for a while.

In the gay community, it's sex, sex, sex. There's a lot of strutting and posturing and carrying on—even though people are more careful because of AIDS. Frankly, if you're not well hung, you're dead. I always found this aspect of being gay so hard to come to terms with. When you live in the middle of that kind of environment, you can't help being always aware that once you're not a young stud anymore, that's it.

—Charles, 39

I had sex for the first time when I was sixteen, and now I'm thirty-four. I don't even remember all the guys I've slept with. It became a habit and I started hating myself because I was having so much sex with so little real feeling. I wanted someone to care about *me,* not just about my body.

—Esther, 34

When I met Richard, I had been celibate by choice for two years. I wasn't even looking anymore. I was just tired of all the pressure. It got to the point where I was not so much interested in having a man to go to bed with as I was in having a man to go to the movies with and to talk to. My loneliness was not the lack of sex, it was the lack of partnership.

—Ginny, 36

People think being gay means you're a sexual deviant. A crazy. They don't want us teaching in the schools because we might not be able to keep ourselves from attacking young boys. Believe me, sex is the farthest thing from my mind right now.

—Todd, 28

Publicly, everyone says that sex is the number-one thing in a marriage. But privately, I'll bet a lot of couples have little or no sex. My parents slept in separate rooms for years because they couldn't stand each other. That's something people can understand a lot better than they can understand Gary and I not having sex because we love each other. Talk about a double standard! It's all right to not have sex and hate each other, but not to give up sex and love each other.

—Cynthia, 37

There is a common theme that is heard from the members of our mixed-up, passionate, struggling ''baby boom'' generation: *There have been fundamental expectations about love, commitment, and family that have eluded them and they are deeply disappointed.* In fact, disappointment seems to run rampant in both the homosexual and heterosexual communities. A particularly poignant complaint was voiced by a young homosexual man who said, "It took me years to find the courage to 'come out' as gay. And I expected everything to fall into place once I did. But it's just as hard, if not harder, to find someone to share my life with now. I'm amazed with how lonely I am."

One woman in her early forties remarked, "If you were to tell me that I would never have sex again, but in exchange I would have a partner who loved me and was committed to me for life, I would be very tempted to choose the latter."

How do people respond to being disappointed in love? Sometimes they withdraw from all attempts at intimacy—thus the many people who live alone and without sexual lives by choice. Others compromise and choose ways of living that are not perfect, but which satisfy some of their needs. They sacrifice one need in the interest of fulfilling another. Still others attempt to create the atmosphere of commitment and sharing that is central to the family ideal—doing so in ways that are not typical.

One interviewee was a woman of fifty who was living with a young bisexual man of twenty-six. She admitted that just about everyone she knew—her friends, her children, her neighbors, and her coworkers—looked askance at the relationship. "When they're not being horrified, they're snickering," she said. "My daughter came right out and said, 'Mother, that's obscene!' Well, what is obscene? That we love and respect each other? That we enjoy each other's company? That I am not living and sleeping alone as a respectable widow should?"

Another woman spent several years with a gay man. At one point they lived together, and while there was no sex involved, they were a couple in every other respect. They "kept house," hosted parties, and shared responsibilities.

"He was someone who was there for me when I dragged myself home at the end of the day," she said. "Someone to talk to—to *be* with. People kept telling me I should be out looking for a 'real' relationship. But those three years were the most content of my life. I felt secure and supported. It got me off the treadmill for a while, gave me a chance to find myself. We both have new partners now—he's with a man—but there will always be a special feeling between us."

CHAPTER FOUR

Married . . . Unconventionally

> Let me not to the marriage of true minds
> Admit impediments. Love is not love
> Which alters when it alteration finds,
> Or bends with the remover to remove:
> O, no! It is an ever-fixed mark,
> That looks on tempests and is never shaken;
> It is the star to every wand'ring bark . . .
>
> Sonnet 116,
> William Shakespeare

THE AIR IN Savannah, Georgia, was thick and sweet, and it hung over my car in a sleepy haze as I drove along the back road that took me from the tiny airport to the home of Robert and Carol Lander. My search for unconventional married couples had brought me to this quiet, conservative community—at first glance, a most unlikely place to find unconventionality of any kind.

Robert and Carol are my age—in their late thirties. He is a pediatrician, she a computer programmer. They have been married for ten years and had moved to this area from Atlanta four years earlier. They have no children.

A friend had put them in touch with me after hearing about my research, and they had filled out a questionnaire. I had chosen them for an extended interview because I read something in their responses that told me they were exceptional—people I wanted to meet.

I neared their address, crossing a short bridge over a swampy river. The grass in front of their old two-story house was a plush, mossy green; my foot sank down into it as I stepped out of the car.

Robert came to meet me, a husky, handsome man with a full head of dark brown hair and clear gray eyes. His hand, when I shook it, was a doctor's hand, smooth and refined. It was also utterly dry, and I apologized for my sweaty grip.

"We're used to the humidity here," he said, laughing, and he took me inside to meet his wife.

Carol Lander was taller than her husband, and pretty, with straight blonde hair that hung down over narrow shoulders. "We're glad you came," she greeted me warmly, motioning me to a chair in the spacious kitchen. We chatted while she finished preparing dinner.

"Robert and I were so surprised when we heard what you were doing," she told me. "And it's kind of strange to have you here. We've never really spoken with anyone before about our lives. People around here would have a hard time understanding. As it is, they see us as a pretty normal couple."

"You're more normal than you think," I said.

She laughed. "I suppose so, if you're writing a book about it. But it isn't all roses."

"So I'm hearing," I said. "There are never easy answers."

She turned from the stove and looked me in the eye. "No. There aren't. I'm not sure I would have chosen this life for myself."

"You did."

Her face softened. "Yes, I did."

After dinner, we sat in the living room, sipping the last of a bottle of wine and talking. Robert told me his story.

"Most people think that being homosexual is a certain thing. You *know* you're gay, and that's that. It was never that way for me, although my first sexual experience was with a male. I was only fifteen, and very naive about sex. But I was wildly attracted to a boy who lived next door—he was sixteen. I don't think he was gay, but he was very horny, as young boys are, and when he guessed my attraction, he

teased me and flirted with me, and finally we had one awkward sexual encounter.

"I wasn't really aware, even then, that I was gay. God
knows, it wasn't something that was talked about. I think I
assumed that all boys experimented like this, to prepare
them for the big event, which was sex with a woman.
Through the rest of high school, I had girlfriends, but none
of these relationships went beyond heavy petting. I noticed
that I continued to be attracted to men, but it was never a
serious consideration. I was going to be a doctor and live a
normal life.

"I moved to Pennsylvania to start college and there had
my first serious girlfriend and my first real sexual relationship. We were talking about getting married when I met
Eric, who worked with me part time in the school library.

"Eric was handsome and funny, and I loved being around
him. We started spending a lot of time together, and I found
that I could talk to him about anything. In fact, I enjoyed
his company much more than my fiancée's, in every way.
She was jealous of our relationship, which I told her was
ridiculous, although it turns out that she had a right to be.

"Eric and I had our first sexual encounter one night when
we were sitting in his room listening to music. It was thrilling for me, not just because of the physical aspect, but because it seemed to be such a fulfilling expression of our
closeness. Eric was very open about being a homosexual,
but I told him I wasn't one. I thought homosexuals weren't
able to have sex with women, and I was. He suggested that
maybe I was bisexual, but I found this definition confusing,
and I was unable to find any literature that defined what a
bisexual was.

"I didn't spend much time wondering about my sexual
identity. I was young, I was enjoying myself. Nobody knew.
It might have been a phase or it might have been more, but
I wasn't worried about it. I felt I had everything under control. You know, college is a rarefied environment. You can
live any way you like, experiment with things, not have to
make decisions.

"My fiancée broke up with me around that time. She could sense my interest was wandering—although it never would have occurred to her to suspect me of having a sexual relationship with Eric. I think she believed I had another woman on the side. I was relieved when we broke up. I wasn't in love with her anymore, and it wasn't as much fun to be with her as it was to be with Eric. At that point in my life, I was very interested in having fun. So I threw myself into the gay world, allowing Eric to introduce me to the subculture that existed in our community. This was the late sixties, so the culture wasn't very open. But occasionally, we'd drive into New York City, and I was astonished by the openness I found there. Men would gather in bars and along the river and in the parks. There were clubs where they danced together. I became completely enraptured with it, and during the next three years, even after Eric and I stopped seeing each other, I visited New York often. In that time, I probably had about two hundred partners, which seems incredibly promiscuous, I know, but that's the way things were then. There was so much sexual freedom, and no big demands the way there were in the heterosexual world.

"I still thought of myself as being bisexual—occasionally, I'd go out with women and I enjoyed their company and could perform well sexually with them. But the period of gay promiscuity helped me understand myself better and accept the side of myself I'd always been embarrassed about.

"By the time I graduated from college and started medical school, I was growing tired of all the anonymous sex and short-term affairs. It gets lonely—I don't think anyone can keep up that sort of lifestyle forever without feeling bruised by it. I had grown up in a very close, loving family, and I wanted something like that for myself. I was afraid, though, because I'd identified myself as bisexual, and I wasn't sure how I could square the two sides of me into one relationship."

He paused while Carol poured coffee, and I commented that his story was fascinating. "I'm interested in your comment about 'knowing' you were gay. Do you think you just adopted the idea of being bisexual to give you permission to eventually settle into a heterosexual lifestyle?''

''At first, maybe. I had always planned to get married and have children, and if I said I was gay, it seemed that this option would not be there for me. But it was also true that I had enjoyed sex with the women I really cared for. I've always been very romantic, and that included the need for lots of physical touching with those I loved. Sex came as a natural extension of other feelings, whether it was with a man or a woman. The period of promiscuity was the least satisfying for me. It was more thrill-seeking than love. After all that experimenting, I was ready to have someone special in my life.''

''You met Carol around this time?''

''Yes—she worked with a gay man I had been seeing off and on, and he introduced us. There was a strong attraction between us from the first moment we met. She knew about my homosexuality, so she was more surprised than I was about our attraction. When we made love for the first time, Carol was very confused because we were so compatible sexually.''

''I was scared,'' Carol interjected. ''I thought, 'Oh, boy, what am I getting into!' But Robert put my early fears to rest. At the time, we were each other's only lovers, and he didn't seem interested in having anyone but me. We spent nearly every night together, and I moved in with him after three months. Besides, our relationship was so diverse. It wasn't just about sex. We were on the same wavelength in so many different ways.''

''Carol was my best friend, in addition to being my lover,'' said Robert. ''I could actually visualize spending my life with her and having her as a partner, something I had never felt for any of the men I'd known. My gay relationships were very *sexual,* more oriented to infatuation than common interests.

''To be honest, I was surprised that I found Carol, surprised that this ever happened at all. I had almost given up on the idea that I would ever have a fulfilling lifetime partnership. By the time I met Carol, I was thirty, and I'd had sex with half a dozen women and maybe two hundred men, many of whom I'd gotten to know fairly well. I'd also had numerous casual acquaintances and several close nonsexual friendships. So I knew something about people and what they're like, and, moreover, I knew something about myself and what I'm like in relationships. I was ready to settle down, and so was Carol. We were just your average couple in so many ways—wanting to get married and have children. What amazes me still about my choice of Carol as a life partner was the superlative rightness of my instincts and rationalizations. I'd had feelings and instincts about people before, and had come up with excellent reasons for selecting them as romantic partners, but I'd been wrong so often and so consistently before that it surprises me, even now, to have been, for once, so very right—and about a woman at that! I guess I just got lucky. The bottom line, in this context, is that the relationship has worked extraordinarily well for over ten years, and I have no intention of ever altering its essential structure.

"Also, in deciding to marry, I was clearly conscious that in doing so I was acknowledging my failure as a homosexual lover," Robert said. "I'd been active as a gay man for ten years and had never lived with a man I loved or who loved me, although that had been my conscious and declared goal throughout scores of tricks and numerous affairs. I was, at best, simply not very good at loving men. At worst, I was unconsciously self-destructive. Something always got in the way—most commonly, dependency, possessiveness, jealousy, promiscuity, or some other irreconcilable incompatibilities. Besides, as I approached thirty, I saw that my second youth was rapidly drawing to a close, and I'd missed my chance. In marrying a woman, and thereby removing myself from the gay matrimonial market, I felt I would be no great loss to the gay community. In this, I was entirely right; with such attitudes as these and such ways of relating, I *was* no great loss to the gay community. Good riddance to me."

"But it wasn't 'good riddance,' was it?" I asked. "You

didn't plan to turn your back on your homosexuality when you married Carol.''

"No, it wasn't that. In fact, before we were married, I was very careful to secure her acknowledgment of my bisexuality and her acceptance of my continued homosexual activities—although I wasn't sure at that time what those activities might be. I was very concerned about being fair to her. We were ready to make the commitment to get married, but the matter of my sexuality had to be addressed directly. Fortunately, Carol was very open.''

"It was a choice I made," Carol said. "I wanted to be married to Robert, and I trusted his commitment to me. But I knew that if I forced a promise from him to give up being homosexual, it would eventually drive us apart. It was a side of Robert that was as real as his relationship with me. This was before AIDS, of course, so that wasn't a factor. And Robert wasn't promiscuous then; he hadn't been with a man during the time we'd known each other, but I knew it might happen. So we agreed that we would be open to a certain amount of sexual exploration in our marriage.''

"For him, not you?" I asked.

"The understanding was that we would both have that freedom, but realistically, it was an agreement that was made for his sake, not mine. I wasn't really interested.''

I observed that it must have been a hard compromise for her to make, and Carol smiled wryly. "It was easier when it was a theoretical point. Not so easy when it was real. Maybe I kidded myself—yes, I'm sure I did—that I would never have to deal with it. When he met Joe and they started having a relationship during the first year of our marriage, I found that I was less tolerant of it.''

"Joe was the perfect relationship for me," interjected Robert. "He was married, too, and also frustrated by exclusive heterosexuality, although he wasn't in the least bit interested in forsaking his otherwise satisfactory marriage of fifteen years. We got together every week or two, and it was very good for both of us. Carol tried hard to keep a perspective on this—she knew that she was number one with me, but she had a hard time dealing with it.''

''It wasn't the sex,'' Carol assured me. ''It was the closeness. I guess I was jealous. I couldn't shake the belief that married people should be close only to each other—that Robert *belonged* to me emotionally. Of course, that's ridiculous. Eventually, out of defiance, I suppose, I began an affair with a man at work. Having an affair wasn't a particularly good idea, but I did care for this man, and it had one positive outcome. It helped me understand, for the first time, and not just theoretically and intellectually, that one can love two people simultaneously. I was able to let go of some of my pain and jealousy over Robert's relationships. I know that, for him, our marriage is the center, but he also needs the love and sex and friendship he has experienced with his male lovers.''

I looked at Robert and Carol, sitting side by side on the sofa, and I thought that they seemed to be a very happy couple, judged against many couples. But certain things about their relationship troubled me.

''It sounds like you're making all the compromises, Carol,'' I suggested. ''I think most people would say that Robert's life is gravy—he has it both ways.''

They glanced at each other briefly, and Carol sighed. ''If you asked me if I would prefer that my husband didn't have homosexual relationships with men, of course I would say yes to that. I have my moments—although they're infrequent—when I wonder if Robert is *really* attracted to me. And I've had times of feeling it wasn't fair that I had to share my husband when other women don't. But I consider those feelings and thoughts to be the lesser side of me. I'm not a victim, you know. This is my choice. Robert has never lied to me. He didn't trick me. And he loves me completely. Of that, I'm sure.'' She smiled at her husband.

''Well,'' I observed, ''some people would say that you have a very enlightened view, but many others would accuse you of just pretending to have a commitment that you don't have. Didn't the ideal of the 'open marriage' fail miserably in the sixties and seventies? And what about AIDS? Isn't this a very irresponsible way to live, given the times?''

"Most people would say the issue is just about sex," said Robert. "They'd consider me this randy guy who has to go out and screw a lot. But homosexuality is not just about sex, and my relationships with men have been necessary to fill a number of different needs. It's more than just physical.''

"I don't quite understand what you mean by that," I ventured. "What are you getting from your relationships then? Is it love? Is it a form of partnership, and, if so, how does that affect your married partnership? Earlier you said that you weren't very good at loving men, and always made a mess of it somehow. How is this different?''

"It's hard to explain," he admitted, "but I'll try. I think the problem I had when I was involved with men before I knew Carol was that I was looking for so much more in the relationships. No matter how much sex I had, I was still alone. I wanted someone special of my own. But I didn't know how to tell the difference between infatuation and the kind of stable love you could build a life on. The kinds of men I enjoyed spending time with were not the kinds of people who could settle into a domestic lifestyle. What I understand now better than I did then is that there are many different ways of loving people. I enjoy the camaraderie that takes place in a gay bar as much as or more than the sexual aspect. We talk about everything—in a way that you can't do with straight men—or at least I never could. They're lovers, friends, buddies, people I care about. My primary commitment is to Carol—she comes first. But my friendship with these men is not inconsequential. If they needed me, I'd be there for them.

"Of course, AIDS has become more of an issue. Partly for this reason, my relationships with men are monogamous—I only have one partner at a time, and only after we've both been tested. And we practice safe sex. I think Carol trusts me that I wouldn't do anything to hurt her by being sexually irresponsible.''

"I do," she nodded.

"Carol and I have a more honest and complete love relationship than many of the people we know who are in so-called traditional relationships," he added. "Who are they to say that we're not committed? Our honesty alone says a lot. I'm not sneaking around behind Carol's back. We're tuned into each other's needs."

"This is a hard question to ask," I said, "but, Robert, if you had a choice—or if you'd had a choice before you married Carol—would you rather be living with a man as a life partner?"

Robert was thoughtful for a moment, formulating his reply. "I've never experienced any second thoughts or regrets about my decision to marry," he said finally. "But occasionally, I imagine how I would feel without her—young women do die sometimes. These thoughts don't stem from any brooding about flaws or disappointments in our marriage, although, of course, there have been some—when you sign on for marriage, you'd better be fully willing to accept imperfection. But every once in a while, I have a moment of fantasy about the imagined road not taken—life in the company of a loving and beloved man. I have to say I find the fantasy difficult to maintain, because, first of all, I would be so grief-stricken to lose Carol. And second, I have no reason to believe that I could ever be more successful at establishing a permanent relationship with a man than I was before. Anyway, the short answer is no, I would not prefer to be living with a man."

On my way out the door, Carol presented me with a bit of proud news—she was pregnant. "We thought it was about time," she said as she grinned, putting an arm around her husband. They stood like that in the doorway. As I drove away, I noted that they looked, in the glow of the porch light, like the prototype of the perfect American couple.

What to make of Robert and Carol? I came away from the evening liking them very much, being impressed with their sincerity and devotion, and acknowledging that I could not have hoped to find a better example of a couple who defied labels. I also had the uncomfortable feeling that comes from being left with a bundle of loose ends. In this encounter and in the many that would follow, I would constantly be forced to confront my own deeply rooted prejudices about relationships. I knew that my discomfort came from the fact that, on some level, I wished Robert and Carol had reached a less ambiguous resolution. I wanted to be able to hold them up as a sterling example—the happy ending to a troubled tale. I knew that many people would read my description of them and immediately mistrust Robert's justifications and Carol's talk of acceptance. Wouldn't most people readily agree that Carol would be better off with a different man?

But "better off" is a tricky concept, or, more to the point, an irrelevant one. Life is not, after all, a buffet table that allows us an infinite selection from which to choose. We only choose from what is available to us, and in the context of Carol's life, she clearly believed that Robert was a happy choice.

Writer Merle Shain articulates this idea well in her book, *When Lovers Are Friends.*

> All of us feel there must be more, but wonder what the more really is, and often the more we yearned for last year isn't enough today. So we wait in vain for something else, something just a little better than what we've got, and often we trade in the thing we have for something we think we should want. We are the "Is this all there is?" generation, waiting for the perfect thing to commit to—the perfect job, the perfect love—and we feel miserable all the while we wait, somehow failing to understand that loneliness lies in the suspended state.

But even giving Robert and Carol the benefit of the doubt, many people would still be confused by the fact that a gay man would deliberately marry a woman—and that a woman would deliberately marry a gay man. It is one thing when it happens by mistake. But to choose such a path stretches the imagination of even the most broad-minded among us. Carol confided to me that she had never told her parents

that Robert was gay. "They just couldn't have handled it,"
she said, "and I figured that since I was happy, there was
no reason to hurt them needlessly. As it is, they adore Robert. Mother has often told me how happy she is that I found
a gentle, secure man like him. This is a clear case of 'what
they don't know, won't hurt them.' " These deceptions are
common among gay-straight couples. It is an unspoken understanding that *people are not going to accept this.* Deception has become their form of being "in the closet."

According to June M. Reinisch, director of the Kinsey
Institute at Indiana University, "Many, many bisexual men
are married. But the problem is that sexual orientation does
not necessarily predict what people do." Reinisch was one
of the researchers at the Kinsey Institute who published a
1987 survey of six thousand men, finding that 20 percent of
those who identified themselves as gay had been married or
had lived with a woman.

Ultimately, marriage is sociological, not ontological. It
is an institution, a design for living that requires only the
commitment of two parties. In these "enlightened" times,
most people have come to understand that many old assumptions about choosing a mate are no longer valid. It is
not necessary, for example, that a couple share the same
background or the same race. They don't have to be of the
same religious orientation, or be educated in the same
schools. They don't even have to live together year-round.
But what about having different sexual orientations?

This is not an entirely new question. The topic of gay
married men appears in popular magazines two or three times
a year, and is occasionally the subject of talk shows. With
the onset of AIDS, it has become something of a paranoid
obsession among some women, who fear they might be
tricked into marriages or sexual relationships with gay or bisexual men. As I was doing research, I came across others
who were preparing material—one of them was a writer for
Cosmopolitan magazine who was searching for resources to
help women who found themselves in this dilemma. Another,
the producer of a "scandal-sheet" television talk show, called

to find out if I could speak to this "problem" on a program they were planning to air. In both cases I questioned the emphasis—"it's a problem"—but I could understand why the contexts were so narrow. There is very little available data that would place the issue in another light. I was particularly surprised to encounter so many uninformed views among professionals and even among experts. It was very hard to find people within the psychological community who were prepared to address the issue. For instance, one psychologist who *specializes* in counseling gay men in a major American city responded blankly to questions about clients who were married. "I have never counseled a gay man who was married," she told me. In fact, she admitted that it had never occurred to her that this was an issue! Another woman, a noted family counselor who had written two books, seemed confused by my questions. "I had always thought that it was not possible for gay men to have sex with women," she said.

More often, the responses I got from psychologists were based on the assumption that these were marriages of "convenience." This, of course, is the most common view, and also the one that people seem most comfortable with. "After all," acknowledged one, "it has long been accepted that people marry for reasons other than love—such as for money or social standing."

The blank walls I encountered when I spoke with professionals underscored the isolation and confusion many survey respondents described. Those who did seek help often reported that there was little understanding of the complexity of the questions they were raising. Only rarely was a deeper appreciation of the issues articulated, and it was usually found outside the popular literature.

In his important book *Loving Someone Gay,* Don Clark suggests a distinction between being homosexual and living a gay lifestyle. According to Clark, the label "gay" is limiting, as are all labels. He writes:

Gay is a descriptive label we have assigned to ourselves as a way of reminding ourselves and others that awareness of our sexuality facilitates a capability rather than creating a restriction. It means that we are capable of fully loving a person of the same gender by involving ourselves emotionally, sexually, spiritually, and intellectually. It may even imply a frequent or nearly constant preference or attraction for people of the same gender, meaning I (as a gay man) might notice more men than women on the street or might notice the men before the women. But the label does not limit us. We who are gay can still love someone of the other gender. *Homosexual* and *Heterosexual,* when used as nouns, are naive and destructive nonsense in the form of labels that limit.

In 1983, Michael Ross, a psychiatric scholar from Australia, published the findings of his research on homosexual married men in New Zealand, Australia, Sweden, and Finland. His analysis, titled *The Married Homosexual Man—A Psychological Study,* was published by Routledge & Kegan Paul in Great Britain and received relatively limited circulation and little acknowledgment in America. Ross conducted two different studies to gather his evidence. The first was conducted in New Zealand and Southeast Australia and focused on three categories of men:

1. Homosexual males still married and living with their wives
2. Homosexual males who were separated, divorced, or widowed
3. Homosexual males who had never been married

His subjects were selected much the same way I selected mine—through advertisements in publications like the New Zealand *Gay News* and the newsletter of the New Zealand Homosexual Law Reform Society. Ross's second study was conducted in Sweden, Finland, and Australia—in what he regarded as more mainstream Western cultures.

There is much that is of interest in Ross's work. What I found to be most fascinating, however, was the portrait it provided of the reasons homosexual men marry, and the eventual outcome of such relationships. Ross outlines five categories of reasons for these marriages. They are:

1. Social pressure from an external source, such as family and friends (including girlfriends)
2. The effort to remove or de-emphasize one's homosexuality, or view it as a passing phase
3. Genuine love for a partner, and the desire for children
4. Lack of awareness of the man's homosexuality at the time of marriage or inability to identify homosexual feelings
5. Companionship—a reason that often occurred with older homosexual men

Ross's study participants revealed that marrying for convenience or even social pressure were viewed as secondary or at least buried beneath other reasons. Here is a breakdown of Ross's findings:

Statement	*Percentage of men offering as main reason for marrying*
You were "in love"	26.2
You thought your homosexuality would go if you were married	16.7
Wife pregnant	11.9
Pressure from girlfriend	11.9
You wanted children and family life	7.1
It seemed the natural thing	7.1
Everyone else was getting married	4.8
All other reasons	12.0

(Ross, Michael W. *The Married Homosexual Man.* Routledge & Kegan Paul, 1983, page 51, table 5.1.)

While elements of social pressure are suggested in several categories, such as the fact that everyone else was getting married, or it seemed the natural thing, other reasons were surprisingly prominent—like being in love or wanting a family. Although Ross acknowledged that "the romantic notion of falling in love, getting married, and living happily ever after has become such a stereotype and goal that it almost reaches the level of a 'social pressure,' " he didn't discount that often both love and the legitimate desire to have children were genuine reasons for marriage. Those who responded that they thought their homosexuality would go away if they married were likewise a mixed group. While some might have been trying to "change" through heterosexual marriage, often the men were not fully aware that they were homosexual beforehand. This reason was common among respondents to my survey who admitted to having some attraction to the same sex prior to marriage but who believed it was an aberration of their true (heterosexual) natures or who denied its meaning because of strong religious or moral convictions. It seems important to emphasize the complexity involved in "knowing" that one is either gay or straight. Much of what we "know" about our sexuality is a learned response that involves a wide range of factors, including cultural and ethnic heritage, social environment, religious beliefs, and personal goals.

Ross further queried his respondents on their judgments of the "best" and "worst" things about being married. The "best" was considered to be "companionship," a response given by 45 percent of those who were still married; the "worst" thing was "loss of freedom." These are answers that might well hold true in any marriage, suggesting that the concerns around which these relationships were centered were not all that different from those of the average marriage.

Whether or not their homosexuality was the primary reason for separation among the men in Ross's study who were no longer married was questionable. Ross reported that 32 percent of the separated group had considered remarriage. He was not able to determine whether this was due to social pressure, the desire for companionship, or other reasons.

Roughly 25 percent of the men and women who participated in my research had chosen to be married with both partners fully aware of the man's bisexual or homosexual identity. These matches have met with varying degrees of success (as is true of *all* marriages). But in most cases, the couples had thought long and hard before taking the plunge, about why they were making this particular choice, what they were hoping to gain, and what they were giving up. Here are some of their thoughts on the subject:

I never thought I'd end up with a woman, but now I can't imagine life without Ellen. She's a wonderful partner and companion. She takes me places I've never been before. Knowing her, I see that life is more than just sex.

—Edward A., 42, married 14 years

For the first time in my life, I'm following my heart, not my head. My head tells me I'm crazy to marry Jack, but my heart speaks louder. He feels the same way, and we're both scared . . . but we're going to do it.

—Susan N., 27, engaged to be married

It sounds greedy, like I want the whole candy store, and maybe I do. But if the woman I love is willing to share me with men, then why should I live differently? Brenda is the solid, nurturing presence in my life. She's the first one I'd turn to if I was hurt or in trouble, or if I had wonderful news to share. She's the only person I know who I can completely trust and depend on, no

matter what. With her, it's love; with the men, it's
something else.

—Frederick G., 35, married 8 years

Sexual preference is not really the issue. The issue is
being happy with what you're doing. I couldn't tell you
that people haven't said terrible things to both Sarah
and me—warning us not to get married. But I think this
will be a good marriage because we love each other and
are committed to honesty.

—Roger C., 26, engaged to be married

We met when I was twenty-five and she was nineteen.
We were friends for almost two years before we became
lovers. Only two of my friends knew I was gay then. I
only told her after we'd been sleeping together for close
to a year. I wanted to give her a chance to get out if she
wanted to. She struggled with it, but she didn't leave,
and we eventually got married. I think it's important
that we were friends first for so long.

—Steve A., 33, married 5 years

We are a gay man and a heterosexual woman who have
enjoyed a monogamous union for three years. Our
experience has been a real surprise, a source of
confusion and consternation. We perceive life to have a
lot more gray areas than it has black and white. We
wonder if categorizing people and lifestyles isn't futile.
We gave up our own labeling, shelved our "what ifs,"
and decided to live and love, trying to accept the
contradictions.

—Natalie J., 34, and Tom S., 34, married 3 years

One woman, Terry, thirty-two, told this story:

"I was sitting in a local night spot, being treated to dinner and drinks by a friend. Paul walked by and my friend, who knew him, invited him to join us. We talked and clicked. We had lots of interests in common. I knew he was gay, so I kind of wondered when he asked me out. I felt attracted to him, but I just assumed he wasn't attracted to me. I didn't quite know what he wanted, but we had a great time, and went out on a couple of other occasions. One night we kissed and discussed the fact that we both had sexual feelings for each other. I didn't understand the phenomenon, nor did he. We spent a weekend together; the sex was loving, but awkward and tentative. He hadn't been with women except a couple times many years before, and I had been widowed a few months earlier and I was still sort of numb, physically and emotionally.

"At any rate, we continued to date and to have sex. Sex became easier and more natural a few months after initiation. We dated for two years, then decided to live together, and now we've been living together for two years and are discussing marriage. We are the best of friends, and we are a wonderful team. We love and support each other, yet we encourage independence in each other. Our sex is wonderful, yet Paul is still more attracted to men sexually. Since he has agreed to be monogamous, I know he sometimes misses having sex with a man. But he doesn't miss *living* with a man. He says, for him, sex isn't the only factor in establishing a loving, committed, comfortable relationship."

Playing Sexual Roulette

The "open sex" clause in many gay-straight marriages is a troubling factor. AIDS is an ever-present concern, but there are other concerns, too, that grow out of the fundamental moralities of our culture. Sexual fidelity, or at least *its appearance,* is a central value in American life. Those in my

study who admitted choosing non-monogamous partnerships might come in for serious criticism for having crossed
the line of acceptable standards. But while most Americans
say they value sexual fidelity as an essential factor in marriage, the statistics tell another story. According to sociol-
ogist Annette Lawson of the Institute for Research on
Women and Gender at Stanford University, 25 to 50 percent
of married women and 50 to 65 percent of married men
now have at least one affair during marriage. The fact that
many, if not most, of these infidelities occur in secrecy
seems to indicate that infidelity itself is not viewed with
unanimous disapproval. Criticized instead is the couple's
decision to be non-monogamous. In other words, dishonest
non-monogamy is considered more acceptable than honest non-monogamy. On the face of it, this double standard is
puzzling. Are we not living in the era of ''open and honest''
communication? Is it not better for couples to have an honest
agreement rather than to be victimized by secret infidelity?
This is an enormously murky topic. I would suggest that although men and women may behave unfaithfully, usually they
don't feel that it is ''okay''—thus, the secrecy. People agree
with the moral standard and, when they do stray, they blame
the circumstances (''I got swept away by the attraction,'' ''I
was under a lot of pressure,'' ''My marriage hasn't been too
good lately'') rather than admit that their actions were a result
of clear volition. The justification that ''all men and women
are sinners'' allows people to be absolved of guilt, even when
infidelity is a continuing pattern. On the other hand, if a
couple agrees that there is no moral imperative for sexual
monogamy within marriage, they shake the very foundations
of our public morality. This is an entirely different and far
more threatening position to take.

   In couples who have agreed to non-monogamous relationships, it is the women who are most often troubled, perhaps
because in general, women tend more than men to equate sex
with love and commitment. Women are less likely overall to
embrace an open marriage; they more often feel forced into

the agreement as the only way to keep their marriages together.

But the issues for women married to gay men are far more complex than whether or not their partners are sexually faithful. In fact, they are so complex that women in these marriages often find it hard to pinpoint the source of their unease.

I contacted Frank and Joanne after Frank sent me a lengthy letter, spelling out his philosophy of marriage and commitment—a philosophy, he assured me, that his wife of sixteen years shared. But later, when they had both filled out the questionnaire, I found that Joanne, who generally spoke of being happy in her marriage, still struggled with many fears related to Frank's sexuality and his male partners.

Frank and Joanne were a pleasant couple, the type one would say looked "comfortably married." He was forty-three, tall and thin with an unmanageable shock of blond hair and wire-rimmed glasses that gave him a professorial appearance. She was forty-one, small and compactly built, a bundle of energy with glistening dark hair, expressive brown eyes, and an easy, wide smile. Throughout their marriage, they had lived in Philadelphia, where Frank was an engineer and Joanne taught high school English. They had a nine-year-old son, Peter.

When they became seriously involved in college, both Frank and Joanne recognized that theirs was a rare kind of love. Their subsequent marriage two years later felt like the right step for both of them.

"When we first met and became friends, neither of us expected it to lead anywhere," said Frank. "I told Joanne right off the bat that I was gay. But we were very attracted, and after we had known each other about six months, we started having a sexual relationship."

"That really surprised me when it happened," Joanne added. "It never occurred to me that Frank would—or *could*—be interested in me that way. But he said that his feelings for me were separate from the ones he had for men.

I didn't quite understand what he meant by that, but I accepted it.''

Throughout their courtship period, Frank, open and comfortable with his homosexuality, continued to engage in occasional sexual liaisons with men. Although he'd never been promiscuous—he'd had about ten male partners when he met Joanne—homosexuality was just a part of his life. Nevertheless, in Joanne he saw something special, and he didn't want to give it up.

"When we started to discuss marriage, it seemed like the most natural thing in the world," he said. "We were both family types, and we wanted children. We loved each other. Why not? By that time, Joanne understood that my occasional relationships with men were not a threat to her. And they're still not. We have a happy and honest marriage. Better than most people we know." He laughed. "You know, a lot of people sneak around and cheat on their spouses. We've never had to do that."

Why did Frank choose Joanne instead of a man? "Maybe if I'd met a man I could share my life with, things would have turned out different," he said honestly. "But I never did. I've never even had a long-term male lover. I've always considered men to be more shallow than women. When it comes to *partnership,* a woman is better."

"But what *is* partnership, if not an exclusive commitment?" I asked.

"We do have an exclusive commitment," Frank argued. "We are committed to love each other above all others and consider each other's needs above all others, and be together for life. I don't have that commitment with any other person but Joanne. But the commitment you make to your spouse does not mean that you are agreeing to forsake all other important relationships in your life. It doesn't mean that you won't have close friends or soul mates or even lovers. I realize this doesn't represent a traditional view, but I don't see how people can criticize us if it works for us."

I asked Joanne how she felt, and she fixed her direct brown eyes on Frank as she spoke. "Frank is my life," she said simply. "I can't imagine not having him there. But I'll admit that he has always been able to adjust to this more easily than I. It's still hard for me sometimes to reconcile this. I trust him, but sometimes I'm scared that he'll fall in love with a man and that'll be it for me."

"Of course, that's completely ridiculous," Frank said, laying a hand on her shoulder.

"Oh, I don't sit around brooding about it or anything. But Frank, you have to realize that for me—and I think for most women—sex is a way we express our deepest feelings of love and sharing. It's harder for me to do that with more than one person at a time, so I don't quite understand how you can, especially when I'm feeling vulnerable about other things."

"Many women have told me that they don't understand how their husbands can have that much emotion to go around—or something to that effect," I said. "It's not simply an issue of physical closeness."

"Emotionally, I've always been closer to women," said Frank. "If something happened to Joanne tomorrow, I'd probably find another woman for a long-term love partner. Sexually, I can give one hundred percent to a man. I can share deep friendships with men. But emotionally, I've never found a man I could relate to in a way that would make me want to live with him the rest of my life. Men just don't seem to be there when it comes to expressing emotional depth."

"It's interesting that you say that," I said, "because one of the things many women say about homosexual men is that they are more sensitive and have more emotional depth because they aren't caught up in the macho image."

"That's true in their relationships with women because they're not trying to put on a front or impress women," he observed. "But when they're with other men, there's the same posturing and pretense that you see in male-female relationships. The macho image is rampant in the gay community."

"And what's different about women?"

"They listen. They're more forgiving. They accept you the way you are. For example, women tend not to be judgmental about appearance, but other homosexuals are very conscious

of it. And once you start to get older, forget it. The homosexual world is really a very insecure place to live.''

"Have you ever sought out other partners?'' I asked
Joanne.

"No. Sometimes I've felt like I needed a second partner,
too, just to make things even, or maybe to try to fill the
spaces Frank doesn't fill. I have romantic fantasies, just like
everyone else. But I do realize, when I think about it, that
none of us should expect another person to fill our empty
spaces, or to be everything for us. Knowing this, I'm able to
put sex and Frank's homosexuality in perspective. I don't
want to give the impression that I'm not happy with my marriage, because that's not true. It's a deeply satisfying relationship. I'm human, so I have fears. But I try not to let them
get in the way.''

I asked Frank to talk about his homosexual partners, and
he said, "I'm not promiscuous. In sixteen years, maybe I've
had six partners. For me, the ideal is to have one steady
partner, not only because AIDS makes it irresponsible to
have it any other way, but also because I hate that shallow
lifestyle. I can't relate to people I don't respect. There have
to be things that click on other levels, and you don't just run
out and find that every day. At the risk of sounding trite, I
consider my relationships with men to be 'male bonding'
experiences.

"As far as safe sex is concerned, if a man and I are attracted to each other, we can wait to have blood tests before
we do anything. That's a firm policy. I'm aware that AIDS
might eventually make it impossible for me to have sex with
men at all—some of my gay friends have become celibate.
I'm certainly not going to jeopardize Joanne's life, or mine,
for sex.

"I agree with Joanne about putting sex in perspective.
People think being gay is just an erotic thing, that gay men
can't help themselves—they *have* to have sex, and that's the
sum total of what it means to be gay. But I don't think anyone
has to have sex. If we said that's what it meant to be human,
that would be a superficial conclusion. Sex is more a gift

than it is a compulsion. I'm fortunate that I have a situation that allows me to explore my sexuality on a number of levels. But sexuality and sexual orientation go much deeper than what two people do when they are in bed together.''

Nancy Friday, in her book *Jealousy,* seems to suggest that the more we love, the greater the chance of jealousy, an emotion born of possessiveness and fear of loss. Says Friday:

> In any love relationship there are good and even pleasurable dependencies. Meeting these mutual needs is part of the magical exchange. But love that is based on the need to survive means you must structure it in such a way that your partner can never leave. The irony of control has mad, Proustian logic. You make the other person your prisoner; you run, control and dominate their lives because you fear they are stronger, can live without you.

This insight may be at the heart of the fears expressed by Joanne and some of the other women in the study. The men they love have a separate life that is very much apart from them, a mysterious engagement they do not understand and therefore cannot control. When we see ourselves as the ''one and only'' in our partner's eyes, we find comfort in his need of us; we achieve power in our hold over him. It is no secret that sexual power plays form the basis of many relationships.

In addition, most women consider sexual fidelity a primary value that cannot be separated from the idea of commitment. Their specialness, which includes their sexuality, is what leads their partners to choose them above others. When the men can achieve emotional or physical intimacy with another person, they feel that their unique position is threatened.

The most common fear expressed by women in non-monogamous relationships is that their men will someday fall in love with a man and leave them. These fears exist over the men's protests, and in spite of all evidence to the contrary.

The women fear the mystery of their husbands' relationships, and they know they cannot control their men's love by creating an environment of sexual dependency.

Many women share the view expressed by Carol and Joanne that these fears exist not because they are valid but because the women themselves are insecure and vulnerable. Nevertheless, their husbands grow impatient when their wives express any doubts. The men remind their partners that they have always been open about their homosexuality and that they entered the marriage fully aware of the circumstances. (This impatience occasionally verges on self-righteousness, as if to make the point, "I'm not one of those gay men who tricked a woman into marrying him.")

If only life were so simple that our rational choices would never be subject to emotional scrutiny! For while the women admit that, yes, they knew the truth, and, yes, they made their choice in spite of it and would do it again, their intellectual enlightenment does not free them from moments of doubt. Here is the way several women put it:

Since I love my husband so much, I want to be enough for him, and it's hard for me to accept that I'm not. He loves me, but he doesn't feel complete with me.
—Sarah P., 29, married 8 years

For me, sex has always been a part of love. He assures me that he's not in love with any of his male partners, but I can't completely get over the fear that he might fall in love with one of them and leave me. Not that he would ever deliberately set out to do this. But falling in love happens sometimes, whether we ask for it or not.
—Roberta T., 32, married 2 years

I don't mind that he's attracted to men, but I guess I don't really understand what being gay means to him.

Why can't he just decide not to pursue it? Is it really that big? I would honestly like to be able to understand how he feels about this, but his homosexual side is a great mystery to me. On the positive side, it means that I'm forced to be more creative in our marriage. The old feminine wiles certainly don't work with my husband.

—Jane R., 40, married 9 years

He can't possibly find my body as attractive as that of a man. He loves me as a person, but I can't believe he'll ever be totally satisfied with me. Because I'm female, I'll never be good enough. Most women try to improve themselves to be closer to their man's ideal. They change their hairstyle, lose or gain weight, wear clothes he likes, do special things for him. But being a woman is something I can't change.

—Mary P., 27, married 4 years

I worry sometimes that he will fall in love with a man and want to leave. If he stayed then, I would feel terrible. I worry that he doesn't always want me sexually, that I don't turn him on, and it's important to me that he is happy and satisfied with me and by me.

—Barbara U., 31, married 7 years

The men generally took a more casual view. For them, the freedom to express their sexuality fully was viewed as a positive and enriching opportunity. As several of them said:

I am very happy in my present situation, which is to be married to a woman I am in love with, and also have a male lover whom I love. My wife and I are dealing with the issues, and we intend to remain married for the rest

of our lives. We share a lot—a lifetime, almost, of rich
and rewarding experiences, good and bad, that bring us
closer together. We have always been close friends first.
                              —David T., 43, married 18 years

---

I love my wife and children and am happy with them.
But I also see that I am a total of many needs. I can't
always understand the forces that drive me or the
feelings I get when I'm with a man. But I am careful
not to hurt my wife or my children or myself.
                              —Jerry T., 40, married 14 years

---

It's so dumb that the sexual nature of man and woman
causes so many problems and hang-ups. The religious
mores and guilt are a large factor in these problems and
must be changed. Otherwise, I think any kind of sex is
great for anyone as long as it isn't forced.
                              —Paul S., 37, married 10 years

I'm in love with my wife in every way—including
sexually. I don't want to end up old and lonely like a lot
of gay men. But I'm not completely resolved about sex.
It's been a long time since I've been with a man, but I
think I'd mind if I thought I could never have that in my
life again. She hasn't asked me to practice complete
sexual fidelity forever, although I know she worries
about it in the back of her mind. I wish there was a way
I could reassure her.
                              —Jack F., 32, married 5 years

The men in the study who have homosexual relationships
outside their marriages are very sensitive to the issue of
AIDS. They do not take the attitude, "My sexual needs

must be met, no matter what." They are responsible and careful—as much as one can be—but determined, nevertheless, to be "true" to themselves and find a balance in their lives. (We will discuss the role of AIDS in greater detail later in the book.)

Still, sexual infidelity is a troubling spectre, regardless of the justifications. As Wendell Berry writes in *The Unsettling of America,* "Domestic order is obviously threatened by the margin of wilderness that surrounds it. Marriage may be destroyed by instinctive sexuality; the husband may choose to remain with Kalypso or the wife may run away with a godlike Paris. And the forest is always waiting to overrun the fields. These are real possibilities. They must be considered, respected, even feared."

And yet, Berry goes on to suggest that the existence of too many restrictions might accomplish the opposite of what is intended, for, he says, the central paradox is that "the natural forces that so threaten us are the same forces that preserve and renew us."

Some of the couples in this chapter might find comfort and hope in his words.

Staying Faithful

When Bill and Paula decided to get married, they pledged sexual fidelity. For Bill, that meant that he would no longer have sex with men. It wasn't a smooth transition.

I met the couple several months after they had married, in a restaurant in Dallas, Texas, where they lived. They sat close together in the booth across from me, enthusiastic newlyweds who talked eagerly of their plans for the future. Like most of the couples I had met, Bill and Paula were bright, straightforward people; they were perfectly willing to share with me both the good side of their relationship and their struggles.

"When I started dating Bill, there was a lot of pressure from his gay friends," Paula, a pretty, thirty-year-old beautician told me. "It was as though they were sending me a message: If women take away all the gay men, what's left for them? They felt I was horning in on their territory, and that I had no right. But Bill assured me that this wasn't true, and he promised that he would be faithful to me. Do I believe him? Yes, but he's close to a number of gay men, and I know they don't think our relationship is valid at all—just a passing phase in his life. Sometimes I think maybe this thing is bigger than both of us, and that eventually Bill might change his mind."

Bill, a handsome advertising writer in his mid-thirties, disagreed. "Nobody tells me how to live," he said boldly. "I love Paula and I want to be married to her. I hope someday we will have children. Maybe it doesn't make sense to a lot of people, but it seems right to me. I don't have doubts.

"I've had a number of relationships with men," he explained. "One lasted seven years. We lived together and I thought it was going to be a permanent relationship—the great love of my life. But it was an emotional roller coaster. We went out a lot and were involved in a big party scene. John loved the fast life, but I was never comfortable with it. It depressed me. I hardly ever saw any stable gay matches, and I wanted John and my relationship to be a stable one. I planned to be with him for life.

"For a long time, I suspected that he was playing around on me, but I just couldn't face it. I kept telling myself I was imagining things, that John really loved me and took our relationship as seriously as I did. Eventually, of course, things came to a head. I confronted John with my suspicions, and his reaction totally stunned me. He looked at me like I was from another planet and said he'd just assumed I had other lovers, too. Didn't everyone? I couldn't even speak, I was so upset. This was before AIDS became a big thing, but even so, it wasn't part of my makeup to be promiscuous, and I would never assume this kind of thing about someone I was committed to. I told him so, but he didn't get my point, so I asked him to leave.

"It took me a long time to get over what happened. I was

bitter, and I was confused, too, because I didn't really know what I wanted anymore. That was a bad time for me. I wondered what it really meant to be gay and, although I never questioned my homosexuality or my attraction to men, I did question whether or not I could realistically hope to find a permanent male partner. Then two years after I broke up with John, I met Paula.''

"Had you ever been with a woman before?'' I asked.

"Yes,'' he nodded. "In high school and college I'd had girlfriends. We'd had sexual relationships, and for a while I had considered the possibility that I might be bisexual . . . whatever that means. I finally decided that no, I was homosexual, but it wasn't this cut-and-dried thing for me. Like, some of the guys I know simply would not or could not have a sexual relationship with a woman. For me, it was always more that I would *prefer* to have a sexual relationship with a man, but I could be happy with a woman if it was the right woman and I really loved her. I don't think that means I'm bisexual''—he grinned at Paula. "Crazy, maybe, but not bisexual. Actually, Paula thought I was crazy at first. She resisted me for a long time, before I finally convinced her that it was going to be okay.''

"I knew that John was the great love of his life,'' Paula said, "and I wanted him to be sure.''

"You thought he might just be on the rebound?'' I guessed.

"Yes, exactly.''

"I saw her point,'' Bill said, "but by the time I met Paula, I was pretty well over John. When I felt myself falling in love with her, I took myself in hand and said, 'Bill, is this what you really want?' and no matter how many obstacles I considered, I kept coming back to the fact that I was willing to make the compromises if it meant I could have Paula in my life.''

"Even though she insisted you give up sex with men?''

He shook his head vehemently. "She didn't insist. That was me. You might find this hard to believe, but I'm a traditional guy. Commitment means monogamy. Period.''

"If he didn't really believe that, I never would have married him,'' Paula added. ''I was very cautious about his not feeling that he was making a big sacrifice for me. I didn't want him to end up being unhappy and blaming me for it.''

''I have talked to many couples,'' I told them. ''Most of them are open to some degree of non-monogamous activity, and they, of course, have their problems coming to terms with the ambiguities in their relationships. However, nearly all of the men told me that they needed to have that door left open; even if they didn't pursue homosexual relationships, they couldn't make a decision to end them. I wonder how realistic you're being.''

''When you get married, you know that there's never a complete guarantee about anything,'' Bill replied. ''I think our chance of making it is just as good, and probably even better, than that of most couples who are getting married today. Commitment implies risk. But I'd rather concentrate on all the good things we have together than worry about the problems that might come up in the future.'' He smiled apologetically. ''I suppose that sounds like kind of a stock answer. But what else can I say? I feel content. I love Paula. I'm committed to make this work. What more is there?''

Many people in the study who said they chose sexual fidelity admitted that sex was not an important priority in their relationships. Others reported enjoying very complete and fulfilling sexual relationships. The bottom line, in every case, seemed to be *choice*. The couples determined that they would not be ''sexual victims,'' that they would invent their relationships based on their needs, and try to ignore what others told them was right or appropriate.

And it's possible that sex is not, in reality, the big stumbling block one would expect it to be in these relationships. Psychologist Don Clark points out that good sexual relationships can and do exist between primarily homosexual men and primarily heterosexual women. Says Clark,

> People are taught, and *believe*, that they should choose one of the two original categories and remain in it, or be

classified in the third [bisexuality] and consider themselves emotionally unstable. For those of us who have
remained aware of our attraction to people of the same
gender there is a pressure to call yourself a homosexual
and believe that you are not capable of any satisfying
emotional and sexual involvement with a person of the
other gender. You would do well not to permit other people to assign you a category. It is you who must decide
the relative strength of each speaker in your stereo system. It is you who must pick your descriptive label, if
any, and who must decide which individuals you will
love.

A number of study respondents shared this view:

I am tired of hearing that homosexuals are *by nature*
promiscuous—that we have to have a lot of sex with a
lot of partners. There's more to life than sex, and
there's more to homosexuality than sex. We have
emotions and intellects and free wills, just like
everyone else.

> —Ben E., 28, married 2 years

I cannot imagine being faithful to my wife in every way
except sexually. It would be a betrayal for me to go out
with men. I'm a husband. I'm a father. I'm not a
playboy.

> —Pat O., 39, married 12 years

For me, sex is the expression of a great many things—
physical attraction, spiritual union, the opportunity for
unspoken communication. It's not just ''doing it.''

> —Gary R., 30, married 6 years

AIDS has a lot to do with my decision to have sex only with my wife. It's time for all of us to be more responsible about our sexual practices. I don't want to die, and I couldn't live with myself if I gave her AIDS. What an awful legacy from a roll in the hay!

—Peter G., 34, married 8 years

Inventing the Unconventional Marriage

When I met them, David and Helen were bursting with excitement, having just signed the papers on a new house. In two months, they would be married.

They weren't youngsters; in fact, it had taken a long while for them to come full circle and reach this point. Both were in their early fifties. Helen had been widowed two years earlier, after a twenty-four-year marriage. David had lived with a male partner for fifteen years, and had been "widowed" himself when his partner died of AIDS. Theirs was a very romantic story, which they told enthusiastically, interrupting each other frequently to add details.

"We met in college," David began, "and we were very close then."

"I adored him," Helen interrupted.

"But I was gay, so it was a big problem."

"We did try," Helen said. "It seemed so unfair that we couldn't be together—we both thought so. Maybe if we hadn't been so convinced that it would be impossible, we would have made it work. But it seemed too improper to consider really having a relationship, much less getting married."

"More so for Helen than for me," David said wryly. "How could I possibly have considered saddling this lovely woman with a gay husband? Helen had everything going for her, and there were plenty of men who were interested. I felt guilty that she wanted me, since I didn't think I would make the best match for her. I was the one who broke it off, even though I didn't want to. It seemed the right thing to do."

"Were you involved with any men, then?" I asked David.

"Things were quite different in those days," he reminded me. "Much more closeted, especially in a place like Virginia. A lot of the gay men I knew were getting married because there just didn't seem to be any other choice. I was interested in finding myself as a homosexual, but it broke my heart to give up Helen. Sometimes I thought I would gladly have said the hell with being gay, just to keep her."

"Of course, he never told *me* that," Helen said. "All that time, I thought that I was the one who was holding *him* back. I never guessed the extent of his feelings for me. I was heartbroken too." She shook her head. "Isn't it silly what we do to the people we love the most?"

"You got married, then?"

"Yes, and I was happy enough. Roger was a good man, although I wouldn't say that ours was the great love of all time. We lived a comfortable suburban life, had two wonderful children, and I don't regret having been married to him."

"And you and David never communicated?"

"We spied on each other for more than twenty years," Helen said, and they both laughed.

"What she means," David explained, "is that we didn't keep in touch, but we kept track of each other through mutual friends. I remember when I heard that Helen was getting married, I went out and got drunk. It was many years before I found any kind of stable relationship."

"I suppose I was glad for him when I learned David was living with a man," Helen mused. "I wanted him to be happy. But there was always this little glimmer of sadness when I thought about David. It never went away."

"How did you get back together?"

"When Helen's husband died, I had been alone for about three years," David said. "My lover, Edward, died of AIDS, and I spent the first year alternately feeling lonely and being scared silly that I might have it, too. I didn't. I think what saved me was the fact that I was never very sexually adventurous—even with Edward. He was different, in that respect."

"David practiced safe sex before it was in vogue," Helen added. "Thank God."

"When Edward died, the thing I wanted most was to talk to Helen, but I never contacted her. After all, she was married. What was I going to do? Show up on the scene after twenty years and disrupt her family? That seemed very selfish. So I kept to myself, and it was a bad time, because I was getting older and I was lonely. But then one day I learned from a friend that Helen's husband had died. I knew I had to reach out to her in some way."

"I was flabbergasted when I received flowers and a note of condolence from David," Helen said. "It was straight out of the blue. I called him immediately, and we met for dinner. What shocked us both was that, after all those years, we seemed to pick up right where we had left off. We started spending a lot of time together, and when he said, almost in jest, that we should get married, I said yes."

"It wasn't in jest," David protested. "I really meant it. But I thought Helen might think it was a ludicrous idea, so I made it sound like a casual suggestion. I was thrilled when she said yes. I was like a kid, dancing all around the room."

"He kept picking me up and kissing me," Helen said as she laughed. "I felt so young."

"How do your children feel about your marrying David?" I asked Helen.

"My son, who is twenty-three, thinks it's a great idea. My daughter, who is twenty, has mixed feelings."

"They know he's gay?"

"Yes, we've been up front about that. Of course, I get all the lectures from them about AIDS and safe sex. They find it a little embarrassing to talk about, but they've been protective of me since their father died—especially my son.

"My daughter would rather I didn't do this. She thinks I'll be unhappy. We argued about it when I first told her. I remember once she complained and said, 'Oh, Mom, what will I tell people?' I said to her very sternly, 'Rebecca, are you saying that you would rather that I be alone and lonely than figure out what to tell people? Tell them whatever you like.'

When I put it like that, she admitted she was being selfish, but she's not very enthusiastic about the idea.''

"Everything will turn out fine," David said, patting her hand. They smiled happily at each other. I left them, thinking how lucky they were.

When I met the couples whose stories appear in this chapter, I was determined to be as objective as possible, fearing I might be "fooled" by the appearance of satisfaction where it really did not exist. I knew they would be judged harshly by those who read their stories, and I wanted to present an honest portrait of both the positive and negative sides of their relationships. I, too, was naturally skeptical, unsure of how I could find anything remotely approaching enlightenment among couples who were not always sexually faithful, and who struggled so mightily.

But it is very hard not to like and respect these couples for their directness, their sensitivity, their love. They are finely tuned to the tensions within their marriages, and their struggles seem more brave than foolish, for although they confront daily the underlying currents of fear and confusion that exist beneath the surface of their relationships, they are determinedly cheerful and optimistic. In a sense, they are the reluctant pioneers of a different family form, and by living the way they do, they are making a statement about the nature of love and commitment in the final years of the twentieth century.

One man summed it up this way: "Society conditions us to define ourselves very narrowly—black or white, gay or straight, blue collar or white collar, Christian or Jew. Finding oneself between the categories requires both time and experience. I would have liked to have been resolved about my feelings before I got involved in a serious relationship, but it doesn't always work that way. Growing means reaching out, and if the one you reach out to is as unsure as you are there can be pain—but not without the possibility of happiness.''

CHAPTER FIVE

Objects of Affection

"I'm sorry," I said after we'd walked a block. "I'm so sorry, Nina."

"What for, George? Really, what for?"

"I don't know." I shrugged. "For disappointing you. I don't know. Sometimes . . ."

"George—" she cut me off. "You don't disappoint me. And I didn't say I wanted to change anything. I didn't say it and I didn't mean it . . ."

. . . Sometimes, sometimes when we were sitting together in the living room late at night or sprawled in our respective rooms doing the crossword puzzles and calling out questions to each other, I wanted to go to her and make love to her, make love to her in front of a fireplace or on an empty beach or in a canopy bed, in a dozen foolishly romantic and artificial settings. I wanted to make love to her with sweet words and tender looks and all the packaged images that have never in my life had anything to do with the genuine lustful passion I've felt. I wanted to feel closer to Nina than I sometimes did, to bring down what often felt like an enormous and invisible wall separating us. And still, I knew that if we ever did make love, it would be the act to consummate the end of our relationship and not the beginning of it. If we ever did make love, we'd be unable to go on with our dancing lessons and our cluttered life together, our safe, celibate relationship. It wasn't what either one of us wanted, and the fact that it never came up was one of the things that held us together.

—from *The Object of My Affection,*
Stephen McCauley

I SOMETIMES still think about a friend I had as a child. Judy was my best friend from the time I was nine years old until I graduated from high school. I can still remember the thrill I used to get, knowing that I had a friend like that—the absolute good fortune of our pairing. Growth, change, and discovery happened fast then; we were propelled into the future by a flood of new experiences, constant physical evolution, and ever-flowing emotion. We shared so much—we couldn't seem to stop talking; my father, who grew hoarse from shouting at me to get off the phone, can attest to that.

Most of our conversations were about the future—that time around the bend of eighteen when we would be *free*. We were in a big hurry to get there, of course, (a trait I recognize in my own fourteen-year-old son) and we simply assumed that wherever we were going, we would be going together.

Today, I don't even know where Judy is, but I imagine that she remembers me as I remember her, from the time before relationships got so complicated and friendships turned so fleeting.

I mention this because, in talking of how we'd always do things together in the future, neither Judy nor I had ever considered the practicalities of such a plan. I suppose we both assumed that we'd get married and have families of our own, but our imaginations conveniently skipped the logistics that would be required if we were to live side by side for the rest of our lives.

It occurs to me now that what many people find missing in their lives is that sense of deep connection that most of us found easy to achieve in childhood, but so hard to establish in adulthood. We are always looking for partners who can satisfy the old itch for telling all without repercussions, and we are disappointed when those who claim to love us most cannot commit to us or listen to our hopes and fears without withdrawing into fears or judgments of their own. Simply put, when we were children, we *loved* the idea of commitment. As adults, we are both callous and afraid.

If, in our innocent youths, we imagined that our dearest

friends would be dear for life, we found in adulthood that friends, no matter how close, could disappear all too easily. They could move away or get married and become less close, or find new and better friends, or any combination of the above. In searching for partners, we placed friends in a lesser category of obligation. Friends were the people who would be *most likely* to help you if you were in trouble, but they weren't *obligated* to. This headier responsibility was delegated to husbands or wives. Marriage was the "bottom-line" relationship. If you moved, he—or she—moved too. There were no loose ends.

It is no wonder, then, that the hordes of single adults feel so unanchored. There is no real context outside marriage for committed partnerships to flourish. Even the newly popular style of "living together" seems a bit unsettling sometimes, for it can be distinguished from marriage only by the fact that the partners have chosen *not* to legalize their commitment. No one ever seems to really explain what is being gained by this choice.

The Object of My Affection, the story quoted at the beginning of this chapter, is the bittersweet tale of a "committed friendship" that speaks directly to the need people have to be together. In the story, Nina is a disorganized young woman with many complications, among them her affinity for difficult men and her inability to complete her doctoral dissertation in psychology. George is a kind, mixed-up kindergarten teacher, trying to recover from a disastrous gay love affair. The high cost of New York living brings them together as roommates, but their relationship blossoms into friendship, and then something more. It's hard to know what to call it. Love, maybe. Commitment. Friendship, in a definition of the term that we can't quite understand. When Nina becomes pregnant and then breaks up with her boyfriend, George decides to stay with her and help with the baby. He does so because he loves Nina, and she lets him stay because she loves him. There are many complications along the way, but it is absolutely clear that Nina and George have found a special place between the lines that people ordinarily draw in defining relationships. And for this reason, it is a lovely, hopeful story.

In *The Third Wave,* Alvin Toffler proposes that the shift from the "de-massified" era to the era of individual potential, while giving people more freedom to achieve personal goals, has also isolated them. "For," Toffler writes, "the more individualized we are, the more difficult it becomes to find a mate or a lover who has precisely matching interests, values, schedules, or tastes. Friends are also harder to come by. We become choosier in our social ties. But so do others. The result is a great many ill-matched relationships. Or no relationships at all." Toffler warns that if the future society is to avoid being "icy metallic, with a vacuum for a heart, it must attack the problem frontally. It must restore community."

The story of Nina and George also brings to light the factor of timing in the development of relationships. Their initial involvement grows out of the comfort they feel with one another. Both feel vulnerable at the end of painful relationships and the absence of sexual pressure is one of the most attractive aspects of the relationship.

Approximately 30 percent of the men and women who participated in my study were engaged in committed partnerships that were not marriage. Some of these were nonsexual and some were sexual, and often the respondents were hard pressed to describe their partner's meaning to them. Many used the description "significant other."

Finding Intimacy in Strange Places

"I hate the word *platonic,*" laughed Marcia. "It sounds so cold and without passion, as though people who are not having sex with one another have no spark between them. Phil and I would be termed 'platonic' friends, in the sense that we didn't have sex. But for two years, we spent all of our time together, went on vacations, held joint parties, shared our dreams, and even slept together. I don't call that platonic, and I resent the implication that if you're not lovers, it means you're stuck with a vague, uncommitted definition like that.''

Marcia is a thirty-two-year-old artist, whose avant-garde style—one earring and about twenty bracelets—is softened by a thin, childlike face, and large, innocent blue eyes. She lives in a New York City apartment with her ''platonic'' friend, Phil.

She told me that she and Phil had met at a party when they both lived in Denver, and were instantly taken with one another. ''He told me right away that he was gay and wasn't looking for a sexual relationship with a woman, and that was perfectly fine with me,'' she said. ''I had just ended a long and awful love affair, and I wasn't looking either. So we just fell into a routine, seeing each other on weekends, going to movies, cooking meals together, and talking a lot about our lives and feelings. We both loved to ski, and we took quite a few skiing trips together, too. Over the course of about a year, a subtle shift began to happen, and people started treating us like an official 'couple.' We laughed about it, but we weren't displeased. It felt good to be grounded somewhere instead of spinning our wheels out in the single world.

''However, I'd be lying if I didn't admit that there was a lot of buzzing in my brain around that time about what was happening between us. I tried to just relax and go with the flow, figuring that Phil was someone I needed in my life at that time. But the nagging thoughts were there. There was something bigger going on than 'just friends' and I was afraid of it, because I didn't want to get sucked into any feelings that would leave me shattered when our time was up. I think we both felt that there was something not very healthy about our closeness, that maybe it was an escape from the 'real' world of more lasting and significant relationships.''

''Did you talk about your feelings?'' I asked her.

''No!'' She threw up her hands and the bracelets jangled. ''That was the frustrating thing. We couldn't, or we didn't,

I'm not sure which. There didn't seem to be any way to discuss it. What would we have said?''

''What happened?''

''After we'd known each other about two years, Phil got the opportunity to move to New York. He had always talked about moving East. He's a financial consultant, and Denver isn't exactly the financial capital of the world. I remember the day he called me on the phone, all excited, and told me that the consulting firm he worked for was transferring him to New York. The news hit me like a blow to the gut. I felt betrayed, though I had no right to be. I told him how happy I was for him, but I didn't feel happy at all.

''For the next couple of months, I watched Phil get ready to leave. At that point, our relationship was very tense. There were a lot of unspoken feelings going on, but neither of us could articulate them. It was one of the worst periods of my life, because I felt as though I was losing something very important and, not only could I not stop it, I couldn't even describe what I thought I was losing. I couldn't tell what Phil was feeling.''

''But you had never really considered your relationship with Phil to be permanent,'' I said. ''It was right for the time, but weren't you ready by then to move on to something else? And wasn't Phil?''

''You mean a *real* relationship?'' Marcia asked, laughing. ''I always thought I would eventually, when it felt right. But it was in some distant future when supposedly I would be more ready. And when the reality of Phil's leaving sunk in, I couldn't think of anything except that I didn't want him to leave.'' She shrugged. ''These things aren't *rational,* you know.''

''Can you describe more fully what it was about the relationship that made you feel so strongly?'' I asked. ''Obviously, it wasn't sexual feelings.''

''No—although, I think all feelings are sexual, in a way, since we're sexual beings. You had a category in your survey called 'intimate, but not sexual.' That stood out for me. We were intimate—more intimate, I think, than most of the

couples we knew. We depended on each other completely.
We could talk about anything.''

"Except your relationship.''

"Right. Maybe we were afraid that if we talked about it,
we'd talk ourselves out of it.''

"But what about sex? Most people want some kind of
sexual relationship. Were you seeing other people?''

"Occasionally. And I know I wasn't planning to give up
sex forever; neither was Phil. It just seemed okay to put it
on the back burner for the time being. It was more important to develop other things. Actually, it was kind of a relief
not to have the pressure. More people should try it.''

I laughed. "You're not alone in that opinion. So, tell me
how you and Phil resolved your dilemma.''

"One night, about three weeks before he was due to leave,
Phil called me up and asked me to meet him for a drink.
He was very agitated, and I kept asking him what was
wrong, and finally he grabbed my hand and said—he was
almost *angry*—'Come with me to New York.' I just stared
across the table at him, and my head was going, 'No, no, no,
I better not.' But my heart was going, 'Sure, why not?' ''

"And your heart won out.''

"Eventually. We had our first totally honest conversation
that night about what we really meant to one another. We
were realistic about the areas that remained unresolved—and
sex was one of them—but we decided that our commitment
was strong enough that we could work those issues through
over time. The important thing was that we wanted to be
together.''

"And now you've been here two years . . .''

"I've never been sorry I came,'' Marcia said. "People
might say I'm crazy, but do you want to know what would
be crazy? For me to have said no and given up the chance to
have what I have now. How many couples are as good together as we are?''

I kept trying to ask Marcia about permanency, but she kept
slipping away from the subject. Once again, I was searching
for something a little bit more cut and dried, because I had

learned to view commitment as something firm and intractable—like the signature on a marriage certificate. Furthermore, Marcia and Phil's relationship seemed to have more black holes than most. In the days following our conversation, I alternated between thinking the relationship was doomed to failure and wondering if maybe it wasn't the sign of a positive trend. I still don't know the answer, although there were many examples of similar commitments among the respondents to my survey. In fact, this unsettling intimacy was the most common theme that emerged from the study, and I only call it unsettling because it came as such a surprise to those who were involved. It was, without a doubt, such a *new* way of approaching partnership. Here is what some of the respondents said:

I am a gay man who is in love with a woman—I have been for some time. She and I have known each other since we were children, and over a period of sixteen years we have built a very loving, understanding relationship. She did not know I was gay until five years ago. Yet after all our tears and fears were spent, we've managed to realize we need each other very dearly. I can't really imagine my life without her being a part of it, and she says I am important to her happiness, too.

—Fred L., 28

I don't know whether my gay friend and I qualify as a "gay-straight love match." We're not lovers, but we do love each other, and it seems that there is some sexual energy between us that is disconcerting to us both. It has caused some problems between us, and I can't say with any certainty that we've come to terms with it yet, although we are both more comfortable with it than we were three years ago. Our relationship has survived a lot of confusion and frustration.

—Pam B., 31

Jay and I have been friends since 1975. He's now thirty-seven and I am thirty-five. We own a house, a car, and three cats together. Over the years, we've managed to incorporate our unusual relationship into the "normal" world around us, and we are now accepted for the way we are by friends, family, and most others.

—Liz P., 35

I met her through a gay friend. She is beautiful, smart, and fun. I gradually fell in love with her and was more fulfilled being with her. We have had good times, but lots of hard ones also. Slowly, we are growing and becoming more understanding of each other.

—John D., 40

I am deeply involved with a gay man. For over ten years now, there hasn't been a day that goes by that I don't think of him. Although it sometimes isn't clear what direction our relationship will take, my intention is always to do what is best. I want to be happy, and I want him to be happy.

For a long time, I fantasized about him sexually, but eventually the lust faded . . . though never the attraction. The realization of how special it is being with him and the happiness it brings, makes the idea of sex both unnecessary and destructive. I feel totally open with him—he's like no other man I've ever known. I have had more intimacy with him than I've had with any other man. Any person who believes that a woman who is involved with a homosexual has a fear of intimacy has a limited view of love.

—Sheila N., 35

I truly enjoy being homosexual, and I enjoy being with women, too, because women are very feeling and

understanding—which most men aren't. I never thought
of having a relationship with a woman, but when I met
Sharon, there was a difference. Maybe it's because I'm
older and more mature. Committed love means caring,
and caring very deeply, for one person in particular.
I've always wanted that, and I hope the relationship will
work out that way.

—Nat P., 48

Profound Choices

What is the difference between loving a person and being
"in love" with that person? I have never heard the distinction clarified; I imagine most people would say that it is not
explainable—just something the heart knows. But on a scale
of importance, "in love" certainly connotes more importance, and a hoped-for permanency, while "love" alone can
imply any number of things. In my experience, the people
most unwilling to express feelings of love are those who
fear they are "in love." People who simply "love" speak
about it all the time. It is a very tangled matter.

Of course, being "in love" is usually considered in a
romantic context. It connotes the idea of being swept away,
since the word "falling" usually precedes the statement—
as in, "I am falling in love with you." Many of the respondents in the study talked of being "in love," even when
their relationships were not sexual, a notion most people
would find confusing. I think it may be possible that emotions exist for which no labels have yet been created. Maybe
the writer and poet Louise Bogan was reaching for this when
she wrote, "I wish there was something between love and
friendship that I could tender him; and some gesture, not
quite a caress, I could give him. A sort of smoothing."

One evening, describing these responses to a friend of
mine who is a counselor for women in transition, I was
almost surprised when she nodded in understanding. I was

becoming so used to people—especially professionals—*not* understanding. "We come from such a romantic tradition," she observed. "Many of the women I counsel are trying to get their lives back together after divorce. They are shattered. Absolutely devastated. It doesn't matter if the men were bastards. People will go to great lengths to maintain the romantic myth. They believe that they will never fall in love again, but what do they mean by falling in love? That they'll never feel dizzy and dependent again? That they'll never cry themselves to sleep five out of seven nights a week? I push them to tell me what they mean. Usually it turns out that they are holding onto a memory, an experience they had once. A romantic feeling. It might not even have been a sexual experience that precipitated it. A large part of my job is to pull them out of that moment into the present. We talk about how they can channel that desire for love in ways that won't damage their self-worth."

"For example?" I asked.

"Learning to love people in different ways, to be a part of the world and the community. You would be surprised to hear how many women don't have really close relationships with people other than the men they are romantically interested in and their children. Oh, they have dozens of people in their lives, but when it comes right down to it, they hold themselves back from being close to others."

I was interested, and I looked at her expectantly, waiting to hear the connection.

"Anyway, the reason I mention this is that I can see how sometimes relationships like these could be good for women. I can also see the downside, of course. Intimacy can be pretended as a form of escape. But it seems that one of the things your people are saying is that they need to have others in their lives they can count on. It gets back to needing a sense of community. Needing to be a part of something. I once counseled a divorced woman who cried and cried because the Fourth of July was coming up, and she and her husband always went to the park and had a picnic and watched the fireworks, and she didn't want to go alone, but she couldn't find anyone else to go with her. All of her friends were busy. This longing had nothing to do with sex. It had to do with having someone who wouldn't be busy on the Fourth of July—or, rather, someone who would expect to spend the day with her.''

"Yes," I sighed. "That seems to be what people are saying. But is it really enough just to have someone who is a companion?''

"Companionship is a loaded concept," she said, smiling. "It can mean many things. True companionship isn't just spending time with someone—you can die of loneliness in a crowded room. I think there's romance and intellectual stimulation and different kinds of pleasure to be found in true companionship.''

Our conversation started me thinking about the times in my life I had felt that close to men who weren't also sexual partners. I remembered one period in particular, when I was in college at the end of the Sixties. Ironically, although sexual freedom was something we enjoyed then without the scourge of betrayal or disease, in retrospect I realized that it wasn't the sex that was so thrilling to us in those days. It was the new ideas and talking all night and doing things we'd never done before. I once told my son that those were the best times of my life; like many people of my generation, I've probably been looking for their equivalent ever since.

The other thing I remembered about that time is that we talked about love a lot. Granted, we didn't even know what we were saying half the time. We rarely equated this love with any kind of long-standing commitment. But whatever our misguided notions or naiveté, for a time we were a community. We had each other. It seemed impossible to imagine a time when any of us would suffer from being alone.

How our generation moved so easily from this expansive environment to the sterile confines of one-person studio apartments is a mystery to me. But our memories have remained intact and that is why it is not such an impossible

leap of the imagination to consider the idea of committed
friendships.

In describing her ten-year relationship with Jeff, Mary
wrote: "It is an exclusive emotional relationship. At times,
it is best characterized as oblique, but ultimately it remains
the primary emotional focus for both of us."

I never met Mary personally, but she has communicated
with me on several occasions in the course of my research,
admitting that it was "therapeutic" for her to try to make
sense of her deep relationship with the man she calls her
"significant other." Since Jeff has been diagnosed as having AIDS-related complex (ARC), her need has carried
more urgency than most.

"We met in 1978 on our college newspaper," Mary
wrote, "and quickly became partners on several projects.
We work together closely, easily, and often. Although we've
never known exactly what our relationship is, we do know
when it started; about six months after we met, we stayed
up all night on the roof of my building in one of those
cathartic collegiate talks that change more lives than people
like to admit. We still exchange anniversary gifts on this
date.

"In many ways, I think I was instrumental in teaching
him about his gay identity, since I introduced him to men I
knew who lived outside the closet. They brought him into a
bigger gay world, although he has never participated much
in gay culture. He stopped denying his sexuality, but has
never wanted to let it define or limit him. We have never
slept together, though there was a phase early on when we
went through a lot of awkward physicality. We each have
our own *petit amis,* but they have never been primary relationships.

"After graduation, Jeff went to the East Coast and found
a good job in publishing. I followed a year later, but I wasn't
happy in New York and returned to California. The year
after that, Jeff decided to chuck it all and go to law school,
but first he wanted to live in Italy for a year. My career
wasn't working out at the time, so I was eventually con-

vinced to go along. We arrived with the vaguest of plans, and ended up staying in Rome for four years. Jeff worked for an Italian publisher, and I freelanced at various international agencies. We usually maintained separate apartments (though we shared a car), but functionally spent most of our time together. It was a very intense bonding experience.

"Last year, Jeff decided he had better go to law school if he was ever going to, and I decided to leave Rome, too, mostly for financial reasons. He is now attending law school in Massachusetts, while I am working as an editor in California. Although he has been diagnosed with ARC, he continues his study and life plans as though this were not a factor. However, he phones me in the middle of the night to tell me his aches and pains and get some reassurance and mordant humor.

"A few months ago, Jeff and I went on vacation together, and I told him about your study. He agreed to reflect with me about what our relationship has meant to him. At the time, he was becoming involved in what I gathered was a rather one-sided, not-(yet)-sexual relationship with one of his classmates. He agonized over this relationship with me, which I found extremely ironic, since the other man's ambivalence toward Jeff so closely paralleled Jeff's ambivalence toward me. As he put it in regard to this other relationship: 'Whoever wants the least, wins.'

"Jeff gave me his version of the history of our relationship. He felt that we had grown steadily closer in college, and in fact had gotten a little carried away with ourselves and some fantasies. The years he stayed in New York and we wrote exquisite poetry to each other, he considered a time of rebalancing. Our first two years in Italy (during which he was often ill and I was often broke), he considered the worst time. The second two years in Italy, when he was healthier and I was more independent financially (and thus emotionally), he had found very satisfying. The past year had been one of retrenchment and reconsideration.

"He asked me what I thought I wanted. He knows I would

like to have a family, and I know he is not remotely interested in having one. He would feel unfairly burdened if he
thought I had given that up for him, but no one else makes
me feel the way he does, not even a little.

"I said I thought one ideal would be for us to be next-
door neighbors—intimacy and privacy combined. I have
seen enough bad marriages to know that what we have is
definitely better than that. I brought up the point that we
had essentially 'grown up' together, not in the sense of having known each other as children, but rather in that we were
very close at the time we were exploring what it means to
be adults. Our own interpersonal negotiations have had a
lasting effect on our overall values. This shared experience
makes us comfortable—even smug—discussing moral and
social questions, in a way I resist with most other people.
In fact, we talk a lot in terms of 'other people' and 'us.'
Our sense of ourselves as a unit is by now self-perpetuating,
and enshrined in certain little rituals and, especially, speech
patterns. We have a lot of family jokes. It has to be real,
but we don't know what it is. There are those special, glow-
ing moments between two people who love each other when
you look up from your reading at the same time and just
smile into each other's eyes with total understanding. What
is that?''

During the period she communicated with me, Mary was
by turns hopeful and frustrated. Often it seemed she was
trying too hard to find an explanation for something that
seemed to stubbornly defy definition. But her inner conflict
was understandable, since she was at the age when she really
did have to decide whether she wanted a family—something
she would apparently never have with Jeff. She was also
painfully aware that Jeff might contract AIDS, and felt an
urgency to resolve her place in his life before he was taken
away from her.

"How did I get into this?'' she asked once, and recalled
that she had always been somewhat different from the norm.
"I've always had a lot of gay friends. As a too-smart, rather
bohemian teenager in suburban California, I always felt out

of the mainstream anyway. There weren't many other kids who were interested in driving into the desert on hot afternoons. I have had sincere and fulfilling relationships with straight men, but I have limited patience with many of the demands of mainstream society. (I think I come by this honestly; my mother expresses her apartness by avidly befriending the few foreigners in the small town where she lives.)

"Jeff and I do some intensely romantic things, like paging each other in airports to say goodbye one last time. We once corresponded for a whole year only in Haiku. Flowers and gifts are frequent. We act out many traditional heterosexual roles when we are together. The years of working, studying, and traveling together have given us an idiolect for being together, a kind of family pattern and inside togetherness that would cost us both a great deal to give up. I could never say why we chose each other at the start, but here we are now."

There were traces of sadness and confusion in Mary's story. It occurred to me that, in this case, perhaps she and Jeff should have opted for a less bonded friendship, since in so many ways they didn't seem to fill each other's needs. As long as she remained so committed to Jeff, Mary would never have some of the things she held to be important, such as children.

I asked my counselor friend what she thought about Mary's story. "Mary is concentrating on the tradeoffs," she said, "which in itself is not bad. But I also hear some hope in her voice that maybe things could be different between them. More romantic, perhaps, or even sexual. One has to wonder why they don't live together, and I suspect it is Jeff's decision. This leaves Mary lonely much of the time."

"Do you think it's possible that Mary could get seriously involved with or married to another man and still maintain the same kind of relationship with Jeff?" I asked.

"I doubt it. She has to leave herself available to him. If she were married, Jeff would no longer be her significant other, would he? Even though she and Jeff don't have a sexual relationship, and don't even live in the same city, based on what I've heard, Mary lives for this relationship. She has quite a lot invested in it. I don't know her, of course, but one has to wonder how she finds the support she needs in this relationship.''

"She thinks Jeff will die of AIDS in the next few years," I said. "What do you think will happen then?''

"If he dies, it will be very hard for her at first. She has no formal status as his partner, so she will find the grieving process very painful. Ultimately, she may experience his death as the release she needs. It is the only circumstance that would allow her to separate from him.''

"It was never my intention to judge the relationships of the people who contacted me," I said. "Society does enough of that—saying one thing is healthy or moral and another thing is not. But a lot of the respondents seem truly confused. They're looking for some kind of direction. Tell me, when you counsel women, do you use any kind of litmus test by which to judge whether a relationship is good for a person?''

She shook her head. "Litmus test is too strong a description. Psychology isn't such an exact science, although not all psychologists would agree. But yes, of course, I have some things I look for—questions I ask. One is, very simply, does the relationship make you happy? Many people are enraptured with the notion of the heartsick lover. I've met women who don't believe they're in love unless they're miserable.

"Another is the factor I mentioned earlier of self-esteem. That is, does your loved one offer support and approval, or are you continually trying to change to fit his or her standards? I suspect that some of the women who are involved with gay men have problems with self-esteem for the simple reason that they love men who do not want them or, at least, do not prefer them sexually. It is a particularly vexing dilemma, since there is nothing they can change to make the men love them more. Their very womanhood is a problem. Also, some of these women may be in relationships as a form of settling. They may feel unworthy of the attentions of a 'normal' man and feel this is the best they can do. A woman who laughs and makes light of the fact that she so often gets entangled in strange relationships may be suffering inside, thinking, 'What's wrong with me?'

"A common point of view and shared goals are important. This does not mean that you have to be joined at the hip and think alike or enjoy doing all the same things. But there is an intimacy and trust that exists in good relationships where the partners know they hold the same values. This manifests itself in different ways for different people, but it has to be there. It's true that opposites sometimes attract, but only on the most superficial level. People feel a vicarious thrill in being with someone who is very different from themselves. But it's rare to see relationships survive when people are truly opposite.

"Ultimately, when women come to me and agonize over whether to stay in their relationships, the answer is never cut and dried. It depends on what their personal priorities are. If a woman deeply longs to have a child and she is with a man who can't or won't have a child with her, she must think seriously about whether it is important enough to leave him. By the same token, a woman may be in a relationship where there is little sex, but sex might not be as important to her as other things. It depends on the individual: What does a person really value? It requires great concentration and self-honesty to cut through the mire and find out what those things are."

Betty, a forty-eight-year-old woman, happily married and the mother of four children, told me about the special relationship she formed with a gay man she worked with in the theater. She never felt that their relationship in any way compromised her marriage, but in many ways it became a primary relationship for her.

"We discovered so many things in common," Betty said, "and over the course of five years our relationship intensified to the point that we had dinner together once a week. I lived about eighty miles from him, and I drove in for these meetings, cooked dinner for him, and spent the night at his house. Many of his friends did not know that he was gay, and some people who didn't know him well thought he was married to me.''

Betty's relationship holds special meaning because during the last year of their relationship, her friend was dying of AIDS. There was no question that she would take care of him during this time, spending many nights with him, nursing him through his pain, and offering all the love and support she had to give.

"When he died, I took care of the funeral arrangements," she said. "I was closer to him than any of his relatives, who lived half a country away."

Now that he's gone, Betty speaks of the emptiness his absence has created in her life, and the intensity of her grieving. "We loved each other," she said simply. "Our being together was the most natural thing in the world. People sometimes act surprised that I continue to grieve and miss him two years after his death. They view friendships as being dispensable—of less value than the bond we have with our husbands and children. How untrue that is!''

I found Betty's story poignant, in part because of the scope of her loss, and in part because, as a friend, she took on the role of caretaker usually reserved for family. She felt the committed obligation that people don't ordinarily take for granted from their friends; in doing so, she became his family.

Betty's story is also interesting because it disproves the version of the great romantic ideal that says one person can fill all of another person's needs. Betty widened her circle of commitment to include her gay friend, and, she says now, their love for each other enhanced her life and enriched all of her relationships, including her marriage.

Emotional exclusivity, when taken literally, can be deadly to committed love, and sometimes relationships develop to fulfill other needs. Marie, a forty-year-old French writer married to a scientist, wrote of how she had found a completion to her circle of commitment through her close relationship with a gay man. However, Marie experienced complications when the relationship grew too intimate.

"I am happily married and my husband and I get along extremely well," Marie wrote, "at least, emotionally and physically. Intellectually, our relationship is a bit more shaky, as we are like chalk and cheese.

"My habit has always been to find friends with whom I can share interests that my husband and I don't share. The only snag has been that there is no such thing as a purely intellectual relationship. Physical attraction tends to sneak into any kind of attachment, not necessarily of a sexual nature, but obviously containing that ingredient too, however subtle.

"Several years ago, at a convention in San Francisco, I befriended a man about my age and we were instantly very close. I didn't make a secret of the fact that I was married, faithful, and doing my best to stay that way. He told me he was gay, but that, while he was more attracted to men sexually, he was more attracted to women emotionally. We both traveled frequently for our work, and during the next two years we got together as often as we could in various cities. We did everything together—visited museums, attended concerts, saw movies, sat in restaurants, and talked for hours. We were perfectly in sync.

"But eventually, the tension became too great, because we wanted to be together very badly, and there was no way to fit a relationship of such intensity alongside my marriage. There wasn't room in my emotions for both. So we broke up. I would have liked to keep him as a friend, but I wasn't capable—and neither was he—of taking such a strong love and turning it into a more casual friendship. Had he not been gay, I might have left my husband to be with him, but I wouldn't live in a nonsexual partnership."

The term "just friends" grates against relationships like this. And, as Marcia argued earlier, "platonic" seems hollow as a way of defining what is for these people the most significant partnership in their lives. There is little status given to friendship in the vast legal network of family and community, and yet the bond often appears less fragile than the one that exists between husbands and wives. Sometimes we love people for reasons we can't explain—we just do. And when this love is nurtured, a connectedness develops that can be deeply satisfying, even when there is turmoil.

The Love-Sex Conflict

In all of these partnerships, the relationship between love and sex became an issue that often proved unresolvable over the long term. While the people involved were able to separate sex from love in describing the depth of their emotional attachments, they were often unable to resolve the many practical issues that emerged as a result of making committed choices. Marcia and Phil temporarily resolved the issue by postponing it. Mary and Jeff's relationship was more clearly in crisis, since they perceived their needs to be in conflict. Mary knew that the home and family she wanted would not be possible with Jeff as a partner. Marie's conflict grew from the impossibility of being together with the man she was growing to love and the realization that she didn't have the emotional flexibility to be deeply involved with him and her husband at the same time.

The conflicts are both practical and emotional. Practically, committed relationships require more planning and compromise than simple friendships. Important decisions about where and how to live deeply affect each person in the relationship, and when these issues arise, they often put the nature of the relationship to the test. Most of the people I spoke with admitted that, regardless of their depth, these nonsexual relationships were unlikely to remain the primary ones in their lives. When sex is part of a committed relationship, that relationship has a greater chance of working because the choices become less complex. This seems to be true even when the sexual relationships are not monogamous. Nonsexual relationships tend to be viewed as less permanent, regardless of their depth, for while most people agree that intimacy is more than sex, they cannot accept the fact that permanent intimate partnerships can exist without it.

It is hard to know, however, whether the absence of sex is a problem because the partners are frustrated or because they assume that spending long periods or even a lifetime without sex is unacceptable. Perhaps one disservice the sexual revolution did us was to foster the idea that a life without regular sex is a lesser life. But historically, there are countless examples of groups of people who chose to forgo sex— either for long periods of time or permanently. Often the reasons were religious—the belief that the "higher self" was distracted by too much concentration on the physical. Nearly every major religious tradition includes a celibate model: the clergy and nuns of the Roman Catholic Church; the "holy ones" in the Hindu tradition; some scholarly rabbis in Judaism; Buddhist monks; certain Protestant sects. Even secular examples exist—the Roman Stoics in the first century, the vestal virgins of ancient Rome, the "courtly love" of the Middle Ages. This is not to say that celibacy is a preferred state; in fact, some of the ideals of the Puritan ethic that equate sex with sin are those of repression. But it does demonstrate that the act of sex is not necessarily a component of love.

While many married couples in the study reached compromises that involved sharing sexual intimacy outside the marriage, the committed couples who were not involved sexually often found that an important point of connection was missing. Normally, both partners had other sexual relationships, which they regarded as "nonprimary," but it was difficult to maintain this lifestyle because it raised too many questions about the permanent nature of their own relationship.

Cheryl, a twenty-eight-year-old-woman who lived with a gay man, described her experience in this way:

"We met and were friends. We had a great time playing together. I moved in with him at his suggestion while he was living with a male lover. We were like a shadow of

each other, did everything together—got up and showered
together in the morning, took the train to work, went to
lunch together, spent evenings together. After a while, he
and his lover split (his lover blamed me), and then we shared
a room and a bed, slept naked and entwined, were one with
each other, and our feelings grew deeper. We were afraid
when we realized that we had fallen in love, and it broke
our hearts when we realized it couldn't work. He found a
male lover who was not tolerant of my presence. A choice
had to be made, and, sad as we were, we knew what that
choice had to be.

"I feel that the breaking point came over sex. We were
very intimate 'platonic' lovers, but for a love of our intensity to survive, there had to be a sexual relationship."

Very often, committed nonsexual relationships grow during a period in people's lives when sex is less primary. This
is what some of the study respondents said:

I met Laura at a time when I was very tired of playing
the games that seem to be a dominant factor in the gay
lifestyle. She accepted me and calmed me and was
someone I felt comfortable with. It was enough for that
time in my life.

—Matt H., 33

I met Mark shortly before I divorced my husband, and
his companionship and common interests, artistic
inspiration, and caring, got me through a painful
period. I didn't want a sexual relationship with anyone
during that period, so what Mark and I shared was
enough for both of us. We were together for two years,
and we had a wonderful relationship. It was just right
for the time.

—Pamela S., 50

When I met Fred I had finally come to the point where
I was tired of meeting new people and getting to know
them and all the dating scene stuff. I finally became at
peace with myself and knew that if I ever found a life
mate, it would just happen. If not, I was okay with that.
Fred had reached the same place in his life. We're still
together three years later. To say that we're taking one
day at a time would not be an accurate description of
our deep love and commitment. Nevertheless, we make
no claims on each other for the future.

—Maura L., 34

Honesty of the Heart

I once knew a gay man who loved women so much that
nearly all of his important emotional relationships had been
with them. The few friendships and partnerships he'd shared
with men had been dissatisfying and, in one or two cases,
self-destructive.

I once asked him if he might not be surrounding himself
with women to create a buffer against the more threatening
choice of intimate love with a man, since his homosexual
affairs had been so brutal. His relationships with women were
deeply emotional and very physical, though never sexual;
might they not, I suggested, protect him against the "darker"
and more tangled engagements of sexual intimacy?

My friend admitted that he was involved in a form of
avoidance, but he asked what was wrong with it. "If my
life is emotionally full and my relationships honest, what
difference does it make if I'm avoiding something that only
caused me a lot of pain?"

The difference, I knew, was that he was not content. He
was often frantic and emotionally on edge. He drank a lot,
and as he grew older, he turned increasingly inward. Because he had a delightful personality and was funny, smart,
and generous, most people found him easy to love. But
eventually he grew to fear that even the most casual rela-

tionships would make more demands on him than he could comfortably meet. His life was a seesaw action between intimacy and retreat.

He was not ambivalent about his homosexuality, and he spoke of it freely. But he had never come to terms with how he would use the understanding that he was homosexual to live a fulfilling life.

Many homosexual men choose to make their primary emotional commitments to women, and there are any number of reasons why they do so. When their choices are motivated by honest love and a clear-headed choice to live one way as opposed to another, they sometimes achieve long-term relationships that fill their most important needs. When their choices are motivated by fear, the turmoil is great.

"By the time I was thirty-seven, I had grown very cynical about sex," Larry said. "Either my sexual partners were the typical anonymous 'faceless' attachments, or they were so deep that they turned jealous and possessive and ugly. There seemed to be no middle ground. I couldn't live like that—it was tearing me up. I wasn't ashamed of being gay, but I grew to resent what that label seemed to imply. The attachments were too dependent on sexuality, most importantly, physical appearance and the more superficial aspects of eroticism. They seemed to place less emphasis on the more subtle nuances of love and growth and commitment. Of course, I don't propose to speak for all homosexual relationships, because I'm sure there are many that are far more fulfilling in those areas than mine have been. But I never had a male lover who could have been a lifetime partner."

Larry was a tall, classically handsome man of forty, a successful sales executive with a large firm in Boston. He had one of those faces you knew would only grow more attractive with age. His thick brown hair showed no evidence of gray. I visited him at his beautifully remodeled brownstone, which was located in the center of the city, a stone's throw from the Boston Common, which he shared with a thirty-seven-year-old woman named Casey. It was a sunny, warm, spring day, and we decided to take a walk along the path lining the Charles River, a point of relative peace in the middle of a bustling metropolis.

"Have you met many people like me?" Larry asked as we walked. "I'd be surprised if you said no."

I shrugged. "Of course. You've met them yourself. A lot of people are running for cover these days."

"Remember when we were all so excited to be part of the sexual revolution?" he mused. "Boy, I thought anything was possible. My parents were stuck together like glue; they only had each other. I imagined myself having this incredibly wide, intense, and loving circle of people who would surround me for the rest of my life. I would be so much happier than my parents were, so much more fulfilled. What happened? I feel shell-shocked."

I didn't answer, and he went on. "Even today, the theory of it seems to make so much sense. If you asked me what I believed was possible, I would tell you the same thing today that I believed twenty years ago. Except that today I'm more cynical.

"I remember that my dad once told me, in one of those awful man-to-man conversations he loved to have, 'The women you really love aren't the ones you're going to marry.' By then, I knew I was gay, or at least bisexual, but the point applied just the same, and it made me so sad. My parents were never in love with each other and it was as though my dad was telling me that real love was too messy to live with. For living, you had to find something different. What scared me was that I was afraid he might be right."

"Maybe we tried to make too great a leap from the rigid structure of our parents' family style to the 'free love' style and got caught in the middle," I said.

"And fell into the abyss," he said, laughing. "Oops— couldn't quite reach. It's not very funny, is it? Sometimes when you bite off more than you can chew, you don't get a second chance to go back and recalculate your distances."

"I gather from what you've told me so far that your homosexual relationships have gone badly."

He nodded. "It's not a very good time to be a homosexual—and not just because of AIDS and social prejudice, although those are very significant factors. Emotionally, everything seems out of kilter. For a long time, there was this intoxicating wildness of having a lot of sex—the slightest spark of attraction and you'd end up in bed. Then, as we grew older and wanted to settle down, we didn't know how to do it. It wasn't part of our *culture,* so to speak."

"How did you meet Casey?"

"Oh, Casey's very special," he said as he smiled. "Actually, she's been in and out of my life for years. We met in high school. I was a loud, nervous, and often obnoxious teenager, and she barely tolerated me during most of high school. Then, in our senior year, we started dating exclusively until we both went away to college. There, I got involved in another heterosexual relationship, but at the end of college, Casey and I got back together again for a while. It was during a time when I was exploring my homosexual feelings, and Casey broke it off when she learned I was having an affair with an older man. After that, we didn't communicate for several years. I continued to have relationships with men, but I was in the closet. The next time I contacted her, it was because I needed a friend—ironically, someone who could support me in my decision to 'come out.'

"For the next two years, both of us were involved in relationships—she with a rather brusque businessman whom I didn't like very much and who seemed to resent our closeness, and I with a somewhat flakey but dear man who was a ballet dancer. Both of our relationships ended badly at around the same time, and Casey and I became closer again, in part because of this. We ended up moving in together about two years ago. We weren't sure what we were doing, but we knew we loved each other, and we were both completely disillusioned with relationships in general."

"Did you have a sexual relationship?"

"This time around, no. We'd had one when we dated in high school and after college, but after all that had transpired, we were a little bit more cautious. I am capable of being—and have been—sexually attracted to women, but at that point I wasn't feeling sexually attracted to *anyone*. I just closed the door. I think, too, that Casey would have been suspicious of sexual overtures at that point. She might have thought I was using her in some way to avoid the truth of who I was. We've lived comfortably together, keeping those issues on the back burner. But we've talked—how we've talked! It's been so nice having someone to talk to who understands me as well as Casey does. We've rehashed all the relationship stuff, what it meant, where we're going. It's been nice. She is my best friend in the world, and I think sometimes, aren't I lucky to live with my best friend?"

We paused to look out at the river. Sailboats and small motorboats were out in full force on this beautiful spring day. "I think you *are* lucky," I said. "There are many couples who live together, but one gets the sense that not many of them could be called best friends."

"I know. That's what's been so special. I'm very dependent on Casey now. I can't imagine being without her. Which raises other issues, of course. The wounds have healed now—we have to deal with our sexual lives."

"I imagine that's a tough place to be," I said. "What are you going to do?"

"I hope we trust each other enough—and I think we do—that we can talk about it directly. I would like to try being lovers. That probably sounds very calculating, but I think these are choices people can make."

"And if you do become lovers, does that mean you will also have relationships with men?"

"I don't know. That will be another bridge to cross. I'll tell you one thing, though." He turned very serious. "I know gay men who get involved with women and even marry them because it gives them a good cover, or it gives them security, or whatever. Then they sneak around and see men on the side, and live a double life. That's not something I could do, or something I would want to do. Whatever I decide, it's going to be right up front and out in the open. No hiding.''

Proust said, ''There can be no peace of mind in love since the advantage one has secured is never anything but a fresh starting point.'' If there is one thing that distinguishes these couples, it seems to be that they are always starting new phases in their partnerships. The lack of definition and insecurity might frighten some, but in making their choices, these couples have agreed to live with an ongoing reformation in the context of their relationships. By the time I had finished the interviews, I was even beginning to wonder if it mattered that these matches might not be permanent. After all, how many things are permanent?

CHAPTER SIX

Faulty Thinking and False Expectations

A certain king decided to tame a wolf and make it a pet. This desire of his was based on ignorance and the need to be approved or admired by others—a common cause of much trouble in the world.

He caused a cub to be taken from its mother as soon as it was born and to be brought up among tame dogs.

When the wolf was fully grown it was brought to the king and for many days it behaved exactly like a dog. People who saw this astonishing sight marveled and thought the king to be a wonder.

One day when he was out hunting, the king heard a wolf pack coming near. As they approached, the tame wolf jumped up, bared its fangs, and ran to welcome them. Within a minute he was away, restored to his natural companions.

This is the origin of the proverb: "A wolf-cub will always become a wolf, even if it is reared among the sons of man."

—from *The Way of the Sufi,*
Idries Shah

WHEN I WAS eighteen, I fell in love with a man who completely dazzled me. At the time, I was ignorant about love and naive about sex, having just come from four years in a Catholic high school for girls. The year I started college, 1968, was a particularly jarring time to be making such a major transition. From my protected high school environment I was thrown into a world of free love, political chaos, casual drug use, and the intoxicating sense that any behavior was acceptable if it felt right.

John was two years older than I and already immersed in the Sixties' university culture by the time I arrived on the scene. He tapped into a part of my psyche that had always been attracted to rebellion. I believed everything he told me and daydreamed about what a marvelous, rebellious couple we would make. Of course, John had no such fantasies. One day he mentioned, almost casually, that he was leaving Seattle to join a community in Oregon. And he wasn't going alone. He was taking Rebecca, a woman I knew by sight, and they were going to get married.

"Wait a minute!" I cried, not understanding. "How can you do this? I thought we loved each other." He answered vaguely that of course he loved me, but he wasn't quite sure of my point.

It was my first big lesson in the experience of unrequited love. And what I had the most difficulty accepting was the fact that I was capable of such strong feelings for a person who felt nothing for me. How was it possible? For a while I was consumed with the idea that if only I had more time, I could eventually bring John around, *make* him love me. Maybe I imagined that a lightning bolt would strike at some point and suddenly he would find that he was head over heels in love with me.

I found myself thinking about John as I considered how I would write about the 18 percent of my survey respondents who seemed to be fighting against the inevitable outcomes of their impossible fantasies. For them, the rightness of their love seemed so compelling that they could not imagine why it did not seem the same way for the person they loved.

This group was the most difficult to place in perspective because it was so hard not to judge them harshly. Most people have experienced, at some point in their lives, that sickening disbelief, the inability to grasp how they could love someone so much and not be loved in return. Maybe these people even thought, as I did with John, that they could turn their loved one's very nature inside out and create a person who would love them back. But love is not a thing that can be forced, and as the Sufi legend so wisely suggests, one's true nature cannot be changed simply by wanting it so.

Women Who Love Gay Men

"Henry is the choirmaster at my church, and I sing in the choir," said Laura, a pretty, nervous woman of twenty-eight. Her deep-set brown eyes looked tired, and she seemed wilted from the efforts of her agonizing. "He is the kindest man I have ever known—everyone loves him, and it's not surprising that most of the women in the church have a crush on him. He's very handsome, too.

"I always felt that there was something special between Henry and me—some kind of connection. I'd catch him looking at me while I was singing, and I knew he was attracted to me. Since I was married, I tried to ignore my feelings, but sometimes I'd find myself daydreaming about him. It didn't help that my marriage was going so badly.

"One night after choir practice I was particularly upset about something that had happened with my husband. Henry found me crying in the back of the church. He immediately put his arms around me and tried to comfort me. He told me that if it would help to talk about it, he was always willing to listen. His warmth and understanding filled me with gratitude. During the following weeks, we became very close. We talked a lot and he gave me the courage to leave my marriage. I thought we really had something special.

"For the next few months, we made it a practice to go out for coffee or a drink after choir practice. Sometimes others would join us and sometimes it was just us. I was living alone by then and feeling much better about myself. The ending of my marriage was not nearly as traumatic as it might have been because I had Henry.

"Henry was a very physical person. He hugged me a lot and always gave me a kiss at the end of these evenings. But nothing more. It was another thing I loved about him. He wasn't trying to rush me into bed like most men. I appreciated his sensitivity to the fact that I needed more time to be whole.''

She stopped talking and stared down into her coffee cup. ''I gather there was more to it than that,'' I said sympathetically.

Laura nodded. ''I'm a shy person, and it's outside my imagination to cook up any sort of seduction scene. But the night I invited Henry over for dinner, I guess I had it in the back of my mind that something more would happen. By then, I knew that I had fallen in love with him.

''We had a great time at dinner. Henry was very entertaining. I drank a little more wine than I normally do, so I was kind of tipsy, but he seemed to think it was funny— endearing, even. After dinner, we moved into the living room and sat together on the sofa. I was leaning my head against him and he was stroking my hair and telling me how beautiful I looked and how much he enjoyed being with me. And then, just when I was expecting him to do something, he kissed the top of my head and told me he had to be going. I couldn't believe it—it wasn't even eleven o'clock. I sort of snuggled into him and said, as seductively as possible, 'Oh, don't leave yet.' But he stood up and started putting on his coat. He was smiling down at me in a funny, almost wistful way, and then he kissed me again and left. I felt crushed, but later I told myself that there could have been a million reasons Henry had to leave.''

''It never occurred to you that he was gay?''

''No.'' She shook her head. ''He had been married once. I never thought of it.''

''How did you find out?''

''For three weeks after our dinner, he acted strange around me and avoided me. He had excuses for not going out after choir practice. I knew something was wrong. Finally, I called him up and said I had to talk to him, and he agreed to meet me. We met at a place we usually went after practice, and I said right away, 'What's wrong?' He was very ill at ease and my mind was going over all the things that might be the matter. Finally, he said, 'I think you've misunderstood how I feel about you.' I froze in my chair, but tried to act casual. He told me he enjoyed me as a friend and liked me very much, but he wasn't interested in me sexually.

"I was embarrassed to hear this. I told him I didn't understand, because it just seemed natural to me after all of our other closeness. He looked down at his drink and seemed to be having a hard time answering, and finally told me that was the point—it *wasn't* natural for him because he was homosexual.

"I didn't believe him, since I knew he'd been married. He said that didn't mean anything. He told me all about his marriage and about his gay lovers, and he admitted that he was frustrated and lonely because he hadn't found anyone special. He said that's why he valued our friendship, but I had to understand that our relationship could never be anything more. I told him it was okay, but I was totally devastated.

"Things got pretty much back to normal after that, but I've been a wreck the past few months because I want him so bad and I can't have him. My only hope is that he's really bisexual—he told me he'd had sex with other women besides his wife. I swear, if I could have him, I wouldn't care if he saw men, and I wouldn't care what people said. I wouldn't even worry about getting AIDS. That's how great my love is."

"Passion will obscure our sense so that we eat sad stuff and call it nectar," William Carlos Williams said, and it seems apparent that Laura's sense was obscured in such a way. She *wanted* Henry, but wanting isn't necessarily loving, since her ideal of the person she wanted was not the person Henry was. And she was willing to sacrifice her own self-esteem, and even her life (if I understand her reference to AIDS correctly) to "have" him.

Many of the women in this segment of my study related

experiences of falling in love with homosexual men, and they spoke of these experiences as being characterized by deep pain and periods of denial. In some cases, the women were able to come to terms with the flaws in their understanding, and accept the men as they were. But other women built castles in the sand, listing their hopes and justifications as Laura had. These included:

- "He's bisexual, not homosexual, so there's a chance he'll choose me."

- "I can give him so much more than anyone else because I love him so much."

- "He will realize that he needs me more than he needs men."

- "This is just a phase."

One woman believed that the man she loved was simply fearful of starting a romance with her—that it was just a matter of his "letting go." She stated with what seemed to be a forced conviction, "He seems to be so attracted to me, and my conclusion is that the largest number of gay men are really capable of being bisexual, and they could enjoy the best of both worlds, if only they'd let themselves."

Still other women seemed almost casual about their affinity for gay men. Some said that they preferred to be with gay men, and they had long histories of repeated relationships with homosexuals.

On more than one occasion, I have fallen in love with a gay man. I find gay men desirable and attractive for a number of reasons. We usually have some interests in common and can enjoy each other's company. Gay men are among the few who genuinely like women. Most men only like women because they can dominate them;

otherwise, they put women down. I don't care to be bullied by ''macho'' men.

Many gay men are exceptionally creative and talented, particularly in the arts. I take an interest in music and theater, and I find that the gay men I know are more sensitive to this world.

But these relationships usually ended with some pain for me, since the men just wanted to be friends and I wanted much more. It's been sad . . . but I can't help the way I feel. What can you do when you fall in love?

—Sharon T., 35

I have often wondered what it is that attracts me to gay men. I find that with the exception of my husband, all the men I've been involved with have been gay—even if they were so far in the closet that they didn't even admit it to themselves until many years later. Maybe it's the quietness and gentleness, which is in such stark contrast to my father, who was argumentative and emotionally abusive.

—Elaine V., 45

Like my close women friends, my gay friends have been people who could share emotions and feelings more openly than many straight men—and without the power struggles and sexual innuendos of heterosexual interactions.

—Kelly S., 36

We were close friends since childhood, and we loved each other very much. I am only now beginning to see how we have both used our closeness to avoid issues of change and family.

—Rena P., 31

I am aware of my own sexual fears that perhaps have
led me into a relationship with a gay man. He was
gentle and loving and he understood me. I avoided the
discomfort of a sexual relationship by being with him.

—Anne R., 50

One woman, Marilyn, age forty-two, sent this poem,
written in a period of despair over her love for a gay man:

I share my bed with books you send
'cause you would sleep alone
and need no heaven to hunger for—
your absence serves for hell.

It might be difficult for most people to understand why a
woman would pursue an unrequited love interest in a homosexual man—not to mention why some women would
repeatedly do so. Every person enters a relationship with a
set of expectations about what they will gain from it. What
do these women hope to gain? Some clues can be found in
the way the women often characterize homosexuals as being
more sensitive and gentle, and less threatening than heterosexual men. Initially, the interest these men take in the
women may seem more authentic, since their gift of friendship doesn't have a sexual price tag. But over time, the
women who expect more than just friendship may become
frustrated when the relationship doesn't move on to other,
more intimate, levels. As one woman, who had become
philosophical about her failed relationship with a gay man,
observed, ''For a long time, I had been looking for a man
who would value me as a person, not just as a sexual con-
quest, someone who would get to know me first before
wanting to go to bed with me. I found someone who wanted
to know me, but never go to bed with me. It struck me as
terribly ironic.''

I was interested to learn that the first gay man many

women were attracted to was a high school teacher or other adult male who took a special interest in them during their teenage years, or who inspired in them a special appreciation for art or literature. It's not unusual for young girls to develop crushes on male teachers—female teachers, too, for that matter. Adolescence is a time when young women feel vulnerable and misunderstood. Several of the women described their early "romances" with homosexual adults (romances that existed only in their own minds) with such fervor that it is easy to understand why they try to restore the feelings with another man.

Marion Rogers, a California family therapist, speculates on the possible reasons some women may have for preferring gay men.

> It is a very different matter from the woman who might learn later that the man she is attracted to or involved with is gay. In that case, her attraction is to *him,* not to his gayness. For some women, the man's being gay is an essential part of the equation. And almost all the reasons they might have for exclusively seeking relationships with these men are embedded in escape, denial, or even masochism. For instance, even though they may have fantasies that the gay man will become sexually attracted to them, it is the impossibility of this happening that makes them feel the most safe.

Experts agree that some men and women subconsciously choose relationships that are impossible and therefore "safe." While few of these women would accept consciously that they were attracted to gay men for this reason, many spoke of having had frightening or abusive relationships with men in their lives—most often, fathers, husbands, and lovers.

"My father was an alcoholic," admitted one woman who, with the help of therapy, was trying to understand why she had so often been attracted to homosexual men. "When he got drunk, he would be rough and abusive. What was especially upsetting to me was that on those occasions he would force my mother to have sex with him, even though she resisted. I would sit in my room with my fingers in my ears so I wouldn't hear them struggling. From this, I learned to mistrust men—they were strong enough to make me have sex even if I didn't want to.

"I was shy in school, and during my junior year in high school, I became friends with this boy, Jerry, who was different from all the rest. Jerry was sweet and gentle, he was involved with the peace movement, and he got me involved, too. We began to spend a lot of time together. He told me he was homosexual, but I was so naive, I didn't really know what that meant. In my mind, Jerry was my boyfriend, with the benefit that he wasn't always pushing me to have sex. When I found out it wasn't like that, I was very upset.

"As an adult, I became involved with two other gay men, with the same results. It wasn't until my therapist suggested it that I began to relate these attractions to my feelings about my father. I had blocked out so much. She helped me deal with it, and now I have gay friends, but I don't fall in love with them or want them to fall in love with me."

As we have seen in other chapters, love relationships can develop mutually between homosexuals and women. But in those cases, the women only rarely sought out their partners *because* they were homosexual. On the other hand, it doesn't seem to be an accident that some women tend to fall in love with gay men, although many would argue to the contrary. One woman who said she was at a loss to explain why she so often got involved with gay men, told me, "It just seems to happen. I don't *want* it." Since this woman had also told me that she had fallen in love with two different men she met in gay bars, I suggested that perhaps it wasn't such an accident after all. What was she doing in gay bars? That's where her friends were, she said; she wasn't necessarily looking for love. But it seemed as though there was a strong element of self-deceit in her claim, and I told her so. She said I wasn't the first to suggest this—she'd been in therapy for three years. "My therapist has almost given up on me. I don't know. If I tried to change things, it would mean giving up a lot of people I'm comfortable being with. I'm afraid I would be lonely. After a certain point, it's hard to start over again.''

Do the women believe that they can ''change'' the homosexual men into heterosexual lovers? Sometimes they do, when they consider homosexuality a choice rather than a fundamental orientation. If the men themselves have any trouble with self-acceptance, it only feeds the seduction. In those cases, the women will take great measures to prove to the men how much happier they'll be with them. June's story is typical.

''We were becoming close, and I was nearly convinced he was interested in me romantically, when he told me he was living with a man. I was greatly disappointed, but I haven't totally given up on him. He was married once, and I don't think he's quite sure of his sexual preference. I am holding up a dim candle, yet anticipate that he will break up with his lover. I do believe in some way he's interested in me, and I have a desire to be with him.''

When June met this man, she had just recovered from a deeply traumatic separation from another gay man. She had been hoping for ten years that the man would begin to see her in a different light, and when he finally moved away, she was in a state of emotional collapse until she met her current object of passion. Further investigation into June's life revealed that she had been married briefly when she was very young (she was now thirty-five), and her husband had been an angry, physically abusive man. She lived with him for three years, tense and on guard against the eruptions of anger that usually occurred when he was drinking. She finally left the marriage, but her self-esteem was at rock bottom. She was unaccustomed to even the most minimal positive feedback—being told she looked nice, being listened to when she talked, being complimented when she cooked a good meal, laughed with when she said something funny. Her first gay friend did all those things and more. She was dazzled to find such warmth directed toward her.

He was the opposite of her husband in every way—gentle, sensitive, romantic. It's not difficult to see why June was attracted. But it was her neediness, not mutual love, that drew her to him.

"June confused the signals," said Marion Rogers, "and this sometimes happens with women who haven't had the experience of being close to men in nonsexual ways. How could a man be so close to her and not be in love with her or want to stay with her permanently? Her problem was that she had never developed an independent sense of her self-worth; she counted on men to communicate her value. We all need close people who give us positive feedback and support in our lives, but June let that feedback control her actions and feelings. And she didn't know how to distinguish her friend's love from sexual love. Women like June tend to fall in love with any man who treats them well.

"She also found that, in comparison with her abusive husband, this gay man was gentle and sensitive. One of the problems for women who are attracted to these qualities in gay men is that they get carried away with their expectations. They think, 'He will always care about me.' And then they feel betrayed when the man 'leaves' them for a man. Of course, assuming he was honest in the relationship, the man didn't really leave them or betray them at all."

The women are not always entirely to blame. Several men wrote to me that they deliberately misled women in the early stages of relationships. Some of their reasons might seem callous—for example, one man started dating a woman in his office he knew was attracted to him, as a "cover." He was so intent on protecting himself from discovery that he never considered that he might be using her in a manner that was cruel. Certainly, given the discrimination that exists toward homosexuals, the temptation to find a cover is understandable. But it is a weak foundation upon which to build a satisfying relationship, and it's bound to cause pain when it reaches its inevitable conclusion.

One man, who worked in a large advertising agency, made a point of dating women in the office so everyone could see he was attracted to women. Ironically, he developed the reputation of being a ''ladies' man'' because he never stuck with one woman longer than a date or two. ''I always cut out before there is any real intimacy,'' he acknowledged guiltily. ''The women think I'm one of those types of men who just plays around a lot but can't make a commitment. They're right about that—they just don't understand how right.

''Do I feel it's wrong to deceive them? Not really, since I never get involved enough to lead any of them on. My biggest problem is wondering what I'm going to do with my own life. I can't keep this up forever.''

In one sense this man felt justified in his duplicitous behavior. ''Am I really to blame?'' he asked. ''Is it my fault I can't pursue my career if I admit to being who I am?''

He seemed to raise a valid question, whose answer was, at the least, ambiguous. Men and women are responsible for their actions, including the hurt they inflict on others, regardless of their motivations. At the same time, the discrimination against homosexuals that clearly exists in many professional settings places men like this in a true dilemma. It is easy to criticize another person's duplicity when you're not the one facing censure. Yet surely the women he is using deserve respect as well. If he feels he must establish a ''cover,'' why not seek one that is less hurtful? He could, for example, ask women friends who know of his homosexuality to accompany him to public functions. There is something offensive about his carrying the coverup to such an extreme that he is viewed as a ''stud'' by his colleagues. While being heterosexual might contribute to his promotability, surely being a stud isn't a prerequisite.

Many people assume that most gay men who are involved with women are using them as covers. I didn't find this to be generally true among the respondents to my survey. More often, the men were either genuinely attracted to the women or had already become involved with them before they recognized the extent of their homosexual feelings. And some men claimed to prefer relationships with women, and their remarks parallel those of the women who preferred relationships with gay men. For those homosexuals who were threatened by the intimacy of sexual relationships with men, or afraid that they may not be accepted by other homosexuals (usually because of their looks or age), relationships with women felt comfortable and safe. Ben was a case in point.

Ben, who was thirty-four, had only had one homosexual encounter in his life, and he believed he could not pursue relationships with men because he was very large—nearly three hundred pounds—and was painfully shy about his body. "I have not had many close friendships in my life," he wrote, "so I was flattered when a woman I work with expressed an interest in me. She said she liked big men. We started going out once or twice a week and our dates led to kissing, but nothing more. She wanted more, and I tried to feel something, but I just couldn't. The crazy thing is, when I finally told her I was gay, it just seemed to make her more determined. She thinks this is a silly phase I'm going through, and I'm tempted to let her keep believing it, because she's the only one who has ever wanted me."

"Some men and women naturally gravitate toward romantic situations that are nonthreatening, even when it means compromising important aspects of their personality," said Marion Rogers. "Unfortunately, they eventually blame their partner when they find their needs are not being met. If Ben marries this woman, it is likely that he will later say she forced him into it, thus abdicating his own role of responsibility. This relationship is a loaded cannon. Neither Ben nor his friend is getting his or her needs met. They're each making intolerable compromises."

The common denominator in all of these situations—and the factor that seems to differentiate them from the relationships that work—is that the two people in the relationship have dramatically different expectations of what they hope to gain. These false expectations are fueled by a distinct lack of honesty, with their partners and with themselves.

And even when the truth is known, many of these people choose to perpetuate the myth and refuse to face reality.

The Disowned Self

Some gay men are so traumatized by their homosexual feelings that they spend their lives in a passionate drive to disown their natures.

Vincent had been a Fundamentalist Christian minister for twenty-seven years, and had been married for twenty-three years. He admitted to me that ''sometimes the pressure is almost unbearable.''

We met under conditions of great secrecy. Vincent looked haggard, and older than his forty-eight years. His gray eyes were watery and tired behind thick glasses. He was also very nervous about talking to me.

''If anyone found out . . .''

I assured him that everything would be strictly confidential, but he continued to be on edge.

''My entire life has been a torment,'' he said miserably. ''I know I'm a homosexual, but I'm also a religious man— a devout Fundamentalist Christian. I struggle constantly with the realization that scripture after scripture says that homosexuality is equal to debauchery. I don't understand how I can be both homosexual and believe the scriptures, and I often blame myself that I haven't prayed hard enough. My religious beliefs tell me that matters of the flesh should be put aside if I am to reach a higher spirituality. But I can't seem to put this aside.''

''Have you ever had homosexual relations?'' I asked.

He nodded. ''Occasionally over the years. You can imagine my guilt . . . and my fear. If I was ever found out, I would lose everything—my work, the love of my wife and children, my friends. Not only that, all the good I've accomplished in my life would be wiped out. That would be intolerable.''

''What is your relationship with your wife like?''

"She is a very devout Christian, and we have a good marriage. But she has never been very interested in sex, and right now we only have sex a handful of times a year. Once, in a weak moment, I tried to tell her about my sexual confusion. She made it very clear that she considers any attraction of men to men to be demonic, and told me I should pray for deliverance." He stared down at his hands. "I have prayed. I have also talked with doctors on a couple of occasions to see if there was anything that could be done to relieve me. I had read somewhere of hormone treatments that could reverse homosexuality, and I was willing to try anything. The doctors suggested I try therapy. Maybe I will."

"To find a way to change?" I asked.

"Yes. I have no choice. I know you must be thinking I'm crazy, but what would you do in my situation? What would anyone do? Being homosexual is ruining my life and threatening my salvation."

Vincent was one of several Christian ministers who contacted me, but I hardly knew what to say to them. They all began from a point of denial and self-loathing, and were terrified by the feelings that they could not seem to control, even with prayer and determination. One religious man, his voice full of confusion and dismay, argued, "Surely, a loving God understands feelings of love." But another said bitterly, "My kind—Fundamentalists—seem to delight in saying God created Adam and Eve, not Adam and Steve. They show ruthless hatred rather than any kind of godly love." Given the choice, these men would readily disown the troubling side of themselves that does not correspond with their beliefs.

The scourge of AIDS has given the anti-gay Religious Right new momentum in our country. AIDS, these people claim, is God's retribution for the sin of homosexuality. New Right spokesman Jerry Falwell has declared, "A man reaps what he sows. If he sows his seed in the field of his lower nature, he will reap from it a harvest of corruption."

Commented Richard Failla, an openly gay judge in New

York City, "AIDS has done more to undermine the feelings of self-esteem than anything Anita Bryant could ever have done. Some [gay] people are saying, 'Maybe we *are* wrong—maybe this is a punishment.' "

AIDS has also created a new activism on the part of gays, and in recent times, many churches have abandoned their homophobic attitudes—notably, the United Church of Christ, the Disciples of Christ, the Unitarians, and the Quakers. But these gestures of support have not been strong enough to counterattack the militant anti-gay forces on the Right. Gay men who are also religiously Fundamentalist are in a double bind. Not only do they fear public exposure, they also fear the wrath of God. Even when they don't practice homosexuality, they are often plagued by guilt over feelings they can't control.

"It's tough," a Catholic priest in New York, who has many gays in his parish, told me. "The growth of Dignity [an organization for Catholic gays] has helped many men, but if you're a devout Catholic, how do you square your practice of homosexuality with your devotion to a Church that regards it as sinful? These people are suffering, and I feel the Church has a responsibility to embrace them. I do what I can, but I see a lot of pain."

Other men talked about wanting to disown their homosexual selves, not because they were in conflict with belief systems, but because they were in conflict with goals and even desires. Naively, I had always assumed that most homosexuals were "in the closet" because, although they accepted themselves they believed they would never be accepted by society. But I learned that many men deeply resented the fact that they were homosexual, as if they had been dealt a very sorry hand of cards. One even told me that he had been visibly homophobic for many years. "I despised gay men because they were what I despised about myself," he said.

The men who tried to disown their homosexuality usually sought out relationships with women, and most of them married. But unlike the gay men who consciously made a choice to marry, while knowing and accepting their homo-sexuality or bisexuality, these men were never resolved about their conflicts. They stayed, rather, on a seesaw, moving back and forth without resolution.

Most of the men in this state who responded to my survey had not told their wives, although several said they thought their wives might suspect.

The former wife of one of these men wrote to me that her ex-husband had committed suicide several months earlier. ''We had been married eight years when I found out my husband was having an affair with a man. He left me to live with his new lover, but their relationship only lasted a few months, and he begged me to take him back. He promised me that he would give up being gay, that it was only a passing phase. But after two years, I found out he had had another affair and I asked him to leave. He begged me to give him one more chance, and promised to get therapy for his problem. But I couldn't handle it anymore, and I told him no. Several weeks later, he checked into a hotel and took an overdose of drugs.''

A psychologist who hosted a radio call-in program told the story of a man who called into the show one day. ''His voice was all choked up. He said he was calling from his car phone, and he was parked near a bridge. He said he'd been driving there with the intention of commiting suicide, but he heard me on the air and stopped the car and called. I immediately knew I had to keep him on the line, but I didn't want to talk to him on the air. I asked him if he could stay on the phone until I got off the program, and he agreed. For the next ten minutes I agonized over what I was going to say to him. I prayed he would be waiting for me on the line when I finished. He was, and he had calmed down. He briefly told me his story. He was fifty-two years old, mar-ried for twenty-six years, with two adult children. He felt as though he had been living a lie for years, and he just couldn't take it anymore. But he believed it was too late for him—he had missed his chance. 'Can you imagine me walk-ing into a gay bar?' he asked. 'I wouldn't know what to do at this point. For me to act on my leanings now would ruin my life and my family's life.'

"His dilemma was pretty far outside my area of expertise. I asked him if he had tried to get counseling from one of the gay organizations in the area. He was afraid to call them. Not only was he terrified of being found out—he was also afraid that he would be pushed into making some kind of a public choice. He came to see me twice after the phone call, and eventually he did leave his wife, although he didn't give her the reason. The last time I heard from him, he was living alone and was trying to work up the courage to go to a church group he had heard about. He was very lonely and unhappy. I don't know what happened after that. He dropped out of sight and I didn't know how to reach him. But he stayed on my mind. Somehow my radio program had saved this man's life, but I didn't really know how to help him. It was the first time in my twenty-year practice that I had dealt with this problem, and I didn't feel equipped to advise him. This was a situation which should have been cut and dried, but it wasn't. In one sense, I felt that he needed to face and accept his homosexuality. But it wasn't as though doing that would solve his problems. It would only create new ones. It would mean giving up everything that was secure in his life. It would mean risking the alienation of his children— something he was terrified of. He was desperately lonely, and worried that he would be alone for the rest of his life. I hope he did finally go to the church group and meet some other men in his situation. I wish I knew what finally became of him.''

It is in these sad stories that we glimpse how powerful the weight of prejudice is against homosexuals. The belief that their behavior is deviant is still widespread, in spite of the fact that the American Psychiatric Association removed homosexuality from its official *Diagnostic and Statistical Manual of Mental Disorders* in 1973. The board's statement read, "Whereas homosexuality per se implies no impairment of judgment, stability, reliability, or general vocational capabilities, therefore be it resolved that the APA deplores all public and private discrimination against homosexuals in such areas as employment, housing, public accommodations, and licensing, and . . . that the APA supports and urges the repeal of all legislation making criminal offenses of sexual acts performed by consenting adults in private.''

In spite of the power of this declaration, discrimination still exists on every front, with the AIDS threat often used to mask a more insidious prejudice. People can say, ''I don't think there's anything wrong with being homosexual, but I'm not going to hire one to cook in my restaurant. What if he gets AIDS and passes it on to my customers?'' And so on.

For those men who feel deep conflict about their homosexuality, this discrimination is a persuasive motivation to bury their gayness. When their self-esteem is low, they might themselves believe that public prejudice is warranted. Not everyone is secure enough or strong enough to take the risks.

Sadly, when these men are driven by fear to take on traditional heterosexual roles, this self-banishment only leads to greater problems. The feelings don't go away. The alienation grows. Ultimately, everyone loses.

CHAPTER SEVEN

Moments of Truth

"What seems to be the problem?"

"It's not a problem. It's something I haven't told you before."

He lifts his eyes questioningly. "Yes?"

I take a deep breath. His eyes will widen with shock. He'll leap from his chair. *How terrible for you. Now I understand.* He might take my hands, or hug me. In his arms I might stop shivering.

"My husband is a homosexual."

The terrible words tremble in the air above us. I clasp my hands.

"I see." His face doesn't alter. It's as if I've thrown a rock into a pond only to see it float like a leaf on the unbroken surface.

"Go on." The same toneless, modulated voice.

"I can't." I gasp. I feel as if a huge beast, trapped somewhere inside me, were struggling to wrench itself free. *"You* have to say something . . . tell me how to feel." I hunch my body around the violent, tearing pain.

"That's not my job," he says. "You have to tell me."

—from *Friend of the Family,*
Natalie Bates

ONE EVENING last summer, Dennis and I met for dinner at a trendy little Mexican restaurant in New York that served blue-tinted margaritas. He was a good-looking man of thirty-five, with an athletic body and the neat, well-scrubbed look of a schoolboy. He wore pressed tan slacks and a white shirt. His blond hair was combed neatly to one side. Dennis was from Salt Lake City, and he looked as though he would fit in well there, although he had long since ceased to be actively involved in the Mormon Church. We ordered chili and Perrier; Dennis didn't drink alcohol, much less blue-tinted concoctions with plastic mermaids floating on top.

"It's nice to be here," Dennis said. "I really look forward to these New York trips."

"You come every summer?"

"We have a place on Seventy-fourth Street and Columbus that belongs to friends of ours. The kids love it—I think they'd like to live here. It's nice for Margaret, too. She's a photographer, and this is a great place for a photographer to be."

"And you, of course, love it."

He flashed a boyish grin. "I'm sure I'd go crazy if I didn't have my annual month in New York."

Dennis has a "deal" with his wife. For most of the year, they live a normal family life in Salt Lake City, and they spend the month of August in New York, so Dennis can be with his gay friends and participate in gay community activities. It is an interesting compromise, and, amazingly, it *works* for them.

"I knew I felt a gay attraction by the time I was thirteen," Dennis said, as we settled into our chili. "It was something I prayed about constantly. I asked God to help me stop listening to the voices in my head that were telling me I wanted these horrible things. It was quite a burden for a young kid. I didn't even consider that this was anything but very wrong. My whole family and everyone I knew was intensely homophobic. I was, too.

"In college, I had my first homosexual experience with my roommate, who was also Mormon. It was horrible and wonderful at the same time. The weight of our combined guilt could have sunk a ship. We told each other that we would never do this again—but, of course, we did. Twice more.

"I was already engaged to marry Margaret then. I loved her completely, and I believed I could overcome my homosexual feelings. It was my great moral challenge to defeat them. I continued to pray about it while Margaret and I prepared for our wedding. It was somewhat confusing, because, from the start, I idolized Margaret. She was physically beautiful and she had a beautiful soul. We used to talk long into the night about the power of God in our lives . . . about the things we hoped to accomplish. Our love was so great that it gave me confidence that I could conquer my mixed feelings about sex. We got married. My college roommate was my best man. Our eyes met once during the ceremony—he knew how I felt. He later moved away, and I'd love to be able to find him now and talk to him.

"The first ten years of our marriage were some of the happiest I've ever experienced. We had two children—Robby after two years, followed by Amanda when Robby was three. The children made me very happy. Margaret made me happy. And by then, I had passed the bar exam and was practicing law, which was what I'd always dreamed of doing."

"During this time, you didn't think about your homosexuality?"

"My homosexuality didn't exist as anything but a temptation. When I thought about it, which wasn't often because our family life was so full and busy, I prayed."

I observed that it must have been hard to carry such guilt.

"It was all right for the first ten years. But gradually—I don't know how it happened—I started thinking about it more. At first, it was just little things. If there was an article in a magazine or newspaper about some gay issue, I'd read it. I read a lot about AIDS, and I remember thinking that ignoring my homosexual feelings had probably saved my life. I was still quite moralistic about it, so I believed, at least on some level, that AIDS was the hand of God."

"An unfortunate viewpoint, shared by many," I said.

He smiled sadly. "You can imagine how it plays in Salt Lake City. Anyway, I started withdrawing from Margaret, and I had a hard time concentrating on my work. It was a very bad time for me and even worse for my wife, because she had no idea what was going on. She loved me, and she couldn't understand what was happening inside me. I was too young to be having a mid-life crisis. This lasted more than a year. You can't imagine how hard it was to have feelings I couldn't control and that seemed so dangerous. But eventually I realized that I had to do something or I would be tormented for the rest of my life. I sat down with Margaret and I took her hand and told her how much I loved her. She was just looking at me; she knew something was happening that was going to threaten our happiness. I said, 'Margaret, trust me and don't ask me why, but I have to go away for a few weeks.' ''

"She must have been scared to death," I said.

"My wife is an unusual woman. She knew something was wrong, and she cared about me so deeply that she was willing to let me go. Margaret is very grounded and she has a deep faith in God. I felt like a total schmuck doing this to her, but I didn't feel that I had a choice. I packed a bag and flew to New York."

"Did you have a plan?"

"No," he responded, laughing. "I was driven by my feelings, but I had never been to New York before, much less inside a gay bar. I was completely out of my league, but I had to do it. Actually, I was smart enough not to go into gay bars. I'm not much of a bar person anyway, and I'm sure that scene would have terrified me. I bought a copy of the Gayellow Pages and found a couple of support groups that I thought might help me. One was Gay Fathers. I called them and went to a meeting.

"I met a man there, Gerald, and he became a friend. We didn't have a sexual relationship, which was good, because I wasn't ready for that. But Gerald showed me around and introduced me to people and talked to me. Through him, I met a gay minister who was instrumental in turning my thinking around about some of the moral issues. I stayed for almost three weeks and when I went home, I knew what I had to do.

"I still remember the look on Margaret's face when I

walked back in the door after my trip. The kids were jumping all over me and I was hugging them and I looked up and our eyes met. I smiled, and I think I tried to put all my love and feeling into that smile. She smiled back, but I noticed her eyes were red, like she'd been crying.

"Later, after the kids were in bed, we sat down in the living room. I told her I was gay, and she started to cry. She cried for a long time and finally she said, 'I wish I were dead.' "

"You must have felt terrible," I said.

"I did. How could I hurt her this way? But I also felt strong. I believed we could overcome this together, that it didn't have to mean the end. I got up and put my arms around her and kissed her, and I said, 'You may not believe it now, but this isn't the worst thing that will ever happen to you.' "

"That's a good line. What did she say?"

"She started laughing—it kind of broke the ice. She was crying and laughing and saying, 'My husband tells me he's gay and it's not the worst thing that will ever happen to me?' "

"We talked all night. I told her everything. And I told her I loved her and the kids and they were the most important thing in my life. I just needed this other part of my life, too. She asked me to give her time to think about it, and I agreed. A couple of weeks later, she told me that she thought she could handle some kind of compromise, as long as I promised to be honest with her. This is our compromise."

"New York?"

"Yes. For the past two years, we've come here in August. We do a lot of things together as a family, but I also have the freedom to be a part of the gay community."

"This is remarkable," I said. "You don't leave your family—you bring them with you."

"We have a great time, too. My wife has made it clear that she'd rather not know the details of what I do, but she doesn't seem too worried about it anymore. In fact, the other day I asked her how she was feeling about everything, and she said, 'To tell you the truth, I don't think about it very much.' I think we're definitely over the hump."

"Do your children understand what's going on? Have you talked to them?"

"They're too young now—but I suppose this is one more bridge we'll have to cross. I don't necessarily think they ever have to know. It's a personal thing between me and Margaret. I have mixed feelings about it, and Margaret definitely doesn't want them to know. Right now I'm taking things one step at a time. But I do make an effort to talk to them about how wrong it is to be prejudiced against people because of the way they live. During our trips to New York, they've seen homosexuals openly expressing affection—something they wouldn't see back home—and we've talked about this. I don't want them to pick up the views that are prevalent in our community."

"How do *you* feel?" I asked. "I'm impressed with the way you've worked things out, but frankly, it doesn't strike me as the kind of compromise that could be permanent. You can't establish any real relationships if you're only here one month a year."

"Actually, I have made some good friends," Dennis replied. "But you're right—this is a temporary measure. Eventually, I think we'll move out of Salt Lake City. It's hard to know about the future. I'm still too busy learning about myself."

"It's possible," I said carefully, "that as you get more comfortable in the gay community, things might change a great deal. Right now, you're satisfied with the compromises, but what if you meet someone you really care for? Do you think you might someday leave your marriage?"

He gave the question a moment's thought. "I'm not naive," he said finally. "But I love my wife and I love my children, and I really can't see that, no."

"Some women have told me," I pressed, "that they fear their gay husbands will leave them when the children are grown and they no longer feel so much responsibility to the family. This is a real fear, I think, because these women know that at that time they'll be older. They dread being left alone when they're old."

"That would be unfair," he said quietly. "I could never do that to Margaret. Besides, I don't think I could live happily without her. You forget that my marriage is not one of convenience. It's not *duty* that binds me to my wife. We're best friends. We're lovers. She's the only person in the world who really knows me. I don't sit around thinking about leaving her. Sometimes she worries about it. She's more afraid of my falling in love—the sex doesn't matter as much. She worries that some force will come and swoop me away. I reassure her as best as I can. I tell her, 'Look, we're never going to be that *normal* picture of a family again, but don't be afraid of it.' "

"Do you tell the gay men you meet that you're married?"

He laughed. "Half of them are married, too. If anything, they're jealous that I have such a good marriage and a supportive wife. A lot of men can't tell their wives at all—these guys are pretty frustrated. Even some of the single men are jealous. I have two beautiful children, and they realize they'll never have children. It's funny," he said, "I always assumed that a married man would be treated like a pariah in the gay community, but it's not that way at all."

"Do you ever feel that you're really two different people?" I asked.

"Not anymore. There was lots of pain making the transition. But things are good now. The tension is gone."

"You're happy."

"I'm excited," he answered, his eyes sparkling. "For so many years, I didn't allow myself to feel what I felt because I thought my feelings would take over and lead me places I didn't want to go. Now I'm at peace. I can be myself, but not be ruled by it. I owe my wife a great debt of gratitude for allowing me that freedom."

Compromise is an essential element in every good marriage. But there are degrees of compromise. Most of the writings that deal with the event of discovering one's husband is homosexual treat this as an insurmountable problem. It is, according to the popular understanding, the *worst* thing that could happen to a woman, contrary to Dennis's belief. The revelation of the husband's homosexuality is considered the automatic end of the marriage, since no woman in her right mind would stay married to a gay man.

Would she?

We've already seen, in previous chapters, countless examples of couples who have established successful relationships that seemed, at first glance, impossible. And we've listened to the stories of women who have married men who they knew at the outset were gay. There is a difference when the choice is made from the beginning of a relationship. But I met numerous couples who, after the fact, chose to remain together, making the necessary compromises to keep their marriages strong.

About 32 percent of the respondents were currently married, and the husband's homosexuality was not known at the beginning of the marriage. Usually, the subject did not arise until much later—ten, twenty, or even thirty years into the marriage. Most of these couples were trying to resolve the issue in a serious, caring way. I was impressed with the way they spoke of taking responsibility for the marriage and for the promises they had made to one another. In their marriages, these couples accepted the idea of the German theologian, Dietrich Bonhoeffer, that freedom cannot exist without responsibility, nor can responsibility exist without freedom. Their lives were not without pain and fear and uncertainty, but the deep love and respect they had for one another was evident in the way they faced reality without pretense or lies.

Did the men know they were gay before they married? In other words, were the marriages based on deception? I rarely found that to be the case among respondents. A 1985 study published in *The Journal of Homosexuality* supports the premise that homosexuality is not necessarily a certainty at every point in life. The study concluded that less than one third of homosexual men thought of themselves as being gay when they entered their marriages. Some considered themselves bisexual, but believed that the duality would disappear with a stable marriage. According to the input of my survey respondents and the current research on the subject, homosexual awareness can evolve in a number of ways:

- In early life, a young man may be sometimes aware of an attraction to men, but does not identify it as sexual.

- A young man feels sexual attraction to certain men, but believes it is of no real consequence, especially if he also feels a sexual attraction for women.

- A young men responds sexually to erotic materials or fantasizes about men, but does not relate his fantasy life to his real life.

- A young man feels sexual attraction to men, but is horrified and seeks to put it behind him. He hopes the feeling will go away if he ignores it.

Many men reported that they didn't know they were gay until many years into their marriages; some reported feeling "more gay" as time went on and they developed sexual maturity. Their feeling more gay did not necessarily coincide with problems in the marriage, sexual or otherwise. It did, however, relate to a conscious decision made at some point in the marriage to explore homosexuality—either by reading available literature or erotic magazines, attending meetings or social gatherings of gays, and/or experimenting sexually. Most often, a period of sexual experimentation took place before disclosure.

Researchers who have studied homosexual disclosure in marriage point out that dissolution of the marriage is not the inevitable outcome, but only one option on a long spectrum of possible courses. In a 1978 study published in the *Journal of Sex and Marital Therapy,* J. D. Latham found that in the cases in which wives were able to gradually understand and accept their partners' sexual orientation, a period of negotiation occurred, leading either to a redefinition of the marriage (usually as more open) or to divorce.

A six-year study currently under way of forty-four members of mixed-orientation marriages (reported by D. R. Matteson in the *Journal of Homosexuality*) suggests that the point of disclosure is normally followed by a period of ambivalence for both partners in the marriage. But, says Matteson, if the couple survives two years of the so-called negotiation phase of the marriage, it is likely that they will stay together.

According to this data, the continuation of the marriage depends first on the wife's willingness to accept the sexual identity of her spouse—even if she is not yet sure she can accept remaining married to him. It is normal for her initial reaction to be one of hurt and rejection, but if she moves beyond this, it is possible for negotiation to occur. When both partners want the marriage to last, and both are willing to accept responsibility for nurturing the marriage, they can more comfortably redefine their options as a couple. Usually, this process requires some therapy.

My survey respondents described their feelings about maintaining their marriages in the following ways:

We've been married twenty-four years and have four children. I told my wife a year ago about my gay side because I knew I was her best friend. We cope with it. We still have sex—not as much as we had twenty years ago, but more than we were having before I told her about me. I guess we're trying harder now. Also I'm liking it more and looking forward to it, because a lot of the tension and fear of the past is no longer there. Our honesty has given us a new closeness.

—Kevin J., 47, married 24 years

At the present time, my husband is in a government job that would make it impossible for him to be openly homosexual. Of course, I fear that after he retires, he will become more open about his orientation and eventually leave me.

"Right now, our children are a binding thread for the relationship. I worry about what will happen when the children leave home. I also worry about how they will accept their father's orientation, and then understand our family relationship and unit.

"I worry about what will happen to me if our relationship dissolves. I have been out of the work force for ten years now. I am almost forty-two years old, and jobs for women that pay well don't allow for family time. Studies show that divorced women with children often live in poverty, and I have no desire to live with my children under those circumstances. Also, medical insurance is more expensive and difficult to get when you're older.

"I have a comfortable lifestyle right now, and I'm not willing to leave it. My husband says he does not want out of our marriage, and we're trying to work out our problems. I don't expect him to bottle his homosexuality and put it on the shelf and forget about it. I'm trying to understand and deal with this lifestyle with the resources I have. I don't know what the future holds, but I work at it day to day, and so does my husband. I hope that we will be together in a loving, understanding relationship until "death do us part."
—Karen, 41, married 14 years

The feelings I have aren't angry feelings, but rather, feelings of awe, wonder, and sometimes dread. We have been so good together that sometimes I know he thinks it would be easier for him to accept it as enough. But I hope he continues to search his soul for what is really good. Time will tell, but we hope to be together forever.
—Pauline B., 33, married 8 years

I am coming to like who I am as a gay man, and I feel a strong identity with the gay community. The

acceptance and support I have received from my wife
has helped me achieve this.

—Jack T., 47, married 16 years

I met my wife when she was dating my college
roommate, and I knew her ten years prior to our
marriage. We had our first child at four years
of marriage, and our second child at nine years of
marriage. My homosexual interest/awareness became
clear to me at around the five-year point. My orientation
became clear to my wife in 1987, and she confronted
me. She works hard to understand and accept me. I
reciprocate by limiting my involvement with men. She
has done an admirable job of trying to understand and
accept and keep the family together, and she earns my
respect in that regard.

Now that I'm in this family relationship, I'm
committed to caring and providing for them. The
question and fear is how my wife and I will cope over
the long term, and maintain our love and respect for one
another.

—Ned A., 42

Taking Care of Each Other

Tom and Ruth Frederick were the kind of suburban couple
everyone loves to have as neighbors. The lawn in front of
their Connecticut house was impeccably mowed, the trees
neatly trimmed. A black BMW was parked in the drive-
way—it was one of the couple's few concessions to the style
they had earned through Tom's successful public-relations
business.

Inside, the smells of cooking drifted out to the hallway.
As Tom hung up my coat, Ruth bustled me toward the
kitchen, her motherly figure covered with a billowing apron.

"I've made a spice cake," she said. "I'm famous for my spice cake." Tom followed us into the kitchen, a trim, tall man of sixty with salt-and-pepper hair. They were old enough to be my parents' contemporaries, and if this surprised me, they seemed to be perfectly at ease.

"Ruth is the best cook," Tom enthused, digging into his cake.

"I learned the way to a man's heart," Ruth confided, and they both laughed. I took a bite and watched them. It occurred to me that they *liked* each other a lot.

"So," I said, when we had all scraped the last crumbs from our plates and were sipping our coffee, "I appreciate your willingness to talk with me."

"We *love* what you're doing," Ruth said. "Tom and I have seen so many people who have suffered so much. So many marriages that have broken up and didn't have to."

"Yesterday, I met a man who had tried to commit suicide," Tom said soberly.

"It was so sad," Ruth said. She poured more coffee. "He was our age—maybe a little younger. Left his wife. How long had they been married, dear?"

"Thirty-four years. She might have been willing for him to stay, but he didn't think he could," said Tom. "But then he didn't know what to do and he was so lonely. It was a very sad story, actually. He told me he wished he could turn back the clock and undo everything—be back with his wife. It wasn't worth it."

"Tom introduced him to a woman we know who counsels gay men and their wives. We hope he'll be okay."

"My God!" I shook my head. "It seems almost unthinkable that a man could make such a change at sixty."

"Yes, well, you don't see it that often," said Ruth. "Usually, they just keep it a secret, which causes them an entirely different kind of pain. You know, Tom was fifty-five when he came out."

"Tell me about your situation."

"I had homosexual experiences in high school," Tom said, "but suppressed my homosexuality in college—this was forty years ago, you have to understand. Ruth and I met in college and dated for two years before we got married. We had a monogamous marriage for about thirty years, and have two grown children—they don't know about my homosexuality. About five years ago, I began yielding to my homosexual feelings. I came out to Ruth about four years ago.''

"I had suspected something for several years before he actually told me,'' Ruth said. "I'm not sure what I saw—it isn't the kind of thing a suburban married woman wonders about her husband. When I couldn't stand it anymore, I confronted him. I could see he was miserable, and I wanted him to know he had a comfortable place and that I understood.''

"That's most unusual,'' I said. "What brought you to such a point of acceptance?''

"I could see that our marriage was deteriorating,'' she explained. "We'd always had such a fine relationship—good sex, shared activities, a quality life with fun and romance. I didn't want to lose it, and I knew that if there was any hope, I had to be the one to initiate the conversation and be willing to keep the marriage alive. I couldn't just stamp my foot and say, 'Don't be gay.' And if I left him, we'd both lose. It worked, too. Our relationship has never been so close.''

"It sounds like you're making all the compromises,'' I said.

Ruth nodded. "At first, I was. I was like this iron woman, determined to hold things together no matter what. There was a lot of tension. But then we got involved in a group and began to see a therapist. She made it clear that if we were going to stay together, we both had to want it. That meant Tom would have to take some of the initiative, too.''

Tom smiled guiltily. "I didn't realize until we were in therapy how much I was taking advantage of Ruth's good will. When she told me she wanted to stay married, I was very happy and relieved. I thought, 'Hey, that's great.' But I was so involved in my own process of self-discovery that

I wasn't doing anything to make the marriage work. Our therapist pulled me up short and made me see that this was a fifty-fifty bargain.''

"Why haven't you told your children? They're adults now. Surely that would make it easier."

"We've talked about it," Tom said. "Ruth says it's up to me. I don't feel strongly about *not* telling them, but I've procrastinated. If I had decided to leave Ruth and go live with a man, I definitely would have told my children. But it's much harder to explain to them why I'm doing what I'm doing. They are very close to their mother and I think they'd be angry and resentful about what I've done to her. Why create a big problem when there doesn't need to be one?''

"I've talked to a lot of couples who don't feel it's necessary to tell their children," I said, "and I can certainly understand that viewpoint. But on the other hand, I would think this duplicity would create a barrier to closeness—especially with adult children. This is who you are. It's something you feel strongly about. You're not giving them a chance to be a part of that. They might surprise you."

"It's something I've considered," Tom agreed.

"And another thing. What if they found out about it and you hadn't told them? Wouldn't it be more traumatic for them?''

"I've thought about that, too. It happened to a man I knew. One of his daughter's friends saw him with a man and told her. She was so upset that she didn't say anything to him for months. It never occurred to her that her mother knew about it. He finally confronted her because he noticed that her attitude toward him had changed so much. She's had a hard time with it. I think she's seeing a therapist now."

"Our children could handle it," said Ruth with a touch of pride. "They already know that we've been involved in gay rights activities. Maybe it's even occurred to them. I've left it up to Tom, but I would like them to know someday."

"Do you mind if I ask you about your sexual relationship?" I asked.

"No. We are warm and loving and affectionate, but we have agreed not to have a sexual relationship," said Tom. "I occasionally have sex with men."

"How do you feel about that, Ruth?"

Ruth blushed. "Sometimes it makes me sad," she said quietly. "I miss it. But we have intimacy in other ways. We have a very *romantic* relationship, if you can understand that. And I'm grateful that we're at a point where we can be so open with one another. I'm not sorry we chose to stay together."

Tom regarded his wife affectionately. "It's given Ruth a whole new cause, and she loves a good cause. She's become the 'mother hen' of the gay community here, fighting for gay rights and doing what she can to help couples who are facing the kind of transition that we went through."

"It's such a shame the way things are," Ruth said. "People are suffering because there has to be so much secrecy— with family, friends, neighbors. The constant need to cover up puts a tremendous strain on people. There's so much pretending, and the ever-present fear of discovery. I've been very disturbed by the homophobia I've discovered in church, family, and society. No one should be discriminated against because of sexual orientation, and I will work to help educate society."

Tom beamed. "That's my wife!" he said proudly.

Tom and Ruth were a wonderful couple, who clearly enjoyed being together. Ruth told me at one point that she supposed their ease with compromise was born of the maturity of thirty-some years of marriage. "We probably would not have succeeded had we been younger," she said. "Sex and freedom are more important then, and relationships aren't so well cemented. When you get older, you tend to take things in stride. You figure maybe you've got fifteen or twenty years left, if you're lucky, and you don't want to spend those years building from scratch."

Christine Henny, a clinical psychologist in Washington, DC, who has counseled gay spouses, notes that the tendency to compromise is common among older couples. "Obviously it's not ideal, but then a lot of heterosexual marriages aren't either," Henny said. "Sometimes the men aren't entirely comfortable with their gayness. They like to go out with gay men, but it's nice to come home and put your slippers on with the wife you've known for twenty-five years who understands you."

Her view was shared by many people over fifty years old. For older couples, the reasons to stay married were often far more compelling than the reasons to separate. Sometimes these reasons were practical, having to do with insurance, security, and the importance of continuity. The couples were respectful of the importance of growth and change, but they preferred to experiment with new ways without wiping out the value of what they had built together over a thirty- or forty-year period. I had the sense, listening to these couples, that they had reached a point of serenity in their marriages that could not be threatened by new revelations. While the younger couples waded through weightier fears, the message from the old-timers was, in effect, "Lighten up . . . it's only life." Here is what some of them said:

The opportunity to freely meet gay men and learn about the gay community is a gift I'm giving myself now that I don't worry so much about what people think. It has little to do with sex and a lot to do with pride. My wife knows what I feel; she stands right there beside me.
> —Sam J., 62, married 39 years

Sometimes I get a flash in my mind of myself running off with some young guy, and I think of how funny it would be to have a cemetery plot with me and this person, whoever he is, who is practically a stranger. And we're stuck lying side by side for all eternity. It gives me a good laugh.
> —George N., 65, married 41 years

To be perfectly honest, we've been through worse things
and survived. We lost a child some years ago. That was
hell. This is nothing.

—Janet M., 58, married 34 years

When you get married, you make a promise until death
that you will love, honor, and cherish this other person.
I couldn't live with myself if I left my wife to live alone
in this house that we've lived in together for almost
thirty years. She devoted herself to me and the kids,
and I always promised her that when I retired, we would
travel and enjoy ourselves. Am I now supposed to tell
her, ''Sorry, dear, but I'm going to enjoy myself with
someone else''?

—Ed Y., 59, married 28 years

I feel very good about myself and my homosexuality,
and I'm glad I didn't live my whole life without finding
myself. But I'm not a teenager. I know how to get
satisfaction without turning the apple cart upside down.

—Pat M., 62, married 35 years

This sounds awful, but I know women who can hardly
wait for their husbands to die so they can enjoy their
final years. They have terrible marriages. Compared to
them, my marriage has been perfect. I can honestly say
that, after working through my initial shock and fear, I
don't mind in the least if my husband is homosexual. It
doesn't change our relationship.

—Sandra, 61, married 38 years

Friendly Partings

The drama of discovering one's spouse is gay unfolds in different ways for different people. Sometimes the revelation tears the relationship apart. One woman spilled out her story with an anger that remained deep, even though her marriage had been over for several years. "I thought I was in a traditional marriage, striving to be happy as a housewife and mother," she said bitterly. "After nine years and two children, I learned he was gay. Looking back, I realize that our marriage was a constant struggle. I tried and wanted it to work, but now, as I look back over all the years, I still feel the pain. I feel that I was cheated—that it was all a lie. I am very angry at him, and I am more angry at myself, because the signs were all there, but I just couldn't see it. There are too many questions and too few answers. He got what he wanted—being out of the closet and free. But what about me? What did I get?"

It is the surprise encounter with unthinkable betrayal that is the more familiar scenario, surfacing every once in a while in magazine articles with provocative titles like "Is Your Husband Gay?" This kind of betrayal was even the subject of a movie starring Harry Hamlin and Kate Jackson. The scenario includes a dreadful moment of truth, ferocious denial, and desperate efforts to hold the marriage together as it unravels thread by thread. In some ways, as we have seen, the scenario is correct: The complicated bonds of love and need do not just automatically disappear because one feels betrayed; rather, the bonds themselves make the betrayal all the more crushing.

However, as we have seen, the end of a marriage is not always inevitable once the truth is out in the open. There are many examples of couples who want to stay together, not just out of convenience but because, in spite of everything, they recognize their commitment to one another as primary. These couples are forced to be brutally honest about their needs, and they must often be willing to make hard compromises. Sometimes it works—and there's no reason why it shouldn't, since people bring to a marriage their own unique set of needs and priorities. One of the most enlightening aspects of my research was the discovery that these marriages didn't automatically have to be dissolved at the point of discovery. There are other options. But staying together isn't always the best resolution. It only works if it's what both the man and the woman truly want. If either or both cannot be satisfied, it is usually best to end the marriage.

Sometimes, the woman is so desperate to keep her husband that she initially agrees to make compromises she is not really comfortable making. In the book *Friend of the Family,* excerpted at the beginning of this chapter, Annie tries to be tolerant of her husband Michael's relationship with their family friend David because she loves Michael so much and wants the marriage to stay together. But no matter how hard Annie tries to be accepting, every moment in the relationship, every word, every look becomes emotionally charged. Michael, who thinks his wife has accepted his relationship with David, can't understand why it continues to traumatize her so much. She doesn't understand, either— the hope that things will return to normal between them burns so deeply inside her that she is not even consciously aware of the extent of her nonacceptance. The point of reckoning only comes after she suffers a nervous breakdown from the strain of pretending.

When a couple chooses to separate, the parting is often, but not inevitably, bitter. Sometimes, with time and counseling, couples are able to let go of their marriages and move on—sadly, but without long-term resentment.

Jeremy and Fran agreed to talk with me together, although they were no longer married. They divorced amicably four years earlier, a year after Jeremy told Fran about his homosexuality. Jeremy lived with a man he met and fell in love with before his divorce. Fran was remarried. Jeremy and Fran had had no children.

Jeremy was thirty-six, a successful commercial artist who had started his own business after he and Fran divorced. He was a comfortable kind of man, tall and lanky, with thinning brown hair and pale blue eyes. We met in the large apartment he shared with his lover, Bill, located on Chicago's "Gold Coast" along Lake Michigan. He was alone when I arrived, but Fran soon followed. They greeted each other with a warm display of hugs and kisses.

Fran was lovely—as tall as Jeremy, she looked as though she could be a fashion model in her figure-hugging dress. In fact, she was a pediatrician. "I love what you've done with this place," she said, looking around.

"Bill's influence," Jeremy said as he shrugged. "You know what a mess I am to live with."

"Jeremy's from the school of 'drop your clothes on the floor and leave them there until they rot,' " Fran told me. "He doesn't have a taste for ambience. If he hadn't met Bill, he would probably be living in someone's garage."

From the bar where he was opening a bottle of wine, Jeremy pretended offense. "I'm not that bad," he declared. He returned with a tray and settled down next to Fran on one of the white sofas. It was late afternoon, and the sun shimmered off the glass of a large picture window.

"You two don't seem any worse for wear," I observed. "I guess it's safe to say that you're friends now."

Fran waved a hand in the air. "It took some time—like a few years—to reach that point. But yes, we are. I even approve of Bill. He's good for Jeremy—a real stable, loving person."

Jeremy reached over and squeezed her hand. "Thanks. That's a nice thing to admit."

She laughed lightly. "Not that there isn't a darker side to this story. Jeremy was the great love of my life. That's how I viewed him. I was always very romantic, and I believed all that stuff about people being destined to be together. We met in freshman year of college. I didn't know what I wanted to do with my life—I had no ideas about becoming a doctor then—but Jeremy knew what he wanted. His art was wonderful, and of course I was very caught up with the romance of being involved with an artist. We fell in love very fast, moved in together after only two months, and got married within a year after we met.''

''You swept me off my feet,'' Jeremy said.

''That was certainly my intention. Once we were married, I thought we had it all. And marriage made me feel safe. There was always something elusive about Jeremy, and I thought marriage would be an assurance that he couldn't slip away.''

''Did you know you were homosexual then?'' I asked Jeremy.

''I saw myself more as bisexual—a side of me that Fran never knew about. I was into free love, and I slept with both men and women.''

''You preferred men?''

He considered this, frowning. ''I wouldn't say I *preferred* men. There was something more thrilling about it because it was so taboo. It took me a number of years to acknowledge that there was more to my attraction to men than thrill seeking.''

''Did you continue to have sex with other people once you were married?''

''Not for the first two years or so. Then, occasionally, I would. When Fran was in medical school and I had more time on my own, I went out more. And over time, I began to realize that there was a lot more going on than just sex. I began to open my eyes to the culture of being gay. The more I learned, the more I realized that this was a part of who I was.''

''Did you tell yourself you were bisexual, or gay?'' I asked.

''Bisexual, since I had a good sex life with Fran. But later, I decided that I was homosexual, since it was clearly my preference. Reading Kinsey's studies helped put things into perspective. I consider myself about a four on the scale—primarily homosexual, with some attraction to women.

''Anyway, for several years, while Fran was in medical school, I experimented. I never intended to do anything serious about it, since I loved Fran so much. Maybe I thought I could have the best of both worlds and just go on this way forever. But then I met Bill.'' He glanced at Fran apologetically. ''Bill was the creative director for the small advertising agency where I was the art director. From the first time we met, there was an electricity between us that shocked me. I was afraid of him. He represented a threat I didn't understand.

''I knew Bill was gay, but as far as anyone at work, including Bill, was concerned, I was a happily married straight man with a beautiful wife. Bill and I became pretty good friends, though. We often had to work late together at the agency, and sometimes we'd go out to dinner. He'd come over to our apartment a lot, and he and Fran really hit it off.''

''I was glad Jeremy had a good friend, since I wasn't around too much those days,'' said Fran. ''I did like Bill.''

''Finally,'' Jeremy continued, ''the inevitable happened one night when Bill and I were working late. I was shaking with emotion by the time I drove home at about two o'clock in the morning. Fran was already asleep. I collapsed on the couch and sat up all night crying. It's hard to explain the feeling of being elated and in despair at the same time.''

''Did you tell Fran then?'' I asked.

He shook his head. ''No. I was a coward. I tried to believe that I could have Bill and Fran both, that I wouldn't have to make a choice. Bill was angry about this. He felt I was being unfair to Fran to keep the truth from her, and unfair to him, too. He warned me that he had worked too hard to be open about his homosexuality to be someone's closeted lover. I kept begging for time to sort out my feelings.''

''I knew there was something wrong with Jeremy,'' Fran said quietly. ''I was so focused on him that I was used to picking up his change in moods. He was very withdrawn, and he was working late almost every night. He'd completely stopped meeting me at the hospital for dinner when I was on the night shift. He kept saying it was his work load, but I was terrified that he was having an affair—with a woman.''

''Did you confront him?''

''No,'' she said. ''I was too afraid that my suspicions were true. I didn't want to know.''

''Looking back,'' said Jeremy, ''I feel like a real creep for the way I treated Fran. I wasn't thinking about how she might be feeling. I was so wrapped up in myself. I even thought I was being kind to her by not telling her the truth. Was I deluded!''

''What finally happened?'' I asked.

''Bill put his foot down. Our affair had been going on for about five months. He told me I'd have to make a decision, or he couldn't continue to see me. He wasn't pushing me to leave Fran—he knew if he pushed for a choice, I probably would have chosen to stay with her at that point. But he said I must tell her the truth, and we'd go from there. He told me he knew men whose wives let them have lovers; maybe Fran would understand. But I knew it wasn't my style to split myself between two people. I was already emotionally exhausted from the effort.

''Finally, on one of Fran's nights off, I told her we had to talk. She gave me such a look of resignation when I said that, like 'Lead me to the firing squad.' It was the first time I realized how much she'd been worrying. We sat down and I told her I was homosexual and had been having an affair with Bill.''

''Talk about shock!'' Fran interjected. ''I had never even guessed. I thought it was another woman, which would have been something I'd have known how to deal with. But this was different. My reaction was violent. I kept screaming at him, 'You're my husband . . . you married me,' as though that were proof it wasn't true. I got hysterical, and Jeremy was holding onto me and trying to calm me down. Finally, I did calm down a little, but I was crying. I told him he was my life, he couldn't leave me. So he said he didn't want to leave me, he wanted to work it out, he loved me. He asked for time.''

"I was too confused to make a decision," said Jeremy, pouring more wine. "Those days, I vacillated. I'd imagine giving up Bill and staying with Fran, then I'd imagine giving up Fran and moving in with Bill. Nothing made sense."

"I had a friend from the hospital who was a family therapist," said Fran. "She was the only one I could think of to talk with. The day after Jeremy told me, I went to see her. I couldn't stop crying when I was talking to her, but she was great—so calm and soothing and unshocked. She told me that she felt sorry for my pain, but that it wasn't all that rare for homosexuality to come up in a marriage. She had known of other couples in similar circumstances.

"She asked me what I wanted, and it seemed like a stupid question. 'I want my husband back,' I told her. I remember she looked at me for a long time and didn't say anything, then she asked, 'No matter what?' I saw what she was getting at, but I was stubborn. I suggested that maybe Jeremy should get some counseling . . . maybe he wasn't really gay. Maybe Bill had done something. I was grasping at straws. She just shook her head and said she was sorry, but she didn't think that was probably the case. She also told me that Jeremy and I could work this out. It might mean the end of the marriage and it might not, but we didn't have to be stuck in this grief. That was encouraging. I agreed to ask Jeremy if he would come with me to a counseling session. He said yes, so we started going together.

"That counseling saved us," she sighed. "You know, it's so awful to feel isolated from the person you love and not to understand what he's feeling. Jeremy talked in those sessions, and I felt closer to him than I ever had. I also learned a lot about homosexuality. He wasn't doing this to hurt me. And it had nothing to do with my desirability. It helped to understand that this was a part of him that he couldn't do anything to change, not a deliberate act of hostility to our marriage."

"I had never been in any kind of therapy before, so this was a brand-new experience for me," Jeremy said. "And it wasn't at all what I'd expected. I thought she would be really tough on me and maybe even try to convince me to give up practicing homosexuality. I figured she would take Fran's side. But there were no sides taken. She was tough on me, but it wasn't about homosexuality. It was about lying to myself and to Fran. I saw how I had been avoiding taking responsibility for the choices I was making.''

"We spent several months in counseling," Fran said, "and the big question always was what we'd do about it. The counselor told us we had options, which was nice to know. It came down to deciding what would make us both happy. She introduced us to a support group for married gay men and their wives, and we met with some of the couples. I was impressed with the fact that some people actually stayed together and were happy. But I was beginning to see that this kind of arrangement wouldn't be right for us. Amazingly, I was ready to accept this before Jeremy was. One night when we were feeling very close, I told him that I would always love him, but I couldn't live this way and I didn't think he could either. We talked all night, and cried some, but in the end we decided to get divorced. He made arrangements to move in with Bill, and it was all very calm and untraumatic.''

"I asked Fran if we could still be friends, and she said she didn't know, maybe eventually,'' said Jeremy. "She didn't want to see me for a while, and I respected her feelings. But after we'd been apart about a year, she called to tell me she was getting married, and we started talking and things moved from there.''

"I was tempted to invite Jeremy and Bill to the wedding,'' Fran said mischievously. "But I knew my mother would just die. Nobody in my family ever knew the truth about Jeremy.''

The door opened and a good-looking, muscular man with thick black hair walked in. He dropped his briefcase by the door and threw his coat over a chair. "Fran!" he cried, and he headed for her as she stood up and hugged him. "It's been too long. How's my favorite baby doctor?''

"Trying to have a baby of her own,'' she laughed. "I

have a feeling, Bill, that I'll be about ten times more nervous than my patients.''

Jeremy handed Bill a glass of wine, kissed him lightly on the cheek, and introduced us.

''I'm glad I met you,'' I told him. ''You've been the invisible presence in our conversation for the past hour.''

He grinned. ''Aren't Jeremy and Fran great? I'm sure they told you every last detail.''

I looked at the three of them lounging on the couch. They were completely relaxed—three people who cared about one another. ''It must feel good not to have those big secrets anymore,'' I said.

Fran leaned forward. ''I feel lucky,'' she said. ''We all feel lucky. When this whole thing happened, I believed I would have the pain for the rest of my life. I couldn't imagine ever being completely happy again. This scene with the three of us sitting here would have been absolutely impossible for me to imagine. When your world falls apart, you feel so helpless, just like a baby. But eventually you learn to crawl . . . then you walk . . . then you run.''

Open communication seemed to make the critical difference for respondents who went through a breakup. ''There was trauma and tears and blaming and all the rest of it, in the beginning,'' one woman explained. ''We were each working out our frustration on the other. But when the emotions settled down, we were able to listen to each other and help each other through the transition.''

When communication was not there, a deadening isolation set in. The men felt trapped and frustrated that their wives could not accept them the way they were. The women felt wounded and betrayed. Because the couples were not open about their feelings, they began to blame each other when, really, neither was to blame. And since neither the husband nor the wife was given permission to grieve about the end of the marriage, the bitterness lingered on. The quiet despair of this fifty-year-old woman was evident in a letter she wrote eight years after she found out her husband was gay:

"We met when we were both eighteen, but did not marry until eight years later, since we were separated by the Vietnam War. When he returned, we were married and had a child. I thought I was the luckiest person alive. He was thoughtful, sensitive, and sexual, and I loved him.

"Sixteen years into the marriage, when our child was eight years old, he came out. Now, eight years after that, I still feel very hurt. I can rationalize everything, but I'm so sad! I'm still trying to make things work, and I try to be positive, but it's getting harder to share my feelings.

"At first, I really thought we could work it out. I was so relieved when he said he didn't want to leave. It took a long time for me to realize that he had already left me emotionally.

"My intention now is to go back to college and try to spend time on myself and stop trying to work so hard on the relationship, because it is too exhausting. I've felt all along that he has never tried to make things work; he's been too preoccupied with his new life. Many times I've suggested that if the other person was really everything he wanted in a partner and was so much better than I was, that he should have that person. My contention was that the greatest act of love would be to let him go, but he never went. Perhaps he felt guilty or safe. I'm sure he's struggling, too, but he hasn't lost anything—only gained. If I were young, I'd never stay.

"Mostly I feel as though my life is slipping away, while he is enjoying himself. Right now, he has a serious relationship going with a man. I don't even think he cares how I feel. It's a very insecure, ego-bashing experience for me."

In a particularly poignant story, another woman related how she attempted suicide. At first, after her husband told her he was gay, she tried to accept it, knowing she would lose him completely if she did not allow him the freedom to see men. As time went on, her husband became more comfortable with his sexuality, and she became more tense.

The breaking point came when he went off with a man he had just met and didn't show up for a family holiday dinner she had prepared. She tried to commit suicide that night. Only after extensive therapy was she able to find the courage to leave him and begin a new life.

Why is it so hard for people to let go of a marriage, even in the face of intolerable circumstances? Part of the reason may be that dissolving a marriage is the emotional equivalent of facing a death—and sometimes it takes a long time for people to work through the stages of mourning. For many, the stage of denial or false hope lasts years. Unlike the physical process of dying, which resolves itself whether the mourners have reached acceptance or not, the death of a marriage does not always feel inevitable, and the denial stage can last for years or even for a lifetime. It may be that the women in Chapter Six who described their attraction to the special qualities they found in gay men and who became involved in repeated relationships with them had simply never finished mourning the end of one particularly meaningful relationship—the first time they fell in love with a gay man only to find he did not feel the same way. Unable to deal with the loss of this love, they seemed to go on looking for its revival in the company of men who were like him.

Sometimes the hurt is so deep that women try to bully their husbands into being somebody different, as if it were possible to reverse the truth. These men reported feeling great despair when they revealed the truth and their wives refused to accept it and even grew spiteful. One man, a minister, told of the way his wife belittled him. "She told me I disgusted her, and it made me feel so dirty," he said. Another recalled the terror he felt when his wife threatened to expose him publicly if he didn't cut off all contacts with homosexuals.

It is hard to hear these stories without concluding that one of the partners is a "bad" person. What other explanation can there be for such neglect and/or hostility? But sometimes what appears to be hostility is really the expres-

sion of vulnerability and a cry for help. And not every couple is strong enough to reach across the chasm to offer
comfort to one another.

Others manage to bridge the gap. Like Jeremy and Fran
in the earlier story, some couples allow themselves the pain
of mourning, then move on. One outstanding characteristic
of these successful dissolutions, as reported by respondents,
is the amount of selflessness involved. Cathy and Tim were
a young couple about to get married when Tim told Cathy
he was gay. She shared her initial feelings and explained
how she reached the point of letting him go:

"We met at a party about two years ago, and we fell in
love. We were going to get married about three months ago,
but Tim got cold feet. When I questioned him, he sat me
down and told me he was having an affair—with another
man. I was deeply hurt and shocked, and I asked him if he
had ever loved me, or if he had just been pretending. He
assured me that he had always loved me and would continue
to love me. In fact, he said if I was willing to marry him,
he still wanted to marry me. He said he would break off his
affair and be faithful to me.

"I thought about it for a long time. I wanted so much to
say yes. How could I let him slip away when he meant so
much to me? I knew that our love was strong enough that
we could make it work, no matter what obstacles we faced.
But even as I was trying to talk myself into it, deep down I
knew it would be far more loving to let him go. Finally, I
told him that I didn't want him to break off his relationship,
that it just wouldn't work because homosexuality is real and
you can't just brush it off. I told him I loved him for being
honest with me, and that we would always be close friends.
And we are."

Another woman shared this experience of coming to terms
with her husband's homosexuality. "We always had difficulties sexually, but neither of us knew exactly what was
wrong. It created many tensions. I finally accepted that sex
was never going to be a big part of our marriage, and I was
able to rationalize the situation. Later, when I found out he

was gay, I was at first extremely angry and felt cheated. But now, a year later, I feel very differently. I have accepted the situation, and I believe he has to be free to be himself. I have met the man in his life, have seen his change, and can now thank his lover for being there to help him. Our marriage is over, and I have accepted that, too.''

No matter what the specific circumstances, the husband's revelation of homosexuality sets in motion a fundamental change in the marriage. Once it occurs, the illusion of the romantic ideal dies forever. Even the most confident couples can feel marooned at times when they no longer have the reliable old ways to depend on. But many of them have taken on the challenge of change and gone ahead, not quite knowing what might happen in the future. In their willingness to grapple with the mysterious joint forces of freedom and commitment, they tell us a great deal about the nature of love.

CHAPTER EIGHT

Choosing Parenthood

It means that your father or mother is different from
other people, different from the way our television
programs say a parent should be. Your parent is
different because he or she is able to love another
man or woman fully, body and soul. Is that so bad?
In a world where grown-ups compete, cheat, steal
from one another, and even kill one another for
what they believe are good reasons, it is not so bad
to have a parent whose "crime" is the
ability to love.

—from *Loving Someone Gay,*
Don Clark, Ph.D.

"A LOT OF PEOPLE don't think you can be gay and still want
to have children," Mark said. "I suppose you've heard that
plenty of times."

I smiled at him across the table. His face was open and
smooth, his black eyebrows knitted together earnestly.
"That's because most people think being gay is only about
having sex," I said. "You know—*normal,* heterosexual
people are more concerned with the serious stuff, like raising families."

His laugh had an edge of bitterness. "Yeah, right. It
seems that people believe what they want to believe. They
don't want to hear about things they can't understand."

Mark and I were having dinner at a quiet restaurant on
the outskirts of Atlanta, a few miles from where he lived
with his wife, Nancy, and their two daughters. His wife had
been unable to join us, but I had arranged to meet with her
the following day.

Mark and Nancy had been married for six years; their daughters were four and two. Mark had written in response to a query I had made for information from gay fathers. To complete my study, I wanted to focus on issues of parenthood; I knew from previous responses that the desire for children was a prominent factor in many of the men's decisions to choose heterosexual partnerships.

"I know being gay is the result of *nature,* not *nurture,"* Mark said. "I never felt there was a choice involved. But for a long time I felt sad because I knew that so many doors would be closed to me. Maybe this is hard to understand, but I really felt an urge to have children. I was an only child myself, and I was always drawn to the families of my friends who had big messy houses and several children. I imagined myself having a family like that someday, but as I grew older, the fantasy became more difficult to maintain. Gay men, I knew, lived alone or with a partner, but the picture didn't include children.

"What surprised me most, as I began to talk with my gay friends about it, was that I wasn't alone in my desire to have children. Many of them shared the same strong feelings. I also knew men who went ahead and got married without telling their wives they were gay, because they wanted children. They rationalized their actions in various ways, but I knew I couldn't bring myself to be so deceitful. I probably would have adopted children, had that option been available to me."

"But you finally did marry. Was having children the reason?" I asked.

"It gets complicated here," Mark admitted, "because at the time I was feeling so many different things. Nancy and I had been close friends almost all our lives. We were each other's main sounding boards during all of our traumas and bad love affairs, and we did important things together, like hike around Europe after college. Once we lived in a house together with several other people for about two years.

"Nancy always wanted to get married, and she came close a couple of times, but it never happened. By the time she turned thirty, I remember how bitter she felt. Here she was, this lovely, warm, giving woman, who just wanted a normal life with husband and kids, and she couldn't understand why it wasn't happening. She thought something was wrong with her.''

"And what was going on in your life during this period?'' I asked.

"I was working on my master's degree and teaching. I had a number of relationships—one of them lasted five years and looked like it might be permanent, but it didn't work out. For the most part, my life was satisfying, but I missed the feeling of closeness that comes with having a family. I was angry that gay men were not allowed to marry and adopt kids. That would have been an ideal solution for me.''

"Did you ever seriously investigate adoption?''

"Yeah, I talked to some people. I know that now it's beginning to happen in some places, but at that time, it seemed completely out of the question—even though there were a lot of kids who needed foster homes, or that nobody else would adopt. I felt angry and humiliated at the same time.

"One day when Nancy and I were in our early thirties, we were having a long lunch to celebrate a job promotion she'd been given. It was one of those lunches that drifts into late afternoon, and we were relaxed and feeling good, drinking coffee and talking the way we always had. The subject got around to Nancy's biological time clock, which she was always talking about, and I said, 'Isn't it funny that you want kids and I want kids and here we are.' It was one of those statements that sticks in your mind—at least, it stuck in my mind. The more I thought about it, the more I loved the idea of marrying Nancy and having children. But I never said anything, because it sounded too crazy.''

"It does,'' I agreed. "You didn't even have a sexual relationship, or seem to want one. And marriage has to have more going for it than just the desire to have children. It sounds like a marriage of convenience—not a particularly romantic idea.''

"Oh, but it wasn't like that," Mark said. He shook his head vehemently. "We did love each other; we spent most of our lives together. If you really think about it, we had more going for us than most couples do. Anyway, we did it, and the rest is history."

"How did you address the issue of sex? Was it a matter of convenience for the sake of having children, or did you actually develop a well-rounded sex life together?"

"I'm not sure what you mean by well-rounded," he said as he laughed. "We've had our share of problems, as any couple does. As our romantic attraction grew, sex seemed more natural. This is just my theory, but I believe that sex can be a different experience with different people. In some circumstances, it is primarily erotic—which is the way I would describe the attraction I've felt for certain men. In other circumstances, it can be the expression of strong feelings of love and kinship. In loving my wife, I wanted to be close to her, to share myself with her in every way, including physically. It was not a forced situation."

"How have your sexual feelings for Nancy changed over time?" I asked. "Many men I've spoken with, who started their marriages with the best of intentions, found that they felt more homosexual as time went on, and other studies support this."

"I am not frustrated sexually, if that's what you mean, because I have not totally stopped having sex with men. Nancy agreed to this in the beginning. And I have no desire to leave my family. I already know how lonely it is out there. To tell you the truth, it's not as great an issue for me as it may be for some men, but I've never been a highly sexed individual. I'm so busy with my job and family, I don't really have the time or inclination to get involved in gay relationships.

"As far as our sex life is concerned, Nancy and I have gone through ups and downs. But are we really any different from other couples in this respect? Most people have periods of being less interested in sex. There are a lot of reasons for that—such as work pressures and being too tired. Actually, we've grown more comfortable with each other. At first, Nancy felt nervous about my true feelings for her or whether or not she could really satisfy me sexually. But as time went on and her worries proved to be unfounded, she relaxed.''

"You make it sound so easy," I said doubtfully.

"It isn't easy, but we allow each other freedom. We understand each other. We're open. We love our girls. In our own way, we're happy. We both acknowledge that maybe it won't last forever, but in that sense we're no different than other couples. I think we've proved that people don't have to be victims of circumstance.''

Mark's story is quite out of the ordinary. I only tell it because it so dramatically makes the point that just because a man is homosexual, it doesn't mean he may not want many of the same things other people want—a home, a family, children. In fact, researchers and demographers estimate that between one and three million gay men are natural fathers, and their offspring may number as many as fourteen million. What drives so many homosexuals into the closet is the conflict between those wants and the difficulty of having them met. They are further fearful that their children will be taken away from them, and that they will be classified as deviants or unfit parents. The idea of a homosexual man as father collides with many cultural ideals. The father, after all, is the child's most prominent *male* role model. How can a homosexual man be that?

Many people believe, erroneously, that when a homosexual adult is in a primary position in a child's life, as parent or teacher, the children will be "at risk" of becoming gay themselves. Most enlightened experts agree that homosexuality is not caused by exposure. Nor are homosexuals interested in converting others. In fact, many gay parents, wanting to spare their children the pain and prejudice that they had experienced, expressed to me their hope that their children would not be gay.

While no definitive studies have been conducted on the

development of sexual identity in the children of gay parents, initial research reveals no real connection between the sexuality of a parent and that of his or her children. In limited studies conducted by Frederick W. Bozett, a registered nurse and professor who has worked closely with the issue of gay parenting, no relationship was seen between parental and child sexual identity. In a 1981 study of twenty-five children of gay fathers, Bozett found no father who reported having a gay or lesbian child, although not all of the children were old enough for their sexual orientation to be determined. In a second study in 1986 of twenty children of gay fathers, Bozett found that two sons reported being gay, and one daughter considered herself bisexual. The remaining seventeen considered themselves heterosexual.

Further, at least five studies have been conducted of the children of lesbian mothers. In no case was there found to be a relationship between a mother's sexual identity and the outcome of her children's sexual identities. Concludes Bozett, "The link between parental and children's sexual orientation appears weak. Thus, the myth that gay parents will raise gay children and that gay parents attempt to convince their children to be gay has no support from research data."

The gay father encounters a unique set of concerns, whether he remains in the family or not. His motivations for marrying in the first place must be examined. A gay man who marries because of a strong desire to have children must face the possibility that he is "using" his female partner—marrying her for her womb. If the desire for children is the basis of a grand deception of this nature, how can it be justified as moral?

But the overt deception is far less frequent than the good-faith partnership, entered into with a commitment to the female partner, and the expectation of parenting as a shared endeavor. In these relationships, the concerns emerge over time; they involve maintaining the integrity of the parenting role while expressing oneself honestly as a homosexual.

Much of the concern focuses on two issues:

- How to create an ethical foundation for children regarding issues of sexual responsibility, the meaning of commitment, and the role of sexual expression in a relationship

- How to foster in children, who are bombarded by prejudice against homosexuality, an open-mindedness about homosexuals and the choices they make

Susan Eckhart, a New York family therapist who has counseled several families of male homosexuals, described what she has seen as some of the most pressing issues for these families.

"Nearly all of the families have been in the process of divorce, and they have come to me to help both adults and children deal with the transition," she said. "When both of the parents have chosen to present a united front, it is much easier for the children to adjust. Unfortunately, it is more often the case that the children observe their mother being hurt and being angry, and they blame their father for this. The mother's behavior communicates to them that their father has chosen to be homosexual and therefore has caused pain in the family. He is seen as being selfish and uncaring. In these cases, the children tend to side with their mother, the wounded party, and they join forces with her against the father. Sometimes the woman encourages this—it's her form of revenge against the man who has hurt her.

"It is always destructive to use one's children as a tool of revenge in divorce," she noted. "But many adults are so hurt and so lost in their anger that they act in ways that are not in the best interests of the children. When I counsel these families, I usually have to bring the parents to a point of understanding before I can effectively work with the children."

"How do you feel about couples who decide to stay together, even though the man is homosexual?" I asked.

"I have little personal experience with these families," she said. "But I can appreciate why some people would opt for this choice. Not every couple has the same priorities, and not every homosexual man is interested in pursuing a gay life. It is easy for us to sit in the bleachers and say, 'They should do this,' or 'They should do that.' But we cannot really know what is best for others. People are very individual in their needs.''

As I listened to gay fathers talk about the strong love they have for their children, and their commitment to parenting, it occurred to me how often we diminish humanity by boxing ourselves and others into singular roles. All of us play many different roles, and have the capability to play many more. We are not just lovers, we are also friends. We are political activists and workers. We are children ourselves of our own parents. And we are parents. In that respect, it is not at all strange that men like Mark would feel the same kind of desire to have children that heterosexual men feel.

Gay Fathers Talk About Parenting

In a separate controlled study, designed to gain insight on specific issues related to parenting, I surveyed ninety-two gay fathers; of these men thirty-seven were currently married and fifty-four had previously been married, but were now separated or divorced. One man was widowed. The men were solicited from the files of study participants, as well as from selected organizations of gay fathers. Depending on whether the respondents were married or divorced/separated, the issues differed greatly. But all were committed, loving fathers.

MARRIED GAY FATHERS
"I hold in my hands the power to turn my family upside down, to hurt my wife, and to alienate my children forever," one man wrote. "I do not want to leave them, and I can't bear the thought of losing the closeness I now have with my children. But I cannot be just partially honest with them. If I'm going to be honest, it's got to be complete."

This man had been married nineteen years; his children were teenagers. He was in the process of coming to terms with his homosexuality and deciding how to let his wife and children know. Like many married men I spoke with, he did not want to leave his wife and family, but he feared they would not accept him. His greatest pain came from the fear that his fifteen-year-old son, to whom he was very close, would turn away from him, and be disappointed and angry.

Of the thirty-seven married gay fathers surveyed, only fourteen were living with women who knew and accepted their homosexuality. The remaining twenty-three were in that difficult predisclosure period, and suffered from the fear that their honesty might cause them to lose everything—in particular, contact with their children. Eight of the twenty-three said they would not tell their wives, at least until the children were grown, and maybe not even then. For the most part, the others were vague or not sure when they would feel ready to "come out" to their wives and children.

In the cases in which the man's homosexuality was known and accepted by his wife, the primary concerns included:

- How to best communicate to the children, in a positive way, what being gay meant

- How to answer specific questions the children might have

- How to protect the children from any discrimination they might suffer if their father's homosexuality became known

Often, in the process of thinking about what to say to children, the couples found that their own understanding and acceptance was deepened. "I always felt strongly about telling our son," one man said, "because I wanted to open the way for him to see that life had options. I don't want him to grow up, as I did, thinking there are no choices in life. My wife didn't want to tell him—she thought he was too young to hear about things that were so adult and personal. But I didn't see this as being a conversation about sex as much as a conversation about being oneself and being free.''

Another man wrote that it had not been their intention to say anything to their twelve-year-old son until he was much older and could better handle the information. ''But one day I heard him out in the yard with his friends, and they were laughing and talking about an 'old fag' they'd seen on the corner. I didn't hesitate for an instant. I called my son inside, sat him down and told him. It was hard. His first reaction was to say nothing, just shrug and try to act like it was no big deal: could he go back out and play? He was clearly embarrassed to be having this conversation with me, and I assumed he was feeling so many different emotions that he just wanted to push them away. I decided to leave it alone for the moment. I told him to think about it and later we'd go out to dinner, just the two of us, and I would answer any questions he had. Later, at dinner, he started to ask things like whether I was going to leave his mom—I told him no—and whether this meant I would get AIDS. Once he realized that our whole life was not going to be turned upside down, he didn't seem to have any problem adjusting to the idea. I later realized that we had been putting off telling him to protect ourselves, not to protect him. Even as we were sitting back and waiting, he was out there picking up all the negative stuff society was only too willing to teach him. It's much easier to believe stereotypes when it's not your friend or brother or father they're talking about.''

Most parents are aware that their children don't live in a bubble. They are going to pick up impressions from a variety of sources, and there is something to be said for them hearing the truth from the parents whom they trust. In the cases in which the mother was openly supportive, the children usually had less trouble accepting their father's homosexuality.

For the most part, the twenty-three men who had not told their wives and children about their homosexuality were deeply fearful of the consequences. Their marriages had not, by and large, been built on deception; self-realization had occurred over time for the men, and now they agonized about what to do.

"I would like to keep my family together," said one man. "It is a part of me that is important. But there are other things that are important, too. My goal would be to find a way to balance both worlds. I take my marriage vows seriously, and my parental responsibilities seriously. My wife is a wonderful woman, and I hope she can understand this and we can stay together. But I honestly don't know what her reaction will be."

Another said, "My son is fourteen—it would be a lousy time for him to find out his dad is gay. He's got enough changes to deal with in his own life and body. I've put off talking to my wife, thinking I should wait until my son is older. But that doesn't seem fair to her. Right now, I'm having trouble figuring out how to be fair to everyone—including myself."

Still another man speculated, "I think my children would accept my gayness, if they knew. They're both adults now, and I know I could talk to them frankly. But I'm afraid if I left their mother, they would feel compelled to stand by her and resent me, and in that way our relationship would suffer."

SEPARATED OR DIVORCED GAY FATHERS

"Although my children are not the only important aspect of my life, they are *the most important*. Their welfare is part of every decision I make. The most difficult part about making the decision to tell my wife I was gay and ask for an end to our marriage was that my relationship with my children would suffer. But after a lot of reading and some counseling, I began to realize that spending less time but happier times with them would be best for all. Because of the pain so many of the people I love are feeling due to the breakup of my marriage, I sometimes think maybe getting married was a big mistake. But then I look at my children and I know if I had to do it all over again, I would. The one thing I always wanted to be when I grew up was a father, and it's the one thing I'll never regret.''

This man admitted, as did many others, that his homosexuality was not necessarily the determining factor in the breakup of his marriage. Marriages don't necessarily break up over the admission by a man that he is gay. Often the couples are having other problems that are totally unrelated to homosexuality.

The man who wrote this letter, the father of two children, reached an amicable joint custody arrangement with his wife when they decided to divorce. Custody wasn't an issue for thirteen of the fifty-five separated or divorced gay fathers, since the children were adults. Of the remaining forty-two, twenty-one had joint custody, five had sole custody, and sixteen had no custody.

Being denied custody and, in some cases, visiting rights, is a devastating experience for any parent. And as in so many marriages, denial of custody to gay fathers is often due to anger or a desire for revenge. The situations I learned of involved hostility from the wife that filtered down to the children. ''My oldest son called me a 'faggot,' '' one man said with pain, ''and my younger son would not acknowledge the situation at all.''

Deciding to leave one's family can involve both emotional trauma and legal nightmares. One young man, the father of three children, told how, even though his wife was supportive, he ran into legal complications. ''My wife told her lawyer she wanted a joint custody agreement,'' he said. ''But he went ahead and filed for her to receive sole custody. It was his attitude that no gay man could possibly be a good father and role model. My lawyer told me that she knows the judge in our court system, and whatever custody arrangements my wife asked for would be granted. She said I stood no chance of fighting because if the issue of my sexuality were brought up, I would surely lose. A friend of mine in a similar situation had to call eighteen different lawyers before he found one who would handle his case.

The first seventeen, upon hearing that he was gay, said, 'We don't handle that type of case,' or just hung up on him.''

Usually, gay men must depend upon the good will of their wives to assure that they are able to share custody or even have regular visiting rights after a divorce. Several men reported that they have only rarely been allowed to visit their children. It is no wonder, given the harsh realities, that so many men go for years without telling their wives they're gay.

Legal issues surrounding custody are very complex and verdicts are often reached subjectively, according to the ill-defined concept of "the best interests of the child." The judge in a custody hearing is given a great deal of latitude in choosing which factors he or she will consider—there is no objective legal standard. It is very frustrating and frightening to know that one's status as a parent might be determined by the personal prejudices of one person. And according to a statistical analysis that appeared in *American Trial Judges,* in 1980, 96 percent of state trial judges were white, 98 percent male, and their average age was 53.4 years. It is probable that the statistics have not changed all that much during the 1980s. The implications are sobering for the gay parent, who must try to educate the judge by bringing to his side social workers, psychologists, and other expert witnesses who will support the premise that homosexuals are capable of parenting and providing a good environment for their children.

The primary issue is how the judge will view the factor of homosexuality—as very important; as only one of many factors; or as generally irrelevant. One approach used in many courts is to insist that the homosexual behavior be directly shown to be harmful to the child—thus giving the parent the benefit of being "innocent until proven guilty." But the custody question remains one of the most confused areas of the law. Without objective legal standards, gay parents are forced to trust their fates to those who often assume that a homosexual household is by definition an unhealthy place for a child. And even when custody is granted, the court often imposes restrictions that seem to be based on fear—for example, that a homosexual partner cannot be present during visitations, or that a parent cannot show open affection to a homosexual partner when the child is present.

Current studies indicate that children brought up in loving households with two adults are generally healthier and happier than children raised in single-parent homes—whether the adults are homosexual or heterosexual. Jane Mandel and Richard Green conducted a study of sixty lesbian mothers and their children to determine the effect on the children of having lesbian mothers. Published in 1979, their study showed that children who were brought up by gay mothers were not statistically different from children raised by heterosexual mothers. Further, the study indicated that children raised in two-adult homes were in better emotional health than those raised in single-adult homes—regardless of the gender of the adults.

Nevertheless, judges frequently ignore evidence such as this and make decisions based on their own arbitrary sets of values. In the 1985 case of *Roe v. Roe,* a gay father and his male partner had been raising his daughter for five years when the mother brought suit. The child was shown to be normal in all respects—bright, happy, and well-adjusted. Nevertheless, the court removed custody from the father, solely because of his homosexuality. The ruling further stipulated that the father's partner, who had been a coparent to the child for five years, was not allowed to be present when the child visited.

Telling the Children

The single most troubling issue for gay fathers and their married partners or ex-wives is whether and how to tell the children about their father's homosexuality. The temptation to keep it a secret is strong, even when the man leaves the family to pursue gay relationships. The issues include:

- A belief that young children are incapable of grasping the implications of their father's homosexuality or will feel threatened by it. Children might conclude that their father is hurting their mother and feel overly defensive of her. They might worry that their father doesn't love them anymore. They may become obsessed with the fear that he—and perhaps all of them—may get AIDS and die.

- The concern in non-monogamous marriages, where the homosexual partner has outside relationships, of communicating the meaning of sexual responsibility to a child. How does one talk about the importance of being free to fill one's needs, while making the point that this is different from a promiscuous "if it feels good, do it" attitude? "I haven't resolved that for myself," said one man. "How do I expect my children to feel, knowing that I am out having sex with someone else while they're home with their mother?"

- A concern for protecting children from the outside world and the many prejudices they might encounter. Fathers I spoke with did not want their children to suffer because of them. For example, one father told of how he struggled with the decision to tell his ten-year-old son. "I knew his best friend's father was anti-gay. He was one of these guys who was always making comments about fags. He had a very narrow attitude. I had mentioned this to my son a couple of times, and he assured me he didn't listen. He also told me his friend was usually embarrassed by his father. My concern, however, was that if this man found out I was homosexual, he would immediately cut off all contact between our sons—and probably even make some nasty remarks to my son. Ten years old is pretty young to have to deal with this kind of prejudice. I wondered: How, in good conscience, can I subject my son to this? I've made the decision to wait until he is older."

- Fear of the children turning on them. Even when there has been a deliberate effort to raise children in an open-minded home environment, many fathers are afraid their children will hate them for being gay. "It's one thing to teach your children to respect the fact that people are different," said one man. "But it's another thing when it is your own father."

Gay and Lesbian Parents, published in 1987, is one of the rare books that addresses this issue. The author, Frederick W. Bozett, presents the research that is currently available on the subject. He strongly advocates "planned disclosure," since too often children find out about a gay parent by default. He also suggests that the younger the children are when they are told, the more accepting they tend to be—especially if they have been taught to be comfortable with their own sexuality. Bozett outlines what the disclosure conversation might look like.

When telling children, choose a quiet place where you will not be interrupted. Keep your tone upbeat and sincere, not heavy and maudlin. Make sure there is plenty of time for explanations and expressions of feelings. Let your children know that this disclosure does not change your relationship with them except to make it more honest. The following are some questions children ask and some suggested answers:

Why are you telling me?
My emotional life is important and, by example, I can teach you to value yours, too. If I'm secretive about sex, you might get the idea that sex is frightening and something to be hidden. Homosexuality is not contagious. Fear and shame are.

What does being gay mean?
Being gay means being attracted to another man. It means being attracted so much that you might fall in love with him and express the love sexually.

What makes a person gay?
There are lots of theories, but no one knows exactly what makes some people attracted to men and some attracted to women. (Caution: The child might really be asking, "Will I be gay?" or "How will I know if I'm gay?")

Will I be gay?
You will not be gay just because I am. You are a separate person. You will be whatever you are going to be because of your own makeup and life experiences. I hope you will find loving relationships and that you will be open to whatever your life has to offer.

Do you hate women?
This question might mean, "Do you hate Mom?" Coming from daughters, this question usually means, "Do you hate me?"

Did your lover make you gay?
My gayness is a function of my own sexual orientation, not something that was forced on me by anyone else. My lover, however, has helped me to express my warm and tender gay feelings.

What should I tell others about this?
If you have friends that you want to tell, try it out. If you have a bad experience, let us talk about it. We can learn together the best ways of sharing this.

Bozett's sensitive approach makes it possible to see how a loving and open conversation with one's children can be a positive experience. Treating children with respect goes a long way toward diminishing their concerns. When you communicate the message, "This is none of your business" or "You're too young to understand," a child is left with his or her private fears—usually much worse than the reality.

Bozett's conversation sample is designed to demonstrate the tone that should be set, rather than actually to answer the many questions that might be raised. For example, he doesn't suggest a way to ease children's unspoken fear that their father's homosexuality means he might hate their mother, or hate all women, including female children. However, by alerting gay fathers to the fact that this fear might exist, Bozett implies that it should be addressed. Often children have trouble seeing the end of their parents' marriage as anything but a personal rejection of them and sometimes even their fault. A homosexual man who is leaving his family to live with a male lover must be careful not to give his children the impression that homosexuals hate women. This might best be handled by talking about the many different ways people love one another. To find help addressing these complex concerns, Bozett urges family counseling with an informed therapist.

Learning New Lessons About Family

Dick, a thirty-six-year-old divorced gay man with sole custody of his four children, offered to have a conversation with them about what it meant to them that their father was gay, and how their views of being a family had changed. He asked if I could send him some ideas about what to ask them. Since his children were quite young—the oldest was ten and the youngest five—the questions needed to be very simple.

It seemed like a wonderful opportunity. I had heard so many concerns and fears voiced about how to tell the children and what the children might think that it seemed logical suddenly to go to the source. What *did* the children think? After much consideration, I sent Dick these questions:

- What are the different things you have heard other people say about gays?

- Why do you think some people say that being gay is bad?

- Why do you think some people say that gay people can't be good dads or moms?

- What is a family? What do you see when you see a happy family?

Several weeks later, I received this letter from Dick:

It was an enlightening experience to ask my children about gay people again. Because they are very young, they have little if any concept of sexuality. But they have heard that faggot, queer, cocksucker, and dyke are names that are meant to hurt. They have heard other children mimic their parents and throw these words around. I am sure that these other children are equally without comprehension of the meanings of these words.

When I asked them why they thought that some people thought gay people are bad, they could not come up with any answer. They indicated that they knew gay people were people like any other. They know me as a father, much like the other parents of the children they know from school and play. As time goes on, I will explain to them about this in more depth.

One thing that came up in the course of the conversation was AIDS. They have heard of the disease. They know that gay men are among its important victims. One of them asked if you could get the disease by being gay. I said firmly that it wasn't who you were but what you did that caused infections.

What is a family? I guess they came to the conclusion that a family is people who love each other. We love each other even though brother or sister might steal our toys, mess up our room, or even hit us when they're mad. We are a family just like any other.

A few months after I received his letter, Dick called me to talk about what was happening with his children and his life in general. The family was about to undergo a major change, as a result of Dick's relationship with his lover, who lived in another state. "We are moving next month to live with him," he told me. "This will be a whole new phase in our life as a family."

"I'm happy for you," I told him. "I can imagine what a burden it is to raise four children alone. I assume you've considered the implications. For example, I know you have told me that the children have no relationship with their mother. Now that you will be raising them as a male couple, are you consciously dealing with seeing that the children—and particularly your daughters—have positive female role models?"

"The kids know that my being gay doesn't mean that I am anti-female. I've always had close women friends, and will continue to do so. But like any homosexual single parent, I am sensitive to the issue. I hope that, especially as my daughters grow older, they will have women they can look up to and talk to. But I don't agree that children need to live with both male and female adults, or are necessarily better off in a heterosexual environment than they are in a homosexual family. That's what many people think."

"How do the children feel about the move?" I asked.

"They have mixed feelings about moving—mainly because they don't want to leave their friends. But I don't think these concerns are any different than other children might have. As for my living with another man, I don't think they mind, since they like Martin. In one sense, they're looking forward to it, I think. It will mean more attention, more money, a bigger house. Children tend to look at things very simply. If it looks like they're going to get more out of it, they'll be all for it. And Martin has worked hard to cultivate their friendship.

"There's another aspect, too. This hasn't been raised openly, but I suspect they've noticed that I'm easier to live with when Martin is around—which makes their lives more pleasant. These last few years have been hard for me. Raising four children by myself has been exhausting. Almost every minute that I'm not at work has been spent taking care of practical matters related to the children. As a result, I've often been tired and cranky and lonely. And there's so much to do that we don't have much time to have fun. With another adult present to share the parenting responsibilities and to support my need for adult companionship, I'll be happier and the children will benefit.''

''I can see that,'' I said. ''It's a shame that many people would view the circumstances of two gay men raising children as a negative for the children. Clearly, in your case, it will be much better for them. Have you prepared them for the community pressure that is likely to occur?''

''Martin and I have discussed it. We know there will be talk. Fortunately, my children are accepting of my being gay, which makes it easier. We'll talk to the children and let them know what they might hear from their friends at school or other people in the community. I've always had an open relationship with the children, so I know they'll come to me with their concerns. The important thing is that we will handle the problems together. Also, Martin and I will take steps to address the issue directly. For example, we'll arrange to speak with the principal and school counselor in advance so they can be aware of any problems that might arise. And we'll be involved in school activities, just like other parents.

''I am optimistic. I think once people see that we are 'normal' loving parents, just as they are, they will grow to accept us. People don't *choose* to be prejudiced. It's only that they're afraid of things they don't understand. It is my hope that people will grow to accept our family and not think twice about the fact that we're two men raising our children, rather than a man and a woman.''

''I'm impressed with how hard you've worked to resolve all of the parenting issues,'' I told Dick. ''I wish that some of the men I've spoken with who are really struggling could talk to you. I think it would give them a new perspective.''

He laughed. ''I didn't set out to be a pioneer in gay parenting, or to be an example to others. I know I haven't always made the right decisions. I see myself as being just like every other parent out there. I do the best I can to give my children the support they need and to provide them with a healthy environment. The fact that I'm gay seems irrelevant most of the time. We have to deal with the same things every other family deals with. I worry, just like every parent worries, about doing what is best for my children. My love for them is no different because I also love another man.''

CHAPTER NINE

Love and Death
in the Era of AIDS

About AIDS: "It must be in some way heartening.
It must improve morale for it to be allowed
a place of honor; otherwise it will be dismissed
as useless, discouraging, immoral, like an art
that accepts surrender during a war . . ."

—from *Ground Zero,*
Andrew Holleran

THE WOMAN'S VOICE was breathless over the phone, and sounded far away. "I hope you don't mind my calling you like this," she said nervously. "I can't believe I'm doing it."

"It's okay," I told her. "Where are you calling from?"

"Oh, I'm sorry. My name is Peggy Greenwood, and I'm calling from Phoenix. Uh . . . you see, the reason I'm calling is that I just got back from signing the papers on a house with my fiancé, and your questionnaire was here, and I wanted to tell someone how happy I was."

I smiled into the phone. She sounded very young. "I'm glad you called me. When are you getting married?"

"In about six months. I've been living with Steve in his apartment for two years—we both just graduated from college."

"So that makes you what? Twenty-three or -four?"

"We're both twenty-four."

"I take it Steve is bisexual or homosexual."

"Yes, he's bisexual, but most of his relationships have been with men. As you can imagine, it took us completely by surprise when we fell in love. We met at a party and neither of us was seeing anyone then, so we started doing things together. We had a great time; I never thought in a million years it would get serious. Neither did Steve. But he brought it up first. When he told me he was falling in love with me, my heart stopped, because I had been having the same feelings.

"Steve had always been very honest with me about his past. I knew he'd had many lovers before he met me, but he said he's never been in love with any of them. The past two years have been so good between us."

"It sounds great, Peggy," I said. "And I'd be interested in hearing about how you worked through some of the issues that usually come up for a couple like yourselves."

"You mean sex?"

"Yes—and monogamy. How do you define your commitment?"

"Monogamy is important to me, but I'm not going to tell Steve he *must* be monogamous. I trust him enough—and I trust his love for me enough—that I know he will do what is right and best. We've talked about it, of course, and he has been very honest with me. Although he hasn't had a male lover for a long time and doesn't want one now, he told me that he can't just pretend his homosexuality doesn't exist. I think he has some unresolved feelings."

"Does that scare you?"

"No . . . well, maybe a little," she admitted. "I don't worry that Steve will leave me for another man, but the sex thing bothers me. It's like he loves me so much that he's willing to make this sacrifice, but I want him to be completely satisfied, and sometimes I wonder if he is. Our sex has been wonderful, but I find myself trying harder. I'm more conscious of trying to please him so he won't think he's giving up too much.

"These are relatively small struggles for me, though. Right now I think I'm the luckiest, happiest woman in the world. I can hardly believe I've found a man like Steve to spend my life with."

"I'd appreciate it if you and Steve filled out the questionnaire and sent it back to me," I said, before we hung up.
"And let me know about the wedding."

"I will," she promised. "I'll send you an announce-
ment."

Her questionnaire arrived in the mail two weeks later,
along with a note mentioning how much fun she was having
getting ready for her wedding. I didn't hear from her for
another six months, but when I sent out a follow-up mailing
to those who had filled out the questionnaires, I added a
personal note with hers, saying I was looking forward to
hearing about the wedding and how she and Steve were coping with married life. Several weeks later, I received a letter
in the mail.

"I'm sorry it took me so long to answer," Peggy wrote.
"My mail is being forwarded to my new address. A month
before our wedding, we discovered that Steve had AIDS.
We are battling this together, but we've separated, and we
won't be getting married. Right now, Steve is living with
his family. It's very hard to talk about. I'll never be sorry
for loving him, but it's very painful right now. Steve forced
the separation because he says he doesn't want to wreck my
life. I want to be with him, but I don't know if I'm strong
enough to watch him die. I know everything seems bleak
and morbid, but I am trying to get on with my life."

As I read Peggy's letter, I experienced the same chilling
sensation that always accompanied news of yet another
young person stricken with AIDS. Life seemed too fragile
in these moments—too impossible. I felt a deep sympathy
for this young couple whose happy plan for the future was
brutally halted. I picked up the phone and called Peggy.

Her voice sounded weary and sad over the long-distance
line, but she said she guessed she was willing to talk for a
few minutes about what she was feeling.

"When Steve pushed me to move out and build a new
life for myself, it seemed very logical," she told me. "We
can't get married, we can't have children, and he knows
these are things I want. He told me that the longer I stayed

with him, the harder it would be when the end came. I didn't want to leave, but he convinced me it was best. But now that I've done it, it doesn't feel right. I should be with him. He should have me there to face this with him, to support him.''

"Have you been in touch since you separated?'' I asked.

"Oh, yes. We talk on the phone, and I've visited him several times. But it seems that he's trying hard to push me away. There's a distance between us.''

"He's trying to be brave.''

"But isn't that nonsense?'' she cried. "What is the point of proving you can face things alone, without the loving support of another person?''

"It sounds like he doesn't want you to be hurt.''

"He's *dying* and he worries about me,'' Peggy said, exasperated. "I wish I knew what to do. This scares me a lot, but it seems that when you love someone enough that you're willing to marry them, the commitment holds, no matter what. We never said the vows, but we would have . . . in sickness or in health.

"I know Steve is thinking that I should be out looking for someone who can be a real husband to me. You know, someone who can fill my needs sexually and emotionally. Someone I can have children with and spend the future with. But that's like saying the only reason I loved him was because he could do these things, and now that he can't, I should just stop loving him.''

"You should try to tell Steve how you feel.''

"I know, but it will be hard to find the words to reach him. And I have to really think this through and ask myself if I'm strong enough to stay with him.''

"There are counselors who help people resolve these issues,'' I said. "Maybe it would be good to talk to someone about this.''

She sighed. "You're right.''

"Peggy,'' I said hesitantly, "I hate to ask this, but how are *you?* I mean, have you been tested?''

"Yes. I'm okay. At least, I'm okay for now. I'm not going to think about it. What's done is done."

"You must feel resentful . . . that he's dying, that you may someday die."

"No. We didn't know. Who am I going to resent?"

"Will you let me know how you make out?"

"Sure," Peggy said. "Wish me luck. Pray for us."

Two months went by before I heard from Peggy. She wrote:

"Steve and I have been through a lot of changes since I talked to you. After doing a great deal of soul searching, I made the decision that my place was with Steve. I told him that I wanted him to come live with me, but he was very resistant to the idea, so I asked him if he would at least be willing to see a counselor with me. I got the name of someone through the AIDS Crisis Center. She was wonderful— the best thing that could have happened to us. We saw her a few times, and finally Steve agreed to move in with me. I've met with his doctor and talked to people at the AIDS Crisis Center so I'll know how to take care of him. He's already had pneumonia once, and he's in very weak condition. His doctor tries to be hopeful, but we are realistic.

"Our life together is very different than it was before. We talk more and are more honest with each other. We spend a lot of time being close, and we sleep together, even though we don't have sex.

"Every once in a while, it really hits me that Steve is dying, and I break down. Sometimes we cry together, and those are our closest moments.

"I know it's right that we're together so that we can share our love for as long as we're given. We're taking things one day at a time."

Steve is still alive as I write this, nine months later. But it is doubtful he will be alive at the time of publication. He's been in the hospital on three different occasions, and is usually too weak to leave his bed. Peggy continues to care for him and love him.

In the course of my research, I encountered eight couples

who were living with AIDS as a daily reality. None of the
women in these couples had the disease—only the men. Like
Steve and Peggy, they were trying to face the bitter reality
bravely. One woman wrote movingly about what she was
feeling:

"Ben and I have been together for nine years, and I never
had any real trouble accepting his homosexuality. He always
made me feel that I was first in his life, that our relationship
was deeper and stronger than any other he might have.

"Within a couple of months of the day we met, our lives
were bound together. It was as though we could read each
other's minds. I felt I knew him as well as I knew myself,
and he knew me—the real me. There was this great sense
of unconditional love, and it has been there as a steady force
through all the ups and downs of the past nine years.

"But now he's dying of AIDS, and it's happening very
fast. He's already been in the hospital twice this year and I
am facing the reality that he may not be alive by year's end.
I worry about his dying and his death, and I try to imagine
how I'll be when he's no longer here. But I find I can't
picture it.

"Now there is no sex between us. We move closer together, then apart. Reaching out and hanging on for a moment before pushing away. It's a strange dance we now do,
where before we moved so easily together. I will stay with
him until the end and care for him. We will do what we can
for one another to make this time in our relationship as
meaningful as all the other years have been."

Being Responsible

When I first began researching this book, AIDS was not yet
the crisis we know it to be today. Many of the early respondents didn't mention it at all, or didn't consider it a
major factor. But as time went on, the subject of AIDS
came up with increasing frequency. Like most people in
America today, these men and women have grown more

serious about protecting themselves from the possibility of contracting the AIDS virus. But obviously it is a more compelling issue when one partner engages in homosexual sex outside the relationship. I asked some of the couples who had non-monogamous marriages or relationships how they were dealing with the issue. They reported that their primary fear was that "safe sex" was not really possible when multiple partners were involved. The AIDS factor raised many new and troubling questions for couples whose commitments had been predicated on the men's freedom to explore their homosexuality. While none of the men appeared to be promiscuous, it was rare to find one who had maintained a single long-term homosexual relationship.

AIDS places a substantial new twist on the issue of sexual freedom. It raises the stakes on all relationships between gay or bisexual men and women, and it changes the dialogue that occurs when one discovers a partner to be gay or bisexual. Before AIDS, women who found that their husbands or boyfriends had had sex with men outside the relationship struggled deeply with what they perceived as emotional and sexual betrayal. But what kind of betrayal is this, that reaches beyond the challenge to one's emotional resources and threatens life itself?

It was difficult for me to understand why the women I spoke with were not more frightened or angry when they knew their husbands or lovers were seeing men, too. The promise of safe sex seems chancey, even with the best of intentions. I had to believe that the women weren't leveling with me—as though by voicing their fears they would make them a reality.

It became a more personal issue for me during the course of my research. When I began, I had never known anyone who had AIDS, so I only understood the disease in the abstract way I thought about cancer—devastating, but not particularly close to home. But during the past year, I have watched a friend become progressively weaker through a series of ailments that have attacked him like hand grenades being lobbed at his center. Each explosion does more damage—just enough to make him weaker and sicker, but never enough to keep him in the hospital or kill him. It is the most tortuous process I have ever seen, made worse by the knowledge that the death sentence is irreversible.

Because I have experienced its devastation firsthand, I have grown more edgy in my interviews when the subject comes up. AIDS is no longer the private domain of the couples who are most at risk. We are all responsible for the risk.

New questions have emerged as AIDS becomes a larger factor in relationships. Since it is now known that the AIDS virus can remain dormant for five years or longer, many more people may develop the disease than currently appear to be infected. For non-monogamous couples, real questions need to be considered, including:

- Is non-monogamous sex even an option?

- If non-monogamous sex is not an option, is the gay or bisexual partner willing to maintain the relationship?

- What specific precautions are being taken for safety—and are these precautions consistent with what authorities agree is safe?

- Will both partners be regularly tested?

- If there is a decision to have children, what assurances will be needed before pregnancy occurs that neither partner has AIDS?

Further, because of AIDS, it no longer seems viable for men to practice gay sex secretively, even when it is with a single tested partner. Because there is a risk to their female partner and even to unborn children, it is no longer men's secret to keep. This is both a moral and a criminal issue. A previous history of gay sex should also be disclosed.

With AIDS as a new given in all relationships, I questioned the men and women in the survey about how it had affected theirs. Here are some of their replies:

AIDS is an ever-present reality for us. Whenever we hear of someone who has become sick or died from it, we experience a new jolt. My husband has been very responsible about his sexual encounters, and I trust him. But we're both aware that this may not be enough. Deep down, I fear that it will come down to the necessity of being monogamous. If that happens, the question is whether he will stay with me, or even if it would be fair to ask him to, since it would mean his giving up a major piece of his identity.

—Cynthia E., 37

One night I returned from having dinner with a man I had been seeing for several months, and found my wife crying. She told me that a dear friend of ours had called to say that he had just been diagnosed as having the AIDS virus. I started to cry, too, and we held each other and cried together. I know our tears were not only for our friend, but for ourselves, as well. We had been so secure, but it seemed that everything was changing.

—Barry, 39

I was 46 by the time I came out to my wife and told her I was gay. That was two years ago. She was supportive, and even said that she was glad I had not been a practicing homosexual when I was young, before the AIDS epidemic, because I might not be alive today. That was a sobering thought.

I had one relationship with a man last year that lasted several months, but none since then. Right now I am looking for a permanent male partner, as I've determined this is the only way I can be safe and protect my wife.

—Roger, 48

My husband practices safe sex with men, and we
practice safe sex when we're together. We've both
accepted this as a necessity, but sometimes I feel a little
resentful that I have to practice safe sex with my own
husband.

—Susan, 27

AIDS was one of the factors that led to our marriage.
We had been having a relationship for two years, and
we loved each other, but monogamy was an issue. She
told me that she could not marry a man unless he could
be faithful to her, and she didn't think it would be a
situation I could tolerate. My willingness now to be
faithful is largely because of AIDS. Exclusive sexual
commitment seems a lot more attractive to me than it
once did. Sometimes I miss having a sexual relationship
with a man, but so far, it hasn't been enough to make it
worth the risk.

—Douglas, 34

In this age of AIDS, I believe firmly that physical
attraction, although still very important, is underlaid
with concern for myself, my wife and family, and those
men with whom I may have sex. I take this
responsibility very seriously.

—Jim, 50

The Lessons of AIDS

Diane and Stewart married young, when they were only
twenty, and had a child six years later. When they had been
married ten years, Stewart told Diane that he was gay.

"That was a very hard time," Diane, now forty, told me.
"I was afraid for myself and for our son that we wouldn't
be able to make it on our own. And I loved Stewart. We

stayed married for five years after he told me, but finally separated. Our parting was emotional, because we cared so much for one another, but we knew this was how it had to be. We didn't get divorced, but we agreed that we would eventually.

"Our separation was very amicable. We wanted our son to experience as little upheaval as possible, and also, we had a lot of respect for each other. We remained very friendly after we separated. In many ways, our communication was more open than it had been during our marriage. I guess it was because we were finally able to let go of our need for each other's approval.

"About a year ago, Stewart showed up at the house one evening, looking terrible. He told me he needed to talk to me. Of course, I was instantly very worried, because Stewart was one of those people who kept his problems to himself—in fact, that stoicism was one of the things we argued about when we were married. I was even more alarmed by the fact that his eyes were red, as if he'd been crying. I don't think I had ever seen Stewart cry, except maybe when his mother died. I asked him what was wrong, and he kind of blurted out that he had AIDS.

"I can still remember the shock of that moment. Everything stood still. I didn't move. I didn't say anything. I just looked at him and he looked at me, and it was like all the hope had been sucked out of us. I wasn't really prepared for this, because I had never given any thought to the possibility . . . no, it's more like I had blocked it out.

"Finally, I recovered enough to go over and put my arms around him. It seemed like such a small gesture. But what else could one do? We sat down and gradually he started telling me the whole story. I tried to think of hopeful things to say about new treatments that were being tried, and maybe he could lick it, but he kept shaking his head and saying that we shouldn't kid ourselves. We had to face it and prepare ourselves and our son, Todd, for what would happen. Then he told me that he needed me and Todd to be with him. He said he knew he had no right to ask this of

me, but he didn't think he could face it by himself. He
wanted to come back home and live with us and be part of
a family.

"I couldn't refuse. He was still my husband—at least,
legally. He was the father of my child. He was a man I had
loved and lived with for fifteen years. And I loved him still.
But I was very uncertain about how things would work out.
We had been apart for four years, and I had built a new life
for myself. Ultimately, I just decided that we'd have to take
things one day at a time.

"Now it's been a year. We've been through some very
bad periods. A couple of times, it seemed he was on the
edge of death, but then he would recover and be strong
enough to get around on his own. His doctor says he's very
strong, so maybe he'll live another year, or even more.

"I have been tested more than one time since we found
out about Stewart's illness, but every once in a while I become literally gripped by the fear that I will die in this
horrible way, too. Only, who will take care of me the way
I am taking care of him? And what will happen to our son?
I try to put these thoughts aside because they only make
things worse. It helps that I have a support group I attend
once a month. If I'm really feeling scared, it makes a difference to know there are people who will listen to me and
understand.

"I've been asked if I'm bitter about what has happened.
I can't really blame Stewart, because I've come to accept
his homosexuality—and he didn't know about AIDS when
he started having sex with men. I feel sorry for him that
this has happened just when he was beginning to feel free.
I'm sad that he won't live to enjoy seeing our son grow up.

"It's funny, in a way. I remember a time when the only
thing I was really afraid of was that Stewart would find a
man he loved more than he loved me. In those days, my
definition of love had to do with sexual attraction. I suffered
constantly over the fact that Stewart found others more sexually attractive than he found me. That all seems so silly
now. Both of us were seduced by sex; we made it the all-

important thing. But our concerns now have nothing to do
with sex, and maybe that's helped us see each other in a
different light. We talk about this sometimes, late at night
when Stewart can't sleep. I sit up with him and rub his
back, and we talk about how these moments are what love
is really all about. I hope it's something I never forget.''

It is not easy to find positive lessons from a disease that
is so ugly. But Diane's insight is echoed by others in similar
situations. It seems that the close encounter with death can
teach people new things about life. The French writer,
Françoise Sagan, once observed that our ability to grasp our
mortality could transform our relationships. She wrote,
''Sometimes I lie on my bed and think, 'I'm going to die.
The people around me are going to die.' That makes me
want to do a thousand and one things. I often hear people
talking to me and I suddenly realize that they're going to
die, too. So I begin to listen to them in a new way. I see
them as they really are. I want to make them stop acting out
roles, to ask them why they're making so much fuss, why
they take themselves so seriously and put on all those airs.
I want to tell them what's really important.''

The complexity of human love may be one of the lessons
we're learning in this era of AIDS. The nature of caring
may be another. Still another might be the need, as Sagan
put it, to cut through the sham and talk about what is really
important.

One of the respondents, a 50-year-old man, said, ''I have
watched three friends die in the past two years, and it's
impossible to have that experience without it changing you
in some way. I used to worry about so many things, but at
some point I taught myself to say, 'How can you worry
about that . . . Bill is dying.' My wife and I have sometimes
talked about how dangerous our lives have suddenly become. We are perhaps more candid than we once might have
been with one another. When I first told her I was gay, I
made it very clear that I wanted to stay married. She accepted that, but she said that she wanted to keep that part
of my life separate from *our* life. In other words, she said,

'Do what you have to do, but I don't want to know about it.' But with AIDS in the picture, that's no longer possible. We have to talk about it. As a result, we have grown closer and more understanding of each other.''

CHAPTER TEN

Life and Love Beyond Sexuality

"All experience cries out to man: Whatever you do, see to it that you don't lose your vital urge; whatever else you lose in life, if only you keep that, there will always be a chance of winning back everything."

–From *The Diary of Soren Kierkegaard*

AFTER WANDERING around the massive church grounds for some time, I found the back door propped open and walked into the light. About twenty-five men and women were standing around in small groups, talking and laughing. Some of them looked up when I came in. They might have been any church study group in suburban America—conservative-looking, middle-aged, the men in the corduroy jackets or business suits they had worn to the office, the women in dresses or neatly pressed slacks and blouses, manicured fingers sparkling with wedding and engagement rings.

A tall man with thinning hair, who looked to be in his mid- to late fifties, and wearing a suit jacket and an open-necked shirt, broke away from a cluster of men and came over to me. I told him who I was and he clutched my hand in a hearty shake. "Great. I'm Jack. We spoke on the phone.

"Rosemary," he called over his shoulder, and a small woman who also appeared to be in her mid-fifties hurried over. "This is my wife, Rosemary."

Rosemary beamed at me and squeezed my hand. "We're all so excited," she said. "This is the first time the men have ever let us come to one of their meetings."

"I guess that means we won't be going to the bar to-night," said Jack, and his wife gave him a playful jab.

I laughed and shook my head. They were a nice couple—

funny, relaxed. The term "old marrieds" popped into my mind. Everyone in the room seemed relaxed. I'm not sure what I expected—a younger group, maybe. More tension. Not this jovial camaraderie.

When Jack first contacted me about speaking to his group, Gay Association of Married Men (GAMMA), I was delighted. I was impressed that groups like this existed—although they were few and far between—and I felt that such a meeting could help me pull my research together. Jack said he thought my presence could help them, too, and the joint meeting of the men and their wives was arranged. Ordinarily, the wives met on their own and were considered a separate organization affiliated with GAMMA. However, although the groups met separately, they socialized together.

People continued to pour into the room—more men than women. Jack and Rosemary scurried around pulling chairs from stacks in the back and squeezing them into tight corners. When they ran out of chairs, several men stood along the wall. There may have been close to one hundred people in the room, and there was the feel of an "event" in the air. It *was* an event. Rosemary told me earlier that she had been on the phone all week, cajoling the wives to come. Some were apprehensive. "They thought you might *make* them say how they felt in front of everyone," she explained. But Rosemary had apparently calmed their fears. In the end, about a third of the people in the room were women.

Jack stood up in front and beamed at the roomful of people. "This is a great showing," he said. "Thanks for coming." He turned to me. "Do you mind if we take care of some mundane business before we begin?" I smiled and shook my head.

He read from a sheet. "We hope everyone plans to attend the November potluck. It'll be November twelfth at seven o'clock at Bill and Florence's. Bill . . . Florence . . . raise your hands so people can see who you are. If you haven't already signed up, see them after the meeting."

He looked down at his sheet. "If you haven't paid your ten-dollar fee for the newsletter, we'd appreciate it. Also,

I'm going to pass the hat now to cover expenses for this meeting. Just put in what you can.'' He started the hat moving down the front row. ''And we're always looking for volunteers for our many activities. If you have any spare time, contact Rosemary. That's my lovely wife. Rosemary, stand up so the people can see you.'' She stood and gave a little wave.

''Okay, I guess that about does it,'' Jack said, turning in my direction. He introduced me, reading from a biography I had supplied him. ''Before Catherine begins, why don't we tell her something about ourselves. Can we go around the room and just introduce ourselves and say a few words? Remember, this will be kept strictly confidential.''

My hands were itching to take notes or tape this part—they were allowing me to tape the rest of the evening—but I was sensitive now to their privacy. I concentrated on remembering as many details as I could. What I remembered the most was the longevity of the partnerships. Twenty years. Thirty years. Forty years. I listened with growing amazement.

Finally, everyone had been introduced and I walked to the front of the room. People were packed in tight—there was less than a foot of space between me and the front row. I leaned against the folding table behind me. ''I don't think I've ever been in a group of people whose marriages had such longevity,'' I said. ''What's your secret?'' They laughed loudly at this, as they would many times during the course of the evening. It was a very upbeat group.

I began by telling them about my study, relating some of the key facts about the people who had responded. ''Tonight, I'm going to tell you some of the things I learned about married people like yourselves,'' I said. ''And share some of my own observations. Then I'd like to spend some time in discussion.

''When I began working on this study, I isolated several underlying themes. These were not *premises,* in the sense that I was trying to prove them—I wasn't trying to *prove* anything. It's more accurate to describe them as assumptions I was exploring. These were: First, that we are drawn to the important people in our lives for a variety of reasons, and there are many different kinds of attraction.

"Second, that knowing one's sexual orientation and preference does not automatically guarantee a set lifestyle. For example, many gay men in my study reported that they preferred to *live* with women, even though they preferred men sexually. In part, this has to do with the realities of our times. Living an openly homosexual lifestyle usually means that a number of sacrifices must be made. For example, many gay men want to have children. Also, there is not yet any acceptable, legal way for gay men to be married to one another.

"Third, sometimes people fall in love, agree to commitment, and even marry for reasons we don't consider 'normal.' And they are satisfied with their choices. But nevertheless, they feel that something is wrong with them because they don't comply with set patterns." I saw a number of heads nod when I said this. "I see that some of you have had these thoughts. Repeatedly, in doing this research, I've heard people say things like, 'I must be crazy to live like this.' Or 'What's wrong with me that I can't have a normal relationship?' Or 'If people knew the truth about how I live, they would be shocked.' "

Many people in the room were laughing now and sharing meaningful looks. "In fact, most people pretend to live conventional lives. It's safer to appear to be just like everyone else. We can't know how many secrets exist behind the appearances.

"My fourth and final assumption was that men and women today—both heterosexual and homosexual—who are not 'involved' are trapped in a *'singles' mentality.* They're looking for Mr. or Ms. Right and meanwhile they're unhappy being alone. Some people choose to be with another person because it gives them a *meaningful relatedness* that is essential—even though it often involves compromises.

"The married people who participated in my study fit into four typical situations. The first knew at the time of their commitment that one person was homosexual, but chose to marry anyway because, very simply, they didn't want to be without the other person. It makes some sense when you think about it. Only marriage or some equally firm covenant gives people permission to say, 'Where you go, I will go.' I've heard from many people that the decision point came when one or the other planned to move away. You can be best friends, soul mates, bosom buddies, but these things don't hold the commitment to be physically present.

"Those who fit into this first category seem generally more content because they worked through many of the issues before they got married. Sexually, some report being monogamous, some non-monogamous, and in some rare case, the marriages are nonsexual. The people in the nonsexual marriages are not necessarily celibate. One or both partners might have relationships outside the marriage. But in neither case are these necessarily marriages of convenience. I rarely found people who took the major step of entering into marriage unless they shared a deeply felt bond. The fact that this bond does not extend to sexual relations should not be taken to mean that it isn't valid.

"In the second category of couples, the woman didn't know at the time of marriage that the man was gay. Usually, the man did not fully know or accept his homosexuality, either. After some years, the truth came out, but the couples decided to stay together."

I told them the story of Dennis, related in Chapter Seven, and when I quoted his comment to his wife, 'This isn't the worst thing that will ever happen to you,' the room broke up. "That's the truth!" Rosemary called out.

"These couples," I went on, "are usually very serious about trying to work things out. They usually reach compromises, and when the marriage lasts beyond the initial revelation, they often go on to have stronger relationships than ever.

"The third category of married respondents are in a similar situation as the second, in that the issue only came up after the couples had been married a number of years. But these couples are having less success staying together. Either the man wants to leave and have a full relationship with another man, or the woman can't accept the situation. Some of these are in the process of trying to work things out. When they really love and respect each other, they're usually able to come to terms with the situation—either together or apart. Not all couples should stay together, of course—only when it's what both partners want. But caring partners will try to diminish the amount of pain for themselves and their children if they should decide to separate.

"The final category is the gay married men who are suffering tremendously because they've kept the fact of their homosexuality from their wives. When such a big secret exists within a marriage, it's a terrible burden. It no longer feels like a choice. In those cases, the men feel trapped.

"Many of these men are in positions that seem to close off all of their options. This is particularly true of clergymen, government officials, and executives of large conservative corporations. One vice president of an international banking firm wrote, 'Society may be more open than it once was, but how many gays do you see in upper management in financial institutions?'

"These situations are sad for everyone concerned. They're usually not happy marriages. The women feel cheated because their husbands are withdrawn for reasons they can't understand. Some suspect them of having affairs—with other women. The men feel cheated because they are stuck. Sometimes they feel bitter toward their wives since they appear as the most visible barrier to their fantasy of freedom. Ultimately, there is a lot of bitterness on both sides and the tragedy is that neither partner, least of all the woman, quite knows why it exists or how to deal with it."

I paused and looked out into the room. "Those are the four categories of married people who responded to my study. Can you identify with these?" Heads nodded vigorously. "Any others you can think of?" There was no response, and I went on.

"I thought you might be interested in hearing some of the main things both the men and women are saying. See if you identify with these feelings.

"The women tend to be less secure, in part because, as heterosexuals they cannot get inside the heads of their homosexual husbands. They don't know how the men feel. The overwhelming mystery of it sometimes leads them to wonder: *Is he a time bomb that's going to explode and leave me at some point in the future?*" Many laughs from women with this point.

"Women are more inclined to equate sex with commitment. Those who have non-monogamous marriages have a hard time understanding how their husbands can truly love them and also have sex with other people. They sometimes take their husband's homosexuality *personally* and view it as a rejection of who they are. Sometimes—usually in their lower, more insecure moments—they wonder if their husbands are only pretending to find them desirable sexually.

"Since most wives really love their husbands, they also worry about the fact that they may be holding them back, and they don't want to do that. It takes guts, and real love, to give your husband the kind of freedom many of these women have. But many report that their husbands are happier and better partners as a result of having freedom.

"Finally, of course, many women talk about AIDS. Several have partners who have died of AIDS or who now have the disease. This is very hard. The reaction is the same as anyone might have, and that is, 'How can I face this?' But in the midst of these terrible crises, the women are often surprised to find new insights about love and caring. Sex is no longer the issue when your husband is dying. Being human is the issue.''

"That's true," a woman near the front of the room said softly. "My husband has AIDS. I had left him, but now I'm back so I can take care of him." Several people turned to look at her sympathetically. "I get a lot of support from this group," she added.

I made a mental note to talk with this woman after the

meeting. "Now for the men," I went on. "Most of the men say they would prefer to stay in their marriages and also be free to have homosexual relationships on the side. This does not mean promiscuous sex. They would like a dual monogamy—their wives and a male partner, with their wives being their primary partner.

"Most of the men surveyed had never had a 'true love' relationship with a man that fulfilled as many of their other needs—for family, companionship, stability—as the relationships they had with their wives. And many found this frustrating.

"And, since people, whether they're heterosexual or homosexual, have different levels of sexual need, the importance of pursuing homosexual sex is more or less important, depending on the individual.

"There is usually great concern about how to really communicate—or get through to—their wives that they are really committed. In all, the male respondents are very responsible people. They are not fleeing their marriages without a backward glance. Even when they know they must leave, they are doing their best to take care of things as well as they can."

 I smiled out at them; they were listening intently, some, no doubt, relating their own experiences to what I had said. "Finally, what it boils down to is this: No matter what labels we place on ourselves, every human being seeks the same thing from a relationship—*that it enhance the quality of his or her life.* That's the only question you have to ask yourselves about your own relationships. Do they enhance the quality of your lives?"

I stopped and asked for questions or reflections. The people weren't shy; about twenty hands went up at once.

"Do you have any data on the patterns of nonsexual friendships?" asked a young bearded man. "I'm curious because my wife has no real friends who are men—except me, of course. But all of my friends are women, and always have been. I have maybe one male friend. Do you have any data on that?"

"Yes," I said, "that's a very common thing. In my study, there are two different categories of these relationships. One is women who prefer gay men and gay men who prefer women. This category represents the extreme. But the more mainstream category is women and gay men who are very close friends or even nonsexual partners. Often the women talk about certain qualities that, while they're not inherent in gay men, are more common with them, maybe because gay men have had to address certain sides of themselves that straight men have not. Women say gay men are easier to relate to and are not as defensive about themselves. Women are attracted to that. The men who are involved with women often say that they are less shallow than the men they've known. They're also less threatening and more accepting. There are people who talk about the other person being their 'significant other'—the person they talk to when they have something important to say."

A professional-looking woman stood up in the corner of the room. "I'm a psychologist," she said. "I counsel many couples in these situations. One interesting point to add to the discussion: I come from Holland and we're talking about uncommon relationships. I think our society is less rigid than America's—of course, you're from New York, so that's a little different." Everyone laughed. "Anyway," she said, "there are many different sorts of arrangements that people have made with each other. And one that's become very popular during the last ten to fifteen years is the relationship that's called 'living alone together.' Those are people who are a little older and maybe they've been married or lost a spouse or whatever. And there's another person they're very close to, but they've decided not to live together. They see each other once or twice a week; often it's an exclusive relationship. They have the bonding and commitment, but they maintain a certain degree of independence in the midst of that."

"That's interesting," I said. "We cut ourselves off from having important people in our lives because we make so many rules."

Jack spoke next. "Recently, there seems to be an increase of media attention on the whole issue of bisexuality and relationships like we have. I read recently that someone said this is perhaps *the* issue of the eighties. Would you call it that?"

"I wouldn't call it *the* issue of the eighties in itself," I said, "unless you broaden it to include the fact that people have many different ways to fill their needs and they choose many different ways of living. And also I think that we have to face the fact that, in the homosexual community, the options are limited. Two men who are together aren't treated the way a married man and woman are.

"That's not totally true," an older man said from the back of the room.

"You do have a lot of things to confront, depending on your profession and where you live," I said.

"We have support groups."

"In some communities. But even when you have the emotional support of a group, you're denied legal rights, medical benefits, that sort of thing. My point is that we can't talk about these relationships without understanding that our cultural arena has a great deal to do with determining our choices."

A man in his late thirties, seated beside his wife, raised his hand. "I wonder what you've learned about talking to children about these issues—and coming out to them."

"That's very difficult," I admitted. "In the family where the parents are together on it, it obviously has the potential of being handled much more smoothly. Most people who answered questions in my survey related to parenting reported that the telling process went very well when they had thought it through as parents and presented a united front. When the parents were not together, it often took many years. I have a few responses from children—this was arranged through some of the gay fathers—and I found that, for the most part, the children had no problem. They didn't understand everything, of course, but they were accepting. That didn't surprise me too much because children pick up the signals that we give them. But I also have to say that those fathers who responded were extraordinarily involved in their children's lives.''

''We're interested in this,'' another man spoke up, ''because we're now involved in trying to decide what to tell our children. Are you saying that your sampling shows that most of the time there's no problem if the parents are together?''

''Not exactly. You know, we put a lot of store in these studies—we're a poll-driven society. And that's not always the best way to evaluate one's own actions. If you read in a book that 90 percent of the parents who talked to their children had fantastic results, you're going to wonder when you don't. The best thing is to pay close attention to your own unique family situation, and to seek help from professionals who understand this issue.''

A youngish man in a gray business suit stood up. He spoke enthusiastically. ''I think one of the most valuable things about a group like this, and about the kind of book you're writing, is that they increase the sense that people in our situation have that there are choices. One of the hardest things in coping with all of this is the idea that there aren't any choices, or that you don't like any of them—that is, that none of the choices have any kind of value for you. Here, we can help people see that there are strategies to make sense of your life. It helps to learn how others have handled similar problems.''

''I agree,'' Rosemary spoke up. ''So many articles and books are so negative. They don't talk about all the different ways that the good marriages work. I think we need to have some positive things said, because all of us here have seen positive things.''

''To start with,'' I suggested, ''most of this press you're talking about treats your situation as though it were a *problem*—and an insurmountable one at that. It's like, 'Watch out, your husband might be gay.' ''

''And they say when it comes out, the marriage always ends in divorce,'' Rosemary said. ''Look at us.''

''I'll bet a lot of people don't even consider the options,'' the man in the gray suit said. "Things are so confused at first—it took my wife and me three years to work things out. But we had this group to help us. And one thing the group said to me when I came to them the first time was, 'Don't do anything now. Don't make any big decisions while things are so emotional.' It was very good advice. I know it saved our marriage to hear that."

"There might be something to that," I agreed. "A lot of women who left their husbands didn't even stop to think twice about it. They thought, 'This has got to be wrong . . . I don't belong here anymore.' And part of that has to do with the notions people have about what a good marriage is supposed to be like. They put their own marriage through a kind of litmus test, and if it doesn't measure up, they assume it's an impossible marriage."

A dark-haired woman who had been sitting in the front row and not speaking, now said, "I'd like to make a statement. I met a woman the other day who told me that she'd had a significant relationship with a gay man, and she thought she was the only person in that kind of situation. I mentioned this group and started explaining about the support, and she was mesmerized. She said, 'You mean there's a *group* that gets together and talks about this?' She couldn't believe it. It's so valuable to be able to see that you're not weird, that there are others like you."

The evening had already lasted an hour longer than planned, but even when it was over, people didn't seem to want to leave. They stood in groups, talking, arguing, sharing experiences. People crowded around me, continuing the discussion. Frequently, I was asked for advice about how to handle one situation or another, as if my knowledge of so many people's lives made me an expert in areas that were clearly beyond my ken.

For a long time, while I talked with people, I had been aware of a young man and his wife standing quietly to the side. I remembered them from earlier in the evening. They looked no older than twenty-one or twenty-two and, unlike most people in the room, they seemed very sober and tense, as though they were straining to hear the right explanation.

Now, as the others began to drift off, the young man came up to me, pulling his wife by the hand. "Can I ask you something?"

I said sure, and he asked, "How do you know if you're really gay?"

I was surprised by the question. "I don't know," I said honestly.

"I don't think I'm really gay," he said earnestly. "And if I am, I don't want to be . . . I really don't want to be." He looked panic stricken, and his young wife's eyes were as wide as saucers. "Have any of the people you've talked with been able to change back?"

My heart went out to this couple. I was beginning to understand the situation. "I don't think you can," I said gently. Their faces dropped. "But there are many things you can do. Have you received any counseling?" He shook his head. I gave him the names of people in the area he could talk to, wishing I could do more. But this situation was far outside my realm. All I could do was deliver the "bad" news and hope someone else could give the good news. They were so young, this couple, almost like babies. I thought of how terrified the woman looked, as though an irreversible catastrophe had been set in motion. In a flash, I realized the truth—that this couple would probably not stay together.

Walking back to my hotel, I played back in my mind the two strongest images from the evening—the certainty and sense of rightness that seemed to glow around Jack and Rosemary and the look of terror in the eyes of the young couple. What very different pictures! It's frightening to feel out of control of one's life, to experience insurmountable contradictions and know that a choice is required. But which choice? "Just be yourself," people advise, as though that settles everything. But which self? The answer could be found, I realized, not in denial, but in exploration. The young man was confused only because he could not bear to listen to what his own heart was telling him. I felt better at the thought. At least the young couple had a support group to help them through some of the rockier moments.

Not long after my evening with the group, I received a note from Jack and Rosemary, proudly telling me that group attendance records had been broken that night. They enclosed a copy of their newsletter, hot off the press, which included an account of the evening. At the bottom was a quote Jack had taken from Boris Pasternak's *Doctor Zhivago.* It read:

> The great majority of us are required to live a life of constant, systematic duplicity. Your health is bound to be affected if, day after day, you say the opposite of what you feel, if you grovel before what you dislike and rejoice at what brings you nothing but misfortune. Our nervous system isn't just a fiction, it's a part of our physical body, and our soul exists in space and is inside us, like the teeth in our mouth. It can't be forever violated with impunity.

Summary of National Survey

[The following is a complete summary of questionnaire data; numbers/percentages of respondents appear in parentheses. Totals do not necessarily add up to 100 percent, as some respondents skipped questions or checked more than one response.]

This questionnaire includes two sections. Answer questions in the first part if you are a MAN, and in the second part if you are a WOMAN. If the person you are involved with/ married to would be willing to fill out a questionnaire too, please give him or her the appropriate section.

The questionnaires are stated in the present tense. If you are describing a past relationship, answer the questions about that relationship, recalling the feelings and experiences you had at the time.

The information in this questionnaire will be strictly confidential. Please use extra paper if you wish to elaborate on your responses.

Return your questionnaire to Catherine Whitney, 84 Charles St., #19, New York, NY 10014.

MEN

Age:
18–25	(39)
26–35	(115)
36–50	(147)

Over 50   (55)
Not known   (19)

Current marital status:
Married   (174)
Separated   (65)
Divorced   (32)
Widowed   (12)
Committed partners   (78)
Not known   (14)

Profession:
Professional   (75)
Business/service   (87)
Arts/
  entertainment   (24)
Government/
  military   (17)
Clergy   (4)
Student   (10)
Not known   (21)

1. How long have you known of your homosexuality?

_____ I have known for many years that I am homosexual and have been comfortable with that. (52%)

_____ I have only recently admitted my homosexual attraction. (26%)

2. How would you describe your homosexual attraction?

_____ I am sexually attracted to both men and women and would refer to myself as bisexual. (22%)

_____ I have felt sexual attraction for women, but my attraction to men is stronger. (64%)

_____ I would like a sexual relationship with a man, but I am afraid to pursue one. (18%)

_____ I am not sure whether I am bisexual or homosexual. (11%)

_____ I am uncomfortable with the idea of my homosexuality. (8%)

_____ Other (Please specify.)

3. Are you openly homosexual?
   _____ Yes (32%)   _____ No (68%)

4. Which of the following reflects your attitudes about homosexuality or bisexuality? (Check all that apply.)

_____ Sexual preference is the most important factor in a committed relationship. (12%)

_____ Homosexuality is all encompassing to me. I cannot conceive of a lifetime relationship that is not with a man. (4%)

_____ I am willing to have a relationship with a woman because of the tradeoffs (e.g., children, lifestyle preference, social acceptability). (50%)

_____ I could have a committed relationship with either a man or a woman; the focus is my love for the individual person. (68%)

_____ I would prefer to have a lifetime relationship with a man, but I am unable to see myself being part of the "gay world." (26%)

_____ Other (Please elaborate.)

5. How would you describe your love relationship with the woman in question?

_____ Intimate, but not sexual (34%)

_____ Sexually exclusive (28%)

_____ Sexual, but not exclusive (45%)

6. How long have you been involved with this woman?

_____

7. Have you had other love relationships with women prior to this one?

_____ Yes (54%)   _____ No (29%)

If yes, please say how many: _____
(average number: 3)

8. You would describe your feelings about this woman in the following way:

_____ I love her and I want to be with her. Sexual preference is secondary. (49%)

_____ I'm confused by my feelings for her and don't know what to do. (35%)

_____ My ideal would be to stay with her, but also be free to have close relationships with men. (80%)

_____ I view my relationship with her as important, but unlikely to last. (27%)

_____ Although I am sexually attracted to both men and women, I am unlikely to form a permanent partnership with a woman. (28%)

_____ The closest people in my life have always been women. (36%)

_____ I feel as if I am living a lie when I am with her. (26%; 92% of those whose partners did not know.)

9. Briefly describe the history of your relationship with this woman.

10. Does the woman you are involved with know you are homosexual?

_____ Yes (47%)   _____ No (35%)

11. **If you answered "Yes" to Question 10, describe her feelings about your homosexuality:**

_____ She is open to pursuing the relationship. (58%)

_____ She is open to pursuing the relationship only if I am sexually monogamous. (27%)

_____ She feels hurt because she loves me and doesn't understand my attraction to men. (46%)

_____ She is confused about how to handle my homosexuality. (43%)

_____ My homosexuality is something she cannot accept. (24%)

_____ She wants to change the nature of the relationship to a more casual one. (12%)

_____ Other (Please elaborate.)

12. **If you are involved with a woman who knows you are homosexual, what are the issues you struggle most with as a couple?**

_____ Monogamy (47%)

_____ Commitment (45%)

_____ Safe sex (42%)

_____ Values/religious beliefs (22%)

_____ Other (Please specify.)

13. **If you are a parent, check the statements that apply:**

_____ My children do not know I am homosexual. (48%)

_____ My homosexuality has been openly discussed with my children. (22%)

_____ Having children is the primary reason I am with a woman. (34%)

_____ My children respect my homosexuality and have no problems with it. (26%)

_____ My children do not accept my homosexuality. (19%)

_____ Other (Please elaborate.)

14. **Please use this space to elaborate on your feelings about:**
    —Being homosexual or bisexual
    —Your relationship with women
    —Your concerns and fears
    —What committed love means to you
    (You may write on a separate sheet of paper if you need more space.)

15. **Would you be willing to be interviewed further over the phone or in person?**
    _____ Yes (79%)   _____ No (16%)
Providing your name is optional. However, if you are open to being interviewed further, please supply the following information:

Name
Address
City/State/Zip
Phone
The best time to reach me is _____

WOMEN

Age:
18–25	(62)
26–35	(87)
36–50	(130)
Over 50	(41)
Not known	(27)

Current marital status:
Married   (185)
Separated   (28)
Divorced   (40)
Widowed   (13)
Committed partners   (60)
Not known   (21)

Profession:
Professional   (89)
Business/service   (62)
Industrial   (18)
Education/
  social services   (85)
Arts/entertainment   (26)
Government/
  military   (7)
Homemaker   (25)
Student   (19)
Not known   (16)

1. **How long have you been involved with a homosexual man?**

   _____

2. **Is he the first homosexual you have been involved with?**
   _____ Yes (67%)   _____ No (26%)

   If no, please elaborate. (17%: one other relationship; 9%: repeated relationships)

3. **How would you describe your relationship?**
   _____ Intimate, but not sexual (28%)

   _____ Sexually exclusive and permanent (30%)

   _____ Sexual, but not exclusive (18%)

   _____ Other (Please specify.)

4. How long have you known he is homosexual?

_____ I knew when I met him. (40%)

_____ I did not know when I met him, but I found out shortly after. (24%)

_____ I did not find out until I was deeply involved. (36%)

5. Which of the following best describes your feelings about your man's sexual orientation? (Check any that apply.)

_____ I accept it and it doesn't affect my love or commitment. (70%)

_____ I accept it, but I am very pained by it. (28%)

_____ I can deal with it in theory, but I would be crushed if I knew he was seeing a man. (8%)

_____ I am bitter and don't understand it. (10%)

_____ I cannot consider having a permanent relationship with him. (28%)

_____ I am happy with him, but deep down I have the fear that he will someday leave me for a man. (24%)

_____ I believe that true love can exist apart from sexual preference. (55%)

_____ Other (Please specify.)

6. If your relationship is sexual, describe your feelings about sex:

_____ Monogamy is essential. (30%)

_____ I am concerned about AIDS. (40%)

_____ Our sexual relationship is good. (35%)

_____ Our sexual relationship is lacking. (34%)

_____ I worry that he only pretends to be satisfied. (19%)

_____ Other (Please specify.)

7. **Briefly describe the history of your relationship.**

8. **Do you feel a special attraction to men who are gay?**
_____ Yes (54%)   _____ No (28%)

If yes, what are the qualities that attract you? List as many as you can think of.

9. **What are the qualities that attract you to the homosexual man you are involved with?**

10. **Elaborate on the concerns you have about your relationship with a homosexual man. Use a separate sheet of paper if you need more space.**

11. **Would you be willing to be interviewed further in person or over the phone?**
_____ Yes (68%)   _____ No (17%)

Providing your name is optional. However, if you are willing to be interviewed further, please supply the following information:

Name
Address
City/State/Zip
Phone
The best time to reach me is _____

ADDITIONAL QUESTIONS FOR GAY FATHERS
(Controlled study: 92 gay fathers)

1. **Please check the statements that apply to you:**
   _____ Married to the mother of your children (37 men)

   _____ Divorced or separated from the mother of your children (54 men)

   _____ Never married to the mother of your children (6 men)

   _____ Currently living with a gay lover (23 men)

   _____ Currently living without a partner (29 men)

   _____ Other (Please specify.) (0 men)

2. **Your daily relationship with your children is:**
   _____ You live with them and their mother. (37 men)

   _____ You have sole custody. (5 men)

   _____ Their mother has sole custody. (16 men)

   _____ You share joint custody. (21 men)

   _____ Your children are adults. (13 men)

   _____ Other (Please specify.)

3. **When it comes to your children, you struggle most with:**
   _____ The attitudes of others that you can't be a good parent to them. (62 men)

   _____ Wanting to be with them, but not willing to be in a heterosexual relationship. (36 men)

   _____ Teaching them to be open to people's differences. (74 men)

_____ How (or whether) to tell them you're homosexual. (42 men)

_____ Other (Please elaborate.)

4. **What is your relationship with your children's mother?**

_____ You are married and your wife is aware of your homosexuality. (14 men)

_____ You are married, but not satisfied, and your wife is unaware of your homosexuality. (23 men)

_____ You are engaged in a battle over custody. (6 men)

_____ You are not living together, but have both tried to create a positive and comfortable environment for your children. (27 men)

_____ Other (Please specify.)

5. **Do your children know you are homosexual?**

_____ Yes (33 men)   _____ No (59 men)

If yes, please describe their feelings.

6. **Please use this space to elaborate on your feelings about:**
   —Being homosexual
   —Being a parent
   —What love and commitment mean to you
   —Societal attitudes about gay parents
   —Other thoughts

References

Altman, Dennis. *The Homosexualization of America.* New York: St. Martin's, 1982.

Bell, Alan P.; and Weinberg, Martin S. *Homosexualities: A Study of Diversity Among Men and Women.* New York: Simon & Schuster, 1978.

Bellah, Robert N.,; Madsen, Richard; Sullivan, William M.; Swidler, Ann; and Tipton, Steven M.; editors. *Individualism and Commitment in American Life.* New York: Harper & Row, 1987.

Bernikow, Louise. *Alone in America—The Search for Companionship.* New York: Harper & Row, 1986.

Boodman, Sandra G. "The Quiet Pain of Gay Men and Their Wives—Some Marriages Endure Despite Fears; Others Exist Within Secret." Washington, DC: *The Washington Post,* October 15, 1988.

Bozett, Frederick W.; editor. *Gay and Lesbian Parents.* New York: Praeger, 1987.

Brown, Gabrielle. *The New Celibacy.* New York: McGraw-Hill, 1980.

Brown, Howard. *Familiar Faces, Hidden Lives—The Story of Homosexual Men in America Today.* New York: Harcourt Brace Jovanovich, 1976.

Bullough, Vern; editor. *The Frontiers of Sex Research.* Buffalo: Prometheus, 1979.

Clark, Don. *Loving Someone Gay* (revised edition). New York: New American Library, 1987.

Coleman, E. ''Bisexual and Gay Men in Heterosexual Marriage: Conflicts and Resolutions in Therapy.'' New York: *Journal of Homosexuality,* 1982.

Colton, Helen. *Sex After the Sexual Revolution.* New York: Association, 1972.

Doell, Ruth G.; and Longino, Helen E. ''Sex Hormones and Human Behavior: A Critique of the Linear Model.'' New York: *Journal of Homosexuality,* 1988.

D'Emilio, John; and Freedman, Estelle B. *Intimate Matters—A History of Sexuality in America.* New York: Harper & Row, 1988.

Doyle, James A. *The Male Experience.* New York: Little, Brown, 1983.

Emerson, Gloria. *Some American Men.* New York: Simon & Schuster, 1985.

Eisler, Riane. *The Chalice & The Blade—Our History, Our Future.* San Francisco: Harper & Row, 1987.

Frankl, Viktor E. *Man's Search for Meaning.* New York: Simon & Schuster, 1984.

Freud, Sigmund. *The Basic Writings of Sigmund Freud.* New York: Modern Library, 1938.

Friday, Nancy. *Jealousy.* New York: William Morrow, 1985.

Gagnon, John H.; and Simon, William. *Sexual Conduct: The Sources of Human Sexuality.* Chicago: Aldine, 1973.

Gallagher, Winifred. ''Sex and Hormones.'' Washington, DC: *The Atlantic Monthly,* March 1988.

Goergen, David. *The Sexual Celibate.* New York: Seabury, 1974.

Green, Frances; editor. *Gayellow Pages*. New York: Renaissance House, 1988.

Gough, Jamie: and MacNair, Mike. *Gay Liberation in the Eighties*. London: Pluto Press, 1985.

Hill, Ivan; editor. *The Bisexual Spouse*. McLean, VA: Barlina, 1987.

Hirshey, Gerri. "Tyranny of the Couples." Washington, DC: *The Washington Post Magazine*, February 14, 1988.

Hite, Shere. *The Hite Report*. New York: Macmillan, 1976.

———.*The Hite Report on Male Sexuality*. New York: Knopf, 1981.

Kinsey, Alfred C. et al. *Sexual Behavior in the Human Male*. Philadelphia, Saunders, 1948.

Koestenbaum, Peter. *Existential Sexuality: Choosing to Love*. Englewood Cliffs, NJ: Prentice-Hall, 1974.

Krantz, Rachel. "Toward a New Definition of Singleness: Building a Life with Close Friends." Cambridge, MA: *Sojourner,* March 1986.

Maddox, Brenda. *Married and Gay*. New York: Harcourt Brace Jovanovich, 1982.

Malone, John. *Straight Women & Gay Men*. New York: Dial, 1980.

McCauley, Stephen. *The Object of My Affection*. New York: Simon & Schuster, 1987.

Masters, William H.; and Johnson, Virginia E. *Homosexuality in Perspective*. New York: Little, Brown, 1979.

Nahas, Rebecca; and Turley, Myra. *The New Couple—Women and Gay Men*. New York: Seaview, 1979.

Norrgard, Lenore. "Can Bisexuals Be Monogamous?" Seattle: *North Bi Northwest,* February 1988.

Olds, Sally Wendkos. *The Eternal Garden—Seasons of Our Sexuality.* New York: Times Books, 1985.

Olsen, Kiki. "Could Your Lover Be Gay?" New York: *New Woman,* November 1988.

Rich, Frank. "The Gay Decades." New York: *Esquire,* November 1987.

Rohde, Peter; editor. *The Diary of Soren Kierkegaard.* New York: Philosophical Library, 1960.

Ross, Michael W. *The Married Homosexual Man—A Psychological Study.* London: Routledge & Kegan Paul, 1983.

Shain, Merle. *When Lovers Are Friends.* New York: Bantam, 1979.

Slater, Philip. *Footholds: Understanding the Shifting Sexual and Family Tensions in Our Culture.* New York: Dutton, 1977.

Sontag, Susan. *AIDS and Its Metaphors.* New York: Farrar Straus Giroux, 1988.

Thompson, Mark; editor. *Gay Spirit: Myth and Meaning.* New York: St. Martin's, 1987.

Thoreau, Henry David. *Walden and Other Writings.* New York: Bantam, 1962.

Toffler, Alvin. *The Third Wave.* New York: William Morrow, 1980.

Watson, Mary Ann. "Sexually Open Marriage: Three Perspectives." *Alternative Lifestyles,* 1981.

Participate in a New National Study on Nuclear and Non-nuclear Family Styles

The following survey has been developed as part of a national study on current "family" styles. Although the traditional nuclear family has long been the pattern for the "ideal" living style in America, it is far from the norm. Some studies indicate that less than 15 percent of adults in America today live in traditional nuclear family structures. Indeed, the conflict between the ideal and the norm has led to a general dissatisfaction among some segments of the population.

According to Alvin Toffler, family living styles reflect the necessities of the times. Toffler says in *The Third Wave* that the traditional nuclear family structure "perfectly fitted the needs of a mass-production society with widely shared values and lifestyles, hierarchical, bureaucratic power, and a clear separation of home life from work life in the marketplace." It is his contention that the so-called crisis in the nuclear family is not a crisis at all, but rather a move from one cultural mode to another.

It is the goal of this study to examine on a national scale exactly how it is that people of all ages and social classifications are living, and what they have to say about the nature of family and community in the postnuclear family era.

TIES THAT BIND
A National Survey on Family Living Styles

This questionnaire is designed to assess national trends regarding nuclear and non-nuclear family styles. Please answer the questions as completely as possible; all responses will be utilized and incorporated into the study. All information will be held in strict confidence. Please feel free to use additional sheets to elaborate on your answers. Return the questionnaire to: Catherine Whitney, 84 Charles St., #19, New York, NY 10014.

1. Sex:

_____ M   _____ F

2. Age:

____ 18–24   ____ 25–34   ____ 35–44

____ 45–54   ____ 55–64   ____ Over 65

3. Occupation:

_____Upper management/administrator/owner

_____Middle management/supervisor

_____Sales/marketing

_____Clerical

_____Laborer/machine operator

_____Craftsperson/artist/writer

_____Teacher/nurse/social worker/clergy

_____Doctor/scientist/lawyer

_____Homemaker

_____Retired

_____Student

_____ Other (Please specify.) _____

Describe your work environment:

_____ Work at home, alone

_____ Work at home, related to larger group

_____ Work at home part time, in office part time

_____ Work full time in a location outside the home

4. Education:
(Check last year completed)

_____ Graduated high school
_____ Attended college
_____ Graduated college
_____ Master's degree
_____ Ph.D.
_____ J.D.
_____ M.D.
_____ Other degrees (Please specify.) _____

5. Income:
(Check combined income of all adults in household.)

_____ Under $9,999　　　　_____ $35,000–54,999

_____ $10,000–14,999　　　_____ $55,000–74,999

_____ $15,000–19,999　　　_____ $75,000–99,999

_____ $20,000–24,999　　　_____ $100,000 +

_____ $25,000–34,999

6. Number of persons living in household:
_____ Adults　　　　_____ Children

7. City and state in which you reside: _____
This residence is: _____ urban　_____ suburban
_____ rural

8. **Check the statement that best describes your current living arrangement:**

_____ Traditional nuclear family. (Married and living together with spouse and dependent children.)

_____ Modified nuclear family. (Married and living together with no dependent children.)

_____ You plan to have or adopt children.

_____ You do not plan to have or adopt children.

_____ Your adult children no longer live with you.

_____ Traditional extended nuclear family. (Married and living together with spouse, dependent children, and one or more blood relations.)

_____ Modified extended nuclear family. (Married and living together with one or more blood relations, and no dependent children.)

_____ You plan to have or adopt children.

_____ You do not plan to have or adopt children.

_____ Your adult children no longer live with you.

_____ Single person living alone.

_____ Single person sharing home with roommate or significant other less than half the time.

_____ Single person sharing home with roommate or significant other more than half the time, but not all the time.

_____ Single person living with roommate or significant other full time.

_____ Single parent living with dependent children, without spouse or significant other.

_____ Part-time single parent, living alone and sharing home with dependent children part of the time.

_____ Part-time single parent, living with spouse or significant other, and sharing home with dependent children (from a previous partner) part of the time.

_____ Living in a community or group. (Check the one that applies.)

    _____ Religious community
    _____ Political/social community
    _____ Retirement community
    _____ Singles community
    _____ Other (Please specify.) _____

Briefly describe the setup of the community in which you live.

_____ Other living style than mentioned; please specify. _____

9. Type of residence:
_____ Single-family home

_____ Multiple-family home

_____ Apartment/cooperative/condominium

_____ Mobile home

_____ Other _____

10. What is your relationship status?
_____ Married

_____ Separated

_____ Divorced

_____ Widowed

_____ Single

_____ Living together with partner

_____ Seeing one partner, not living together

_____ Other (Please specify.) _____

11. **How would you classify your sexual identity?**
_____ Heterosexual

_____ Homosexual

_____ Bisexual

12. **How would you characterize your current sexual behavior?**
_____ Sexually active/monogamous

_____ Sexually active/non-monogamous

_____ Celibate by choice

_____ Not sexually active (because no current partner)

_____ Other (Please specify.) _____

13. **How would you describe the nature of your current most significant relationship(s):**
_____ Permanent

_____ Transitional

_____ Not sure

_____ Other (Please specify.) _____

14. **How are roles assigned and tasks distributed in your household?**
_____ Traditional. (Male works outside the home; female responsible for household.)

_____ Modified traditional. (Male and female work outside the home, but female the primary homemaker.)

_____ Informal. (Tasks are done by the person most available to do them.)

_____ Structured. (Tasks are assigned to members of household.)

_____ Other (Please specify.) _____

15. Check the statements that best reflect your feelings about your current living style:

_____ I am living the way I most want to live.

_____ Right now, I am living the way I want, but I don't see this as permanent.

_____ My living style is comfortable, but not perfectly satisfying.

_____ I would not have chosen to live this way, but circumstances make it necessary.

_____ I am very dissatisfied with my current living style.

_____ Other (Please elaborate.)

16. Do you foresee that at some point in the future you will have a different living style?

_____ Yes   _____ No

If yes, please describe:

17. How do you think other people would describe your current living style?

_____ Traditional

_____ Nontraditional

18. What, if anything, makes your household or living style different from a traditional household or living style?

19. **Which factors do you believe have had the most impact in changing styles of family and community? Check all that apply:**

    _____ Women entering the work force

    _____ Social changes of the 1960s and 1970s

    _____ Change of religious values

    _____ The sexual revolution

    _____ Economic circumstances

    _____ Electronic era

    _____ Greater health and longevity

    _____ Other (Please specify.) _____

20. **What is your personal definition of "family"?**

21. **Describe in your own words the living style you would be most happy with, either now or in the future.**

    Use this space to elaborate on other thoughts you have about family and community.

Optional

Name _____

Address _____

City _____ State _____ Zip _____

Telephone _____

Would you be willing to be interviewed further?

_____ Yes   _____ No

Do you know others who would be interested in participating in this study? List names and addresses:

_____

_____

_____

_____

Return this survey to:
Catherine Whitney
84 Charles St., #19
New York, NY 10014

Afterword
by Christine Henny, Ph.D.

Christine Henny, Ph.D., is a clinical psychologist and family therapist, practicing in Washington, D.C. A native of Holland, Dr. Henny formerly practiced at the Human Sexuality Institute in Washington and is certified by the American Society of Sex Education Counselors and Therapists. Dr. Henny is uniquely suited to discuss unconventional relationships. Approximately 30 percent of her practice is devoted to helping married couples where one partner is gay.

It is often difficult for men and women to explore unconventional relationship options because the cultural constraints in this society are very rigid. Everything is seen in black and white, and there are many prejudices against people who do not conform to the accepted patterns. But prejudice is always based on lack of understanding and fear. In my practice, my first goal is to help people move beyond their rigid assumptions and their fears so that they can really evaluate their relationship on its own merits.

I have seen many people in my practice who are struggling with the issues described in this book—in particular, married couples dealing with the revelation that the man is a homosexual.

Often, when these couples come to me the wife feels that the situation is impossible. She will say, "He likes men. I can't handle it." That's fear. I try to objectify things by saying, "What you need now is to make a new contract. You thought you married someone who was heterosexual, and now things have changed. They're not the same as they were when you made your first contract.'' And I help the couple develop a new agreement. That might mean ending the relationship, or it might mean staying together. If they stay together, they have to decide on new rules. Every relationship has rules, and these are no different.

However, before I can address the issue of homosexuality directly, I must first look at what kind of marriage it is. One couple in their forties came to see me after the man admitted to his wife that he was having homosexual fantasies. After looking into the marriage and talking with them at length, both together and separately, I came to the conclusion that they had a lousy marriage—and that it had nothing to do with the man's homosexual fantasies. So I said, ''Let's leave the issue of your interest in men alone for a while, and examine your marriage.'' After six months, their relationship with one another was dramatically improved. He grew up, and she stopped being so moralistic. Then I helped him become more accepting of his fantasies about men. I told him, ''It's okay to have these fantasies, and you have a choice. You can act on them, or you can choose not to act on them.'' Since his wife was adamant about their marriage being monogamous, he had a big choice to make. He finally decided that his homosexual interests were not that great, and he stayed in the marriage.

I place the emphasis on choice, because choice is a dominant factor in our lives. When we decide to have one thing, we often can't have another, and we must make a decision. I think this so-called Me Generation encourages people to think, ''I must give in to everything I feel. I must express myself in every way.'' Now, many homosexuals get angry with me when I say this, because they do not understand the dual roles of nature and nurture in influencing our sexual expression, and they think I'm dismissing or denigrating their sexual preference.

Most professionals agree that all human beings are *capable* of bisexual behavior. But sexual behavior, in my experience, is a combination of nature and nurture. Although there may be prenatal, hormonal influences that create a predisposition for being homosexual, the other half of the mix is the environment. Not all people who have such a biological predisposition end up practicing homosexual behavior; some of them never even think of themselves as being homosexual. My work has taught me that sometimes people who classify themselves as bisexual are reluctant to make a commitment to a relationship that is either homosexual or heterosexual. I also think that many people go through phases during their lives when their behavior is primarily heterosexual or homosexual, but then change. Finally, you have to remember, when talking about human sexual life, that our brain is the largest sexual organ we have. There are a lot of decisions that we can make.

It's also important to place sexuality in perspective. In Abraham Maslow's hierarchy of human needs, sexuality appears as number sixteen out of twenty. This helps to explain why some men will stay in relationships with women even though they are homosexual. They're looking to have other needs met. However, men generally find that they can separate the erotic and the emotions, while for women, it's a little more complicated, since sexuality for them is generally more closely tied to the emotional expressions of loving and caring. In part, that has to do with cultural conditioning.

When I am working with couples where the man is homosexual, I always consider carefully whether or not one partner is settling for less because she doesn't feel good about herself. This is definitely an issue with some of the wives. They've grown too dependent and they're scared of leaving, so they put up with anything. Ultimately, the questions for anyone pursuing a relationship are these: Does the relationship enhance your life? Can you grow in the relationship? Can you express yourself? If both partners can honestly answer yes to these questions, who are we to judge whether their relationship is good or not?

I admit that many of my colleagues disagree with me about this. They say, "Come on, tell the women to get out of these relationships. They're just staying because they have low self-esteem.'' But this is not always true. I support the plea for tolerance that is reflected in this book. We are, generally speaking, a very puritanical country and there is much prejudice against people who are different or who make unconventional choices. But when we say that those who are not like us are bad, or that they should be ashamed, we are responding out of ignorance.

Index